FAMOUS
by Default

M.K. HARKINS

Famous by Default

Dedicated to

NANCY BAILEY

May 6th, 1953 - March 29th, 2013

Light

Beautiful

Kind

Patient

Humor

Compassionate

Dedicated

Loyal

Empathetic

Determined

Positive

Nurturing

But what I remember the most is:

Love

PLAYLIST

"*Unsteady*"—X Ambassadors

"*Secrets*"—OneRepublic

"*Talk Me Down*"—Troye Sivan

"*Let It Go*"—James Bay

"*Little Do You Know*"—Alex & Sierra

"*Starving*"—Hailee Steinfeld

"*Let Me Love You*"—DJ Snake/Justin Bieber

"*Something*"—The Beatles

"*Come On Get Higher*"—Matt Nathanson

CHAPTER One

JAX

SCREAMS ECHOED BEHIND ME.

Dear God, if you get me out of this, I'll never ditch my bodyguard again.

"There he is!" squealed a high-pitched voice. A twelve-year-old girl, like the others in her mob, chased me. And I feared for my life. I'd think about that charming fact later.

I darted around the corner and came face-to-face with a brick wall. Dead end. My chest heaved in ragged breaths, and sweat seeped from every pore. Where to escape? I backed into a small alcove to assess.

A rabid herd of crazed, stampeding tweens, all wanting a

piece of me—hair, t-shirt, shoes, whatever they could rip off—were too close. I needed Ray, my bodyguard, like, this second.

But I'd ditched him this morning so I could have a "regular" day at the mall. The type of day I'd enjoyed only six months before. A lifetime ago. I hated my life now. However, focusing on survival was the wisest choice right now.

With a lowered head and a tug on my baseball cap, I rounded the corner back into the main corridor and ducked into the nearest store.

"Can I use your bathroom?" I asked the clerk.

She let out a squeak and dropped something lacy and pink.

Not again.

"Quick. They're coming." My hand tapped an impatient rhythm on her counter. Temporarily shielded by a rack of nightgowns placed at the front entrance, my time was running out. The excited voices from just outside came through loud and clear.

"Did you see which store he went in?" a breathless voice asked.

"I think he went into Victoria's Secret."

The stunned clerk pointed to a back hallway. I dashed past bras and crashed into a half-naked mannequin, veered sideways, and managed to lock myself in the closet-sized employee bathroom.

Frustrated, I ripped off my cap and threw it across the small room. It bounced off the wall and plopped into the toilet. Figures. My favorite hat splashing in the toilet was the perfect metaphor for my life. No way was I fishing that out of there. I kicked the door and swore under my breath.

It was *their* fault. Why shouldn't I swear at the top of my lungs? Why not scream obscenities through the door for all the fans to capture on their cell phones? I'd love to see the headlines: *Brother of the chart-topping rock band, The Jaynes, has mental breakdown at the Bellevue Square Mall.*

My mom's voice floated through my head. *Don't embarrass your brothers. They need your support right now. Just because you didn't want to join the band doesn't mean you should turn your back on music. They've cleared the path if you ever decide you want a solo career. You can record that artsy Indie stuff you like so much.*

I paced back and forth in the small room, rubbing the stubble on my chin. It didn't matter anymore because I hated music, well, for now anyway. My entire seventeen years spent surrounded by the guitar, piano, violin, and drums didn't matter anymore. My history wasn't enough to make me want to play again. What I wanted was an eraser, or maybe time travel. I'd go back and tell my twin, Gage, not to form that stupid rock band with our two older brothers. I'd tell them it would make my life a living nightmare, and it wasn't worth it. I never wanted it. I never enjoyed it. I wanted my life back.

Although, *they* were enjoying the hell out of all the attention.

Famous by default. A genetic twist of fate. Either the girls thought I was my twin brother, Gage, or they were intrigued because the media had labeled me "mysterious." The fact that I refused all interviews that included our family fascinated the public. Because, in our media-hungry culture, who didn't want their fifteen minutes? Who didn't want to be a rock star? Not me. No thanks. I wanted nothing to do with the music industry or the fans.

Correction—fanatics.

A loud rap on the door made me jump back. "Mr. Jayne? We have mall security here."

I let my head fall back against the wall. Once, then twice, pounding harder each time. Mall security? What a joke. They couldn't help me. With a groan, I pulled out my cell. Ray would rant for an hour and then probably kill me.

Think.

Out of the two possible death scenarios, Ray would be the lesser of two evils. The thought of girls ripping and shredding my clothes did not appeal to me, even if it meant I could escape Ray's wrath.

My parents had hired him for this very reason. He was tough, he was mean, he had a temper. And all of that would be aimed at me in five seconds. I pushed speed dial and waited.

"Why are you calling me?" His gruff voice sounded mildly irritated.

"Hey, Ray. How's it going?"

Silence.

"Okay. Well, I have a little situation."

"How can you have a situation if you're home, behind a locked gate and security? You know, like we agreed yesterday."

I looked around the small bathroom. Maybe there was an air duct I could crawl out of. Nope. I closed my eyes and jumped into the proverbial lava. "I didn't stay home. I'm at the mall."

"What the hell? No, no, no. Tell me you aren't that stupid?"

He didn't ask. He didn't yell. He screamed at the top of his lungs.

"Yes. I mean, no. But, yes I'm at the mall."

"Holy shit. What's going on?" In the background, keys rattled and doors opened and shut.

"I'm in a bathroom, somewhat, uh, surrounded?" I don't know why it came out as a question.

"I'll call mall security and the team. We'll be there in less than ten. Which store?"

Sweat dripped from the back of my neck. I wiped it and answered, "I'm not sure, there's lace everywhere. Victoria's Secret?"

Ray groaned. "Your mom is going to kill you when these headlines hit."

"She can join the club." I almost didn't care.

Almost.

The car ride home was quiet. Oppressively so. Ray and his eight-man team had extricated me from the bathroom and escorted me through the mall. Eight full-grown men to remove my clueless ass.

My favorite cap—gone.

Anger sizzled inside my chest, the heat expanding to every part of my body. Covered in sweat, frustration took over. Correction, I was *pissed.* How dare they take away my freedom? My last year of high school—ruined. No one had asked my opinion. No one wanted to hear how their fame affected me.

I pounded my fist against the car door, unable to contain the festering, out-of-control emotions I'd kept bottled up since May, when The Jaynes' smash hit, "She Doesn't Love Me," broke all sales records, changing my life.

"Hey, kid. Take it easy on my door."

Kid? The car rolled to a stop at a sign a few blocks from our house. I grabbed the door handle, determined to make an exit, and yanked. Locked. Letting out a deep breath, I rested my head against the back seat and squeezed my eyes closed.

I can't even get out of the damn car.

After passing the security gate and guard, we pulled up to the front drive. The massive, brick Tudor loomed ahead. I wanted to move back to our other house in the normal neighborhood instead of being forced to live in this overpriced, pretentious shell.

Mom stood outside with her arms crossed, and a scowl spread across her wrinkle-free face. At forty-five years old, she still looked like she was in her twenties. On occasion, people would mistake her for my sister. She would throw her head back, laugh, and say, "Fooled them!" She loved it.

Me, not so much.

She wasn't laughing today. A red face, flared nostrils, and clenched fists were the first things I noticed. Yeah, that was exactly how I felt, too. Not a good combination. We both had a temper, but, luckily it rarely appeared at the same time. Today promised to be epic.

She shouted at me as I climbed the stairs to the front porch. "What were you thinking?"

Not answering, I stomped past her into the large foyer and kept going.

She followed me down the hall that opened to a gigantic chef's kitchen. It was the only good part about this house. A kitchen could never be large enough, especially with my three brothers and father. But the rest of the house was enormous and too formal.

The price of fame. Security came with the mansion. Five acres surrounded by a ten-foot wall. Or barricade. Same thing.

"Don't you dare walk away from me." Her voice was low, but her tone stopped me in my tracks.

I turned to face her and attempted not to shout. "They aren't even in town, and I still can't go out of the house. I'm a prisoner here." The mall had always been my go-to place to hang out and chill. By myself or with friends, I'd hit a restaurant or movie to waste the day away. Now it was in the no-go category unless I took a bodyguard.

Her eyes flared. "Don't you raise your voice with me."

Voice control unsuccessful. I crossed my arms and nodded.

She inhaled. "Listen, they'll be done with their tour next month. When they get home, we'll all go on vacation somewhere remote. Okay? Next year when you're away at college, this will all die down."

Out of sight, out of mind.

I frowned, unconvinced. The Jaynes' security team thought the recent interest in me might be because of the over-exposure by the local television stations here. Seattle was proud of their hometown boys, and, as a result, the band was featured almost daily on various entertainment news shows. Most of the time, I was included in their speculations about the band and our family. *Why didn't Jax join the band? Was he going to start a solo career? Why doesn't he do interviews?*

Why couldn't they just leave me alone? My brothers' breakout stardom had spread fast, without a breather in sight for me. The band, too huge; their fans, insane.

"Tell me, why did you put yourself at risk today? All you had to do was take Ray with you. Is that too much to ask?" Her face flushed, and she blinked rapidly.

Not the tears.

"Mom," I groaned on a long breath. "Don't do the guilt thing." I jerked open the refrigerator door, looking for the orange juice. Anything to distract me from this conversation. I didn't do tears.

I poured some juice and walked to the window overlooking the grounds. "I feel like a child when Ray is around. He even calls me 'kid.' Did you know that?" Mom liked to live in her bubble where "everything is going to be okay." She didn't want to acknowledge her youngest son wasn't happy. Her goal in life was to pull her family into a make-believe cocoon and protect us from everything. That way, she wouldn't have to admit her grand plans for success weren't working for everyone. I was the thorn that kept popping holes in her illusion. The one piece that refused to fit, no matter how hard everyone tried to force it.

"No, I wasn't aware he calls you 'kid.' I can ask him to quit. Okay?"

"There's more. I was supposed to meet Robbie at the theater, but he ditched me. Take one guess why." Robbie used to have my back, but not anymore.

Mom pinched the area between her eyes and let out a sigh. "What did Robbie do now?"

"The girls he was with wanted a *real* Jayne. Not me, but the band. I'm the baby. Did you know that's my new name in the media?"

"That's ridiculous. You're six-foot-two, and the star quarterback. You were voted Most Handsome Teen. What's wrong with girls today?"

Ugh. "You've been reading those stupid teen magazines again."

She bit her lip and looked out the window. *Busted.*

I closed my eyes and shook my head. She didn't have a clue.

"You're like your brothers, handsome and talented." She tried to toss me a calming smile.

Not working.

"I'm not *them,* Mom. They think I'm Gage, or their fans are curious about me. I risked going today to hang with Robbie, see a movie. No harm, no foul."

"So he didn't show because your brothers weren't with you? Are you sure?"

"The only thing I'm good for is what I can do for them. Tickets to one of their shows, gossip about the band. Oh, and the clothing—it's a hot commodity. T-shirts or jackets, anything they've worn will do. A girl once asked for underwear. I think she probably wanted to sell them on eBay." *Gross.* I shook off the visual.

Should I keep going and tell her everything? That all the kids at my school thought I was stuck up, too good or something—and now Robbie didn't even want to hang with me. Something about his street cred taking a hit. My only friend left at Prep turned out to be fake.

I set the glass of orange juice on the counter and rubbed my forehead. "I know you don't want to hear it, but this is my life now. I know you have to manage the guys, and that's a full-time job, but I'm left here holding the bag of crazy."

"I'm sorry. We can fix this. I promise." She reached over and smoothed my hair.

Here we go again. Empty promises. I'd heard all this before. She was wrong, and the fury built inside me like an out-of-control forest fire. The denial needed to stop.

Without thinking, I swept my arm across the counter and knocked the glass of orange juice, along with a dozen eggs, onto the floor.

Oh, hell. That wouldn't go over well.

I wasn't backing down, though. I was done pretending. Mom positioned her hands on her hips, and our eyes locked. Hers widened, then narrowed. We stood like that for a good thirty seconds before my dad walked in, interrupting our silent battle.

He took in our stare-down, the broken glass with cracked eggs, and said, “Time for Aunt Betty?”

Mom sighed and repeated, “Time for Betty.”

I looked back and forth between them. They couldn’t be serious. “Crazy Aunt Betty? The one who lives out in Boondocks, Iowa and adopts anything that breathes?” My heart rate doubled.

They both nodded.

“You can’t make me go.”

CHAPTER Two

Sivan

THE CAR SMELLED OF NEW leather and spearmint gum. The landscape flattened as we drove across Highway 3, heading east. I usually loved these car rides, mainly because it meant I had escaped another disastrous foster home, but, this time, even the beautiful fall colors of the Iowa landscape couldn't calm my racing heart.

Relax, Sivan.

"It'll be different this time," my caseworker, Sharon, assured me.

I nodded and adjusted my skirt.

"I visited the farm myself. You don't have to worry about—" Sharon pursed her lips and shot me a glance.

"That's okay. I'm used to . . ." My throat tightened as I sought the right words. "Sharon, I don't blame you for any of this." The foster homes she'd placed me in had a score of zero for three. If I were naïve, I'd think I was in the wrong place at the wrong time. But I knew better. Foster care? No. Take the "care" out and add "dump as fast as you can."

But Sharon tried. One person couldn't be everywhere, doing everything.

She reached over and patted my hand. "Thanks. It makes me feel better, but. . . ." After straightening her shoulders and giving me a quick look from the corner of her eye, she asked, "Did you change your appearance because of all this?"

Ah. Knew she'd ask. "You mean all the blackness?" I swept my arm up and down my outfit.

"Well, yes, your clothes. There's also your hair, fingernails, and lipstick." Her eyebrow rose. "You went all out. Are you trying to send a message?" She turned her eyes back to the road.

I shrugged. Was I? I did want people to keep their distance.

Well, maybe not everyone.

"Anyway, no males live at this house. There's Betty, the foster mom, Alice, who's three, and Emily, who just turned five. Oh, and five goats, three horses, and a multitude of other furry creatures. I lost count when she started to name the ducks." She chuckled.

"You sure she's okay with me doing the online courses to finish high school?"

A crease formed between her brows. "Are you positive that's the way you want to go? Homeschooling? I'm sure the kids in the farm community will be a lot different than those from the city."

"I'm not worried about the bullying anymore. This is my senior year anyway. By the time I got in and said hello, bam, it'd be goodbye again."

"It's September. I'm sure you could make friends in nine months. But I won't try to talk you into it. Betty said homeschooling is fine by her. She's a retired teacher."

"How old is Betty?"

"She's in her late forties."

"She retired at forty?"

"Yes. Unfortunately, her husband died three years ago. He was this famous, world-renowned heart surgeon. It was a huge loss, not only for Betty, but the medical community. Soon after, she decided to take in foster kids. Must be her way to give back and stay busy at the same time." She smiled. "I think you'll really like her."

"That sucks about her husband." My stomach twisted, and a familiar sense of loss tried to rip through the blockade I'd built. *Nope. Not happening*. After shoving it down I asked, "You don't think I'll scare her off, you know, with my black soul?"

She smirked. "Oh, you won't scare her," she said while covering her mouth with her hand. "And you, my dear, have the un-blackest soul I've ever encountered."

Was she trying not to laugh? "Oookay, anything I need to know?"

"Look. Here's our exit. It should only take another twenty minutes."

Not so fast. "I'll rephrase the question. What are you *not* telling me?"

"I've told you everything you need to know."

The info did nothing for my racing heart. I bit my lip as I

tucked a lock of hair behind my ear. Breathe. Once. Twice.

Relax, Sivan. Don't lose it.

Why was she being cryptic? "No fathers, sons, brothers, or boyfriends, right?"

Her expression dropped. "I'm so sorry about what happened. It doesn't seem fair after what you've been through."

I rubbed my chest where a stabbing sensation made my breath catch. "It's okay. I'm not afraid. I've learned I can be strong and take care of myself."

"Yeah. He won't forget that lesson anytime soon. I'm really proud of you, you know."

Creep. The thought of that pervert made my stomach churn.

"Sivan, wake up. Daddy's here."

Balled up in my bed, pulling the blanket tight around my neck, I squeezed my eyes shut as his footsteps drew near. The doorknob clicked as he locked it. My hands formed into fists.

"Remember, you're mine now. If you keep quiet, I won't tell anyone it was your fault your family died." He pulled back my blanket, exposing my boy shorts and t-shirt. "You're my beautiful girl." He grabbed my shorts and pulled. "Now, you're to do everything Daddy says."

"Daddy" didn't know about the self-defense classes I'd taken. I pounced, giving him a black eye, and I was pretty sure he still walked hunched over. His junk would never be the same. Or so I hoped.

Ronald and Marcy Kent. Ugh. The biggest phonies on the planet. They were all, "We are so humbled to serve others," or, "Our foster children fill our lives with joy." Three to four foster children lived with them on a rotating basis. All girls from the ages of thirteen to seventeen. The red flags were there, but no one had noticed. Or they didn't want to believe it. I know I hadn't wanted to.

"Is he still standing trial next week?" I asked.

"Yes. The video testimony you provided should strip him of his foster care license at the very least. If convicted, he'll have to register as a sex offender for life, and we're banking on jail time."

I let out a sigh. "It's still his word against mine."

Sharon scrunched up her face and pulled over to the side of the road. "I've been avoiding something."

Uh oh.

"We haven't had time to discuss this. But a few more girls have come forward since the news hit." Her eyes gentled. "Sometimes, it takes a person like you, someone brave enough to take action. The other young women will add validity to your testimony. The prosecutor said this should be a slam dunk."

"I still don't know if he would have followed through. You know, rape." Rape. A horrid word for an unspeakable act. I rubbed my sweaty palms along my jeans.

Relax, Sivan. It's over.

"The two young women who came forward prompted the DA to press charges of rape against Ronald Kent."

My stomach dropped. "Those poor girls."

Sharon grabbed my hand and squeezed it. "See? This is what I love about you. Instead of thinking about yourself and what could have happened, you're concerned for the girls. You don't deserve this. Any of it. If only I could—"

"Really, Sharon. I'm okay."

"Now you are." She slapped her hand against the steering wheel. "Damn the state and all their rules restricting me from taking you in. Ethics are more important? Yeah, right. Instead, you ended up with a pedophile."

"I'm not there anymore. That's all that matters."

"That's true." She paused. Then a slight smile formed on her lips. "Betty will be a welcome surprise."

"You're going cryptic on me again. What type of surprise?"

"The good kind. Now let's get back on the road. She's expecting us."

We drove down a dusty dirt road and pulled up to the farm fifteen minutes later.

"Wow," I breathed. "It's . . . it's a farm on steroids."

Wrap-around decks encircled three massive stories. The architectural style was . . . different. Maybe it was a cousin to some type of castle because it had a huge turret attached to the right side.

"Where's the moat?" I asked. Instead of water, a garden bed of multicolored flowers bordered the house on all sides.

"It's fabulous, isn't it?" Her eyes drifted up and down, back and forth. "Before interviewing Betty, I knew she'd be great based on this building and land alone. There's a huge barn out back with all sorts of creatures."

Sharon was a city girl. She probably wouldn't know a goat from a donkey.

"How many acres?" I asked.

She grabbed the file sitting between us and flipped through a few pages. "Okay, here we are. Seven thousand square feet for the main house. The barn is another three thousand, and it sits on sixty-seven acres. It isn't a working farm; she just cares for the animals."

Homeschooling would be no problem. I'd tuck myself away

in a cubby somewhere. Or maybe I'd wander around the grounds. I could be invisible here.

Rolling hills in vivid shades of green covered the countryside. Stunning. I opened the car door and stepped out, breathing in the fresh air, hoping it would steady my rapid pulse.

Relax, Sivan. This is nice.

Sharon walked to my side of the car to help with my luggage. I turned and gave her a smile. "You've outdone yourself, Sharon."

She dropped my suitcase and grabbed me into a hug. "I wasn't going to stop looking until I found the right place for you. You know that, right? I'm sorry—"

"Don't be. I knew you'd come through."

She slung her arm around my shoulder. "Let's do this."

We each grabbed a suitcase and wheeled them up the steps onto the huge deck where lots of flowers were scattered about in pots of different sizes. The many colors almost blinded me. "Do you think maybe she likes gardening?" I laughed, gazing around at the endless shapes and sizes.

The door flung open, and a woman burst out in a whirlwind of fabric and bright colors. "You must be Sivan!"

I nodded. Speechless. This was a forty-eight-year-old? Betty was beautiful, that was for sure. Only a few laugh lines fringed her eyes. Everything else indicated youth: bright and colorful clothes, a pair of clunky Doc Martens, a long, patchwork skirt, and t-shirt with a picture of a boy band—One Direction, maybe?

And her hair. Fascinating. It appeared her stylist went for the entire rainbow, with streaks of blue, green, violet, and magenta. Someone might say she had overdone it, but with the brown to balance it, she totally pulled off the Boho-chic style.

Betty approached and put her hands on each side of my face, squeezing my cheeks. “Aren’t you cute as a button!” She turned to Sharon. “You didn’t tell me what a beauty she is.”

The blood left my cheeks. “Yoth sthwishing ma fash.”

“Oh!” She dropped her hands and laughed, the sound almost musical. I closed my eyes briefly to block it.

“Just look at you in all your black!” She picked up a lock of my hair. “I simply love this color. It’s so black, it’s almost blue. And look how you’ve matched everything. Every stitch is black. I love those jeans. Where’d you get them?”

I gave Sharon a *what the hell am I doing here?* look, but she just returned a crooked grin.

“A thrift store,” I replied.

“All the best things come from thrift stores. You’re a smart girl.”

No, just poor.

Betty gripped me by both arms and continued her inspection. “Wow. You have the bluest eyes I’ve ever seen. All the black makes your eyes pop, and my goodness, your eyelashes are so long. And those high cheekbones. You’re a classic beauty.” She laughed. “I’ll have to keep a bat handy to swat the boys away.”

Sharon cleared her throat. “Have you read Sivan’s file yet?”

“Nah. Gordon was sick last week and closed the post office.” She turned to me and said, “You’ll find that everyone who lives out here in the boonies is on a different time schedule. And by that, I mean slooooow.” She laughed again, still gripping my arms. “We don’t need a few sheets of paper to help us get to know each other. A cup of tea and a long chat in the kitchen should do it.”

I stifled a groan. I didn't do "chats."

I shot Sharon a *help* look.

Sharon cleared her throat. "I think we should have a quick talk inside." She turned to me, "Will you be okay waiting for us out here?"

"Sure." I flopped onto one of the six lounge chairs on the porch.

While waiting, I played through their likely conversation in my head.

Sivan has a tragic past. She's been in three different homes, all with a horrible outcome. Don't talk about men around her. It's a sensitive subject. She might be trying to send a message of 'stay away' with all the black.

My therapist had brought up my clothing and style choices numerous times, taking stabs at the possible reasons for it. Was I depressed? Did I want people to stay away? Was I rebelling or doing drugs? No, no, and no. It was simple. I just felt like wearing black.

Thirty minutes later, they returned to the deck. Betty's eyes still sparkled, but her smile was more subdued.

Betty gave Sharon a little rub on her arm. "I've got it from here. Everything will be good." She turned to me and winked.

I smiled to ease Sharon's worry. This part was always the hardest. We both knew things could go bad. But Betty wasn't the typical foster mom, so maybe that'd be a good thing?

Relax, Sivan. Let things play out.

Sharon tugged my arm, and we walked down the steps to her car. She grabbed me into a tight hug. "Things are changing for you. I can feel it."

I patted her back. "Sure." My hope for *different* had gone

splat on the floor so many times, I'd lost count. But a part of me wouldn't let it die.

She released me. "You have my cell number and email. You can call or text whenever you need me." She lowered her voice. "Any little thing. I don't want you waiting too long this time."

In the past, my philosophy had been "wait it out." But I was tired of always being on guard. Tired of everyone thinking the poor, little foster girl wouldn't fight back. They were wrong. "Okay. I'll call this time."

"Good. Now I've got to go before I start blubbering all over you." She wiped under her eye.

"Okay. Thanks for everything. I'll be fine. Don't worry."

One more hug, and then she moved next to her car, gave another look, and climbed in. As she backed out of the driveway, her hand popped out the window for one last wave.

"It's just you and me, kid," Betty said from the porch. "The girls, Emily and Alice, are at our neighbors, the Thompsons, for the afternoon. I thought it would be nice for us to have a little time to ourselves. You know, to chat."

Ugh. I thought Sharon had stopped that train.

"Let's go inside and get that tea. I put some on while Sharon and I had our talk." She motioned me inside.

I stopped as soon as I walked through the front door. *Wow.* The foyer was three stories high with a huge multi-colored glass chandelier. Didn't I see something like this in a YouTube video? "Is this...?" I pointed to the beautiful blown glass.

"Chihuly? Yes, he owed me a favor." She laughed and kept walking.

I followed, taking everything in. A messy look by design. Distressed wood furniture, rich patterns, and vibrant colors. Lots of throws, pillows, rugs, and tapestries. Vases and planters were placed around the windows, in corners and alcoves. It smelled like baked scones and lavender.

We entered a large farmhouse kitchen. Rustic, with white painted cabinets, vintage handles, and an apron sink. Wood countertops, mason jars that held wildflowers, and black stained wood floors. It was spacious and cozy at the same time.

Could a person fall in love with a house? I smiled a little.

She motioned me over to the long table that sat a few feet from the kitchen island. Painted a pale yellow and flanked by white chairs with painted daisies on the seats and backs. As I sat down, a cup of tea was placed on the table in front of me. Betty plunked down opposite me. "I lied," she blurted.

My body tensed. *Sharon's only ten minutes away; maybe she could come back and get me.*

"It's nothing bad," she said while waving her hand back and forth. "Gordon wasn't really sick. I have your file right over there." She moved to a built-in desk, pulled open a drawer, removed a manila envelope, and gently laid it on the table. "I haven't read it, and I don't plan to."

My eyes widened a little. What? She didn't want to read the file top to bottom, backward and forward, to make sure I wasn't too *bad* or wouldn't be too much trouble like the other foster parents had?

"Here's the deal. I have a core belief we are not defined by our past. We are what we are now, today, and what we'll become in the future. I want to respect the person you are today."

"But—" I started.

"Sharon's already told me you're a great kid. I trust her. Also, I wouldn't put Emily or Alice at risk. But beyond that, everything that's happened in your life will be yours to tell. Does that work for you?"

"Yes." An unfamiliar lightness lifted from my core. I got to skip the invasive and humiliating part. What happened to me when I was eleven shouldn't be splashed like blood on paper. The worst part? When people found out, they either concluded I was damaged or weak—someone they could take advantage of. Of course, they were wrong. Sure, I kept a low profile, but when things went south, I was more than able to take care of myself. "That works for me."

"That doesn't mean I won't try to get you to talk." She grinned. "But it will be your choice. The only downfall with this plan is if you have any triggers I may not know. You can either tell me about them now, or, if I say or do something you don't like, you'll have to agree to let me know."

I loved this plan. Something warm fluttered in my stomach. "I have one thing," I started. "My foster father was not a good man. So, um, if you decide to date, I might be a little nervous about it." My hands twisted in my lap.

"Oh. That's an easy one. I'm not going to date."

What? Why not? Not asking though. "I'm okay with it. I can, maybe, not be around?"

"It has nothing to do with you and everything to do with my late husband, Henry." She smiled warmly and said, "Let's go check out your room. I have you in the turret on the top floor. It's a room fit for the princess you are."

A princess? That was a stretch. I shook my head, and a laugh escaped. I didn't think Disney had my version. But, oddly enough, the little girl inside me started to wake up.

CHAPTER Three

JAX

A SOLID WEEK OF ARGUING did nothing to sway my parents from their grand plan to ship me off to Aunt Betty's after the New Year. They thought the break would be good for me. Me? Not so much.

It was the first part of October, so three more months until Farm Prison. I didn't have a choice. Well, technically I did. But the thought of Ray moving and shadowing my every move twenty-four-seven until college was even worse. It'd be a complete and total loss of freedom. At least at Aunt Betty's, I'd be able to breathe. No security, and I'd be homeschooled. So, the agreement was made. Reluctantly.

Mom folded a shirt and placed it in the open suitcase on my bed. "Our media advisor told me the interest in you here in

Seattle has spiked. Maybe it's a hometown thing. No one is quite sure why." Her brow furrowed. "This little break will be good for you. Once you get to Phoenix, you can relax and spend a few days having fun with your brothers. I just hope the press doesn't find out."

"You booked my flight for three a.m. Everyone will be half asleep. Your strategy will work." I flopped onto the bed, too tired to give any more reassurances.

"Ray will be here in a few minutes. He'll be with you the entire trip."

Great.

"Do you have anything else you want to take?" Her eyes shifted to my guitar.

I hadn't played for almost seven months. Mom noticed, and I knew she worried about it. Did I want to take it? Not really, but it'd make her happy. "Maybe I'll ask Ray to grab it before we leave." Mom turned to hide her smile.

The doorbell chimed, and Mom grabbed my hand. "He's here. Remember, Ray is going with you for your protection. Don't make his job harder than it already is."

"I'm always good." I pulled out my best angelic expression.

"God help me," she said under her breath.

"I heard you. You know I hate having a bodyguard following me around."

"I know, but—"

Ray poked his head into the room. "You ready?"

"Not quite." I turned back to Mom. "Ray doesn't need to shadow me this entire trip, right? I'll get a couple hours to myself?"

"No. Absolutely not." She turned to Ray. "Don't take your

eyes off him."

"Why don't I just go to Aunt Betty's now? I can't have any fun with Ray trailing me around." Maybe the threat to leave early would work. I knew she wanted me around for the holidays.

"Don't test me." She folded her arms across her chest and glared.

In an obvious attempt to break the tension, Ray grabbed the largest suitcase, flexed his bulging muscles, and power lifted it above his head.

I picked up the smaller one, muttering under my breath, "Show-off."

Mom rolled her eyes. "You two better get going before someone gets hurt."

Ray nudged me. "Let's hit the road, ki . . . I mean, man." He turned and started down the stairs.

"Don't trip on the way down," I called to his back. Always trying to be the manly man; I was almost certain he had a hidden thing for my mom.

"Have fun, but not too much." Mom ruffled my hair.

I gave her a hug knowing she meant well. This would be a long couple days.

Airports were the most boring places on the planet. I pulled out my iPad from my backpack and searched for a book to fill the hour wait for my plane. Bradbury? Golding? Koontz? Focused on my decision, I hadn't noticed the gasps and giggles at first.

I peeked over the top of my tablet. A small group of girls had gathered at the kiosk next to Starbucks. Ray, slouched next to me, was absorbed with his expert-level Sudoku puzzle. I scanned the group, searching for a potential threat. Around twenty teens formed an all too familiar fan-mob. They wore Hawaiian print shirts, leis, and some volleyball logo on their jackets. Not what I'd call menacing, but they were looking right at me.

I elbowed Ray. "Hey. Stalkers at three o'clock."

He straightened up. "What? Where?" He grabbed for his weapon, but apparently forgot he'd checked it with his baggage. "Don't make any sudden movements. I'll call airport security for backup." He pulled his cell out of his back pocket. "We'll need to get into the closest VIP suite."

The VIP section of the airport sucked. It always smelled like booze and leather. I didn't want to admit it to Ray, but those rooms made me claustrophobic, and I hated them. We'd argued for a good twenty minutes about sitting out in the terminal. I had logic on my side—it was the middle of the night, and we'd taken a flight three weeks earlier without any problems. Ray had finally relented, but now, with his eyes darting around and his body tense, he probably regretted letting me win the argument.

"It is him!" one of the girls shouted.

Ray latched onto my arm and yanked. "Move it."

The group of twenty increased within a few minutes, but they hadn't made a move toward us yet. Though thanks to cell phone cameras and social media, my location would be common knowledge in seconds. "Who travels this early?" Stupid question.

"No time. I shouldn't have let you talk me into this. The band has become too popular." He shook his head and continued to guide me down the hall.

The Band.

"I'm not in the band," I groaned. "I didn't choose this."

"Get over it," Ray snapped. He pulled me toward the elevator and stabbed at one of the buttons.

"Don't get all mushy on me. Your sympathy overwhelms."

"One of these days, you and I are going to sit down and have a long talk." He tossed a look back at the gathering crowd.

"Have two parents, thanks." Ray was probably in his mid-forties, and an intimidating presence, so I decided to back off. For now. No need to distract him while he went into warrior mode.

One of the girls left the group and bolted toward us.

Ray stepped in front of me with his hands up and shouted, "Don't come closer. Security is on its way, and you *will* be arrested." The girl froze, her eyes wide. "I said, do not come any closer," he growled.

Her hopeful eyes turned to me. I shrugged and said, "I'm not Gage."

She jumped up and down and yelled to the group, "It *is* Jax!"

"Now you've done it." Ray took hold of my arm, but it was too late. The mob surged, and everything went to hell. He thrust his body in front of me and yelled, "Stop! Back the hell off."

The girls broke through the one-man barrier and latched onto my clothes from all sides. I moved back, tripped, and hit the ground with a thud. Oh hell, that hurt. Ray threw his body over mine, shielding me.

It was a free-for-all. An elbow crashed into my eye, hands pulled my hair, clothes being tugged apart.

Was this how it would end for me?

Just as I was giving up hope, airport security arrived and

forcibly removed the screaming girls. I sat up, sleeveless, my eye hurt, and I'd lost a shoe. Crazy.

Ray helped me to my feet, and a burly, tattooed TSA agent whisked me down a long hallway into a secure room. Adrenaline shot through me, like a supercharged firecracker, buzzing and crackling. I paced and waited for it to drop back to normal. After a few minutes, I sat, feeling a little better, but couldn't stop my hands from shaking. *That's humiliating*. The secure room swarmed with security, so I clasped them together, hoping no one would notice.

"Damn!" Ray shouted. He ran his fingers through his hair, and, in a lower voice, said, "I should be fired for this."

Ray annoyed me on a consistent basis with his gruff and bossy orders. *Do this, don't do that.* But I knew he was just trying to do his job, and I didn't want him taking the rap for this. "My fault." I shoved his shoulder. "I won't tell if you don't."

"Not an option." He pulled his cell out of his back pocket and pushed one of his speed dial numbers. Mom.

"Hi." A gorgeous, smiling brunette broke through the commotion and stood directly in front of me with an ice pack.

Whoa. I didn't usually go for the security-types, but this girl could easily be a *Sports Illustrated* model. Tall, with gorgeous brown eyes. Her body, holy crap, filled out her uniform in a way that made me stupid. I nodded, mute. I'd even toss my usual preference for blonde hair and green eyes. No way I'd say no to this girl.

"I'm so sorry about your injury." She handed me the ice pack. "This should help."

"This? It's nothing." Good. Speech had returned.

"Let's go, Casanova." Ray stuck my missing shoe in one of my hands, grabbed me by the other arm, and pulled.

"Wait. Hold on a sec." I tried to yank my arm free, but he had me in a vice-like hold and continued to tug me out of the room. "Thank you." I managed to say before we left. "Ray. Stop!" I yelled. That slowed him a bit. "Have you gone blind or something? Did you not see that girl?"

"Now isn't the time. They've cleared the path to the tarmac. The airline has transferred your ticket to Iowa."

"No." I shook my head. *Oh, hell no. Not yet. I'm not ready.*

"This situation is out of control. You'll be so far out in the boonies, you won't even need me. Your parents have arranged for a private flight for both of us. I'll go with you to Iowa then head back to Phoenix for extra security for your brothers. It's settled. Don't argue."

"Not so fast." Two could play this game. I hit speed dial as I slipped on my shoe. "Mom?"

Her first words were, "Don't argue. It's settled." Ugh. Sounded familiar.

"I don't have any of my stuff. What about Thanksgiving and Christmas? You don't want me around?"

"That's exactly why you're going to my sister's house. I want you safe. You could have—"

"It wasn't that bad." *Think.* "I promise not to ditch Ray. Okay?"

"No. It's escalated to the point where Ray isn't enough. You're all over the news in Seattle. We need to tuck you away on Betty's farm until this settles down. I'll send some warm clothes tomorrow."

She wasn't going to budge. "Whatever. I have to go now," I said and clicked off. I gripped my cell and looked for a wall to smash it against.

"You'll regret it," Ray warned.

The memory of my favorite hat in the toilet charged back, so I decided to shove it into my pocket instead. I raised an eyebrow in Ray's direction.

"I read people for a living. Now, let's get going."

Six armed security guards flanked each side, escorting us from a side door to the jet bridge, then onto the waiting plane.

Ray looked me over and sighed after we took our assigned seats. "This is my fault. I screwed up." He leaned forward and rubbed his face.

I couldn't be mad at him. It wasn't his fault. Damn. I didn't have anyone to blame but myself. Not even my brothers.

A change of subject should do it. "The only thing you messed up is tearing me away from that agent. She was hot!" When he didn't respond, I added, "It was almost worth having my clothes ripped and having you cop a feel while we were on the floor."

"Smart-ass. Don't try to make me feel better." He shook his head.

"Listen, Ray, I'm the one who talked you into sitting out in the open. Hell, I thought SeaTac would be mostly empty at this hour."

"It usually is. My first mistake."

"If you get me the security guard's number, I'll forgive you."

"She's too old for you. Besides, you can have your pick of any girl. All you really have to do is point your finger. Game over."

My stomach sank. "Why? I haven't done anything to earn it."

"It's the Kardashian effect. They're famous for being famous. You're famous because you're related to the Jayne brothers. It's also being fueled because of your refusal to step into the spotlight. People are curious. The fact that your brothers are photographed everywhere doesn't help either. You're an enigma. Fans want to know your story, especially why you aren't in the band." His eyes shifted around the plane. "I didn't realize it had exploded like this."

"It's probably good I'm going to Iowa then."

"Maybe. But you'll still need to be careful. Keep a low profile, and no social media. I wouldn't put it past an overzealous fan to try to track you down when you completely disappear from sight."

"Are you trying to make me nervous?"

"Yes."

A young, pretty flight attendant leaned over Ray and touched my shoulder. "Can I get you anything, Mr. Jayne? Anything at all?" Her eyelashes fluttered, and she bit her lip.

I turned in time to see Ray roll his eyes. "No, thank you. I'm good," I said while jabbing him with an elbow. "You need anything, Ray?"

"Oof." He grabbed his side. "I've had about enough."

Good. I turned with a smile to look out the window.

A few minutes before takeoff my cell vibrated. Mom. I clicked, knowing she'd blow up my phone if I didn't.

"Don't hang up again!" she yelled.

"I didn't hang up before. I had six TSA agents waiting to get us on the plane."

"So, you're not angry?"

Didn't want to admit it, but she was right about taking a time-out from all this. Two things I asked myself: would I miss my friends? No. Would I get a break from all the madness? Yes. I'd let them win this one. If they wanted me gone, so be it.

"I've accepted it for now. I'm tired of being chased around." I turned away so Ray couldn't eavesdrop. "You know how I feel about security."

"Will you change your mind about Ray? I'd feel better if he stayed with you on the farm."

"Mom, we've talked about this a zillion times. I won't need him, and besides, Mr. Bouncer would go crazy on some farm out in Nowhere, Iowa."

She sighed. "Okay, but I don't like it. You'll call if you have any problems?"

"Yeah. I have to turn off my phone. We're taking off."

"I'll miss you, honey."

"I'll miss you, too, even though you're sending me into exile. Oh, and Mom? If the plane goes down in a ball of flames, I forgive you."

She laughed.

I wasn't really kidding. But, whatever.

After a tornado warning and a mechanical malfunction on the plane, we landed in Chicago and remained grounded for most of the day and night. Twenty-four hours later, we arrived at my Aunt Betty's farm. The entire house was dark with only the outdoor lights on. Not surprising since it was two in the morning.

I exited the car without my suitcases or guitar. Because of the last-minute switch, my luggage was sitting somewhere in the Seattle airport. I made the journey to Nowhereville with just the clothes on my back and a hundred in cash.

Ray got out and leaned against the car. "Safe and sound on

the farm as promised. Look at this place." His head swiveled from the house to the barn. "Your mom hasn't been able to reach your aunt yet. She mentioned something about landlines and no voicemail."

"Yeah. I guess my aunt doesn't like technology." This would be a long eight months.

"It looks like everyone's asleep. I'll wait until you get in, then take off. You be good." He said it in his usual tough-guy way, but he smiled and punched my arm.

"Your affection overwhelms." I groaned and laughed at the same time.

"Really, all joking aside, if you need anything, let me know. I'll fly right out. Okay?"

"Sure, Ray." I gave him a nod. He'd be the last familiar face I'd see in a long time. A twist of discomfort settled in my chest. Would I miss him? No. Just tired. I gave him a wave and climbed the stairs. After knocking on the door, I waited. Nothing. Mom probably hadn't reached her yet. Exhausted, jet-lagged, and hungry, I tried twisting the door handle. Locked. Now what? As I turned to go back down the steps, I spotted an envelope sticking under the door mat. I snagged it and ripped open the top. A note and key fell out.

Welcome, Jax. Just found out you're coming for a visit. Make yourself at home. Security panel to your right—070758. Your room is top of the stairs, third on your left. I'll look forward to catching up with you tomorrow. xx Aunt Betty

One last wave to Ray and I unlocked the door, found the panel, and punched in the code. It flashed green, and I let out a sigh of relief. Bed. My stomach would have to wait.

I crept up the stairs and counted the doors. Didn't want any surprises. I turned the handle, opened the door, and flipped on the light. The huge, four-poster platform bed perched against the back wall was exactly what I needed. Twenty feet away and I could pass out. I turned the light off and crept through the room, counting the steps until—Damn, stubbed my toe.

I sat on the bed and groaned. What was an okay idea twenty-four hours ago, didn't feel so great now. Sleep deprived, my eye hurting, a headache, missing and torn clothing—nope, not in a good place. I was a stranger on a farm with an aunt I barely knew. Oh, couldn't forget the good part. Two young girls lived with her, both below the age of five.

And no girls my age for miles, probably not even in the county, guessing by the long stretches of back roads to get here. It didn't matter anyway. I couldn't trust girls anymore. Any girl. I didn't want "Game Over" as Ray called it. Would any girl ever want me for just me? Or would it always be about my family? I wanted it to be real. But now, it would probably never happen. Fame was a bitch.

My eyes started to close as I slipped under the soft cotton sheets. The last thing I remembered before drifting off was Ray's mini-lecture, a feeling of dread, and the smell of lavender.

CHAPTER Four

Sivan

I COULDN'T SHUT DOWN THE shame and embarrassment shooting through every inch of my body.

The conversation started off like usual. Betty and I, hanging in the library, talking about ordinary things around the farm. Only a couple weeks in and we'd slipped into a nice routine. Until she noticed my fingers.

Busted.

The heat from my cheeks betrayed me as I searched my brain for a way to get out of the library.

Betty reached over and grabbed my hand, giving it a gentle squeeze.

My stupid habit of rubbing my thumb against my forefinger had worn some of the skin off. I tried to pull back. She gripped it tighter.

"It's nothing," I stuttered out. My breathing uneven.

"If this is the worst thing that's come as a result of your childhood, I'd say you're doing great. If it isn't, well, we can talk about that later." Her gentle brown eyes were such a contrast to her hair and clothes.

Betty deserved an explanation. I looked down at our joined hands, and my shame notched up to horror. "Oh no, I'm so sorry! You have blood on your hands."

"Don't you dare be sorry. This," she held up my hand, "is your war wound. I know what it's like to battle against life, against darkness. I'm here to tell you this: you can win."

Her words calmed me. I'd never thought about it like that. It had always been something to hide. A habit that showed weakness. "It's embarrassing. I want to quit, but I do it without thinking." My cheeks cooled, and shame loosened its hold a little. I hadn't even told my therapist about it. What was it about Betty that made me want to confess all?

"I'll help you quit. First, we'll get it washed up and put a Band-Aid on it. Then I'll attach a rubber band."

What? I took a deep breath. "Why? Where?"

She laughed. "Don't look so panicked. I'm not going to rubber band your entire body. Just the two fingers. You're lucky it's your left hand. You'll be able to wear it all day without it interfering too much with daily activities. But, nighttime is the most important. I'm sure you're doing most of the damage while you sleep, because I haven't seen you do it before now."

I nodded. My finger throbbed every morning when I woke up.

"But, Sivan?"

"Yes?"

"We'll need an alternative."

"What do you mean?

"This habit has been serving a purpose. It's called self-soothing. You're going to need another, healthier activity to replace it."

Oh.

"Measured breathing and self-talk are the two I've had the most success with when I taught high school. Have you tried them?"

"Um. Like all the time."

She clapped her hands. "Wonderful. You have an excellent start." She tapped her forefinger against her lips. "Hmmm. How do we keep those hands busy?"

I shrugged.

"Hang on a sec. I'm thinking."

The warm feeling I always had around her swelled inside. No one had ever paid this much attention to me. Not even my therapist.

"Do you knit or crochet?" she asked.

"No. I tried once. I managed to wrap more yarn around my arms than the needles." Tenth grade Practical Life class hadn't turned out so well.

"Oh, I know. I could teach you to play the piano. I have a music room with a Steinway." Her face brightened.

No!

Cold dread snaked through my body. I bit my lip, but before I could stop myself, the words "I hate music" tumbled from my mouth. I ripped my hand from hers, turned, and fled up to the turret where I could hide away. I couldn't talk about playing the piano. Or anything else.

I curled up into a ball on my bed and willed myself not to remember.

"Do you like it, Sivan?" my mom asked.

"It's . . . it's the most beautiful thing I've ever seen." My wide-eyed expression reflected from the black polished surface of the brand-new Steinway in our living room. I reached out to touch the glistening ivory keys, but waited until my mom nodded.

"Here." She handed me a blue polishing cloth. "This is yours. Will you keep the keys and wood dusted?"

"Yes!" I clapped and jumped up and down.

"Can I help?" Danny asked.

"Of course," my dad answered. "Right, Sivan?"

I rolled my eyes and said, "Sure." Brothers could be so annoying.

Pain seared through every cell. I gasped and tried to catch my breath.

Shove it away, Sivan. Don't remember.

About an hour after burrowing under my blankets, a soft knock sounded on my door. It crept open, and Betty's face appeared. "Are you okay?"

Betty had tried to be helpful, and how did I repay her? Shouting and running away. I should be at kindergarten with Emily. Ugh.

I sat up a little. "Sorry." I tried to smile.

"I will tell you—again. There's no reason." She stepped in a few feet. "A trigger?"

"Yeah. Guess I should have mentioned it." Another humiliating fact. I couldn't listen to some types of music.

She sat on the end of my bed. "I just remembered our code word. Why didn't you tell me?"

"Oh, you mean 'boy band'? Words are totally okay. I'm just not a fan of that type of group." I took in a breath. "It's only some genres of music, mostly classical."

No more questions. Please.

She smoothed the blankets. "I love how Emily has bonded with you."

Good. A change of subject. Emily had taken to me like "a hotdog to a bun," as Betty liked to say. Cute as a squirming, playful puppy, she shadowed me when she wasn't off doing her thing in kindergarten. It was fun. Even though most all my evenings were filled with her questions—Why is the sky blue? Who makes the dirt? Why do flowers smell good?—somehow, it didn't bother me. Her curiosity made me think she'd grow up to be some sort of scientist. Alice, a curly blonde, was much shyer than her outgoing, dark-haired sister. Alice loved to follow Emily around, which meant I had two little shadows on and off throughout the day.

Betty had said, "I can distract the girls so you can get a breather. You're not here to babysit, you know."

"I enjoy them." I'd told her.

She'd studied me. "I may be old, but I'm not that old. I can keep up with them."

I laughed. Betty had more energy than anyone I'd ever met. "That's an understatement."

We'd made a deal from the get-go. If the girls became too much, or I needed a break, I'd say the code word "boy band." As far back as I could remember, I'd always hated boy bands, but Betty's face had lit up when we discussed the idea, and I didn't want to disappoint her. That woman had a strange fan-girl thing going on. She had five or more t-shirts with some band, I thought maybe One Direction or The Vamps, but they all looked and sounded alike to me. I could live with the code word if I didn't have to listen to that annoying music.

"Emily is my little buddy. I enjoy my time with her and Alice, and, as you know, I haven't needed to use the code once." I smiled.

Betty nodded, but a crease formed between her eyes. "I have music lessons for them starting next week. Will that be a problem?"

Yes. "No."

Her eyebrow rose.

"Maybe. But I'll deal."

"As you know, I'm a great talker. But I'm also a terrific listener." She took my hand again. "We still have to get this fixed up."

Betty was a good person to talk to. What was the worst thing that could happen if I did talk to her? *I could start crying and never stop.* My eleven-year-old self never had the chance to cry or grieve for her family. Too busy trying to survive. I wanted to hug that little girl, tell her it was okay. But I wasn't convinced of it. Not yet.

"Okay. Can we get started on this," I held up my fingers, "and work on the other, um, issues later?" *Please let it drop.*

The seconds ticked by, seeming like hours. Betty's eyebrows knitted together and then relaxed. "Sure. C'mon. I've got Band-Aids in the kitchen."

I jumped out of bed; this part would be easy. I hoped. "Lead the way."

We circled down the spiral staircase as the landline started to ring. "Telemarketers," she groaned. "Go on to the kitchen. I'll join you in a minute."

I wound down the rest of the way and hurried down the hall into the kitchen to give her privacy. I couldn't help but smile when I thought about Betty and her aversion to cell phones. She had three landlines in the house, and two extensions in the barn and outdoor areas. None of them cordless. She told me she hadn't wanted to become a slave to technology, but she answered the phones anyway.

Her words filtered in from the hall. "Sure, the girls would love a new dog."

A long pause.

"Yes, honey. Don't worry about it. I'd be happy to help."

Warmth settled within my chest. Betty had adopted three chickens and a goat since I'd arrived. All that needed to be said was, "They need you," or, "We could use your help." Well, if anyone needed her, she'd be there. She reminded me of a cotton ball—soft and squishy.

The Band-Aids were laid out on the table, so I rinsed, then dried my finger and put one on quickly.

"You're adopting a new dog?" I asked as she entered the kitchen.

"A border collie. He can herd the goat."

A loud crash boomed as the kitchen door flung open and bounced off the wall. "Betty, look! I drew a picture of our family." Emily pushed forward a slightly crumbled piece of paper with a colorful crayon drawing. Alice bounded in right behind her.

On closer inspection, I was able to make out Betty in the drawing. I stifled a laugh. She was located on the left side, a stick figure, but, wow, the hair. Emily had done her justice. Colorful rainbow spikes covered not only her head but her entire body. The two girls were in the middle, a smaller size. And then, me? I was on the right, black hair, blue eyes that took up my entire face. But, right in the center of my chest, a huge red heart had been colored in. I blinked back my surprise and caught Betty's eyes.

She nodded once and said, "That's lovely, Emily. You've captured our little family just right."

Family?

I blinked rapidly, hoping to shut out the memory trying to barge in.

Messy, curly brown hair, freckles, and a huge eight-year-old grin framed Danny's face. "Look, Sivan. I made this picture of our family. See? There's Mom, Dad, me, and you!"

No. No. No. Why does this keep happening? Why now?

I wiped my sweaty palms against my jeans. The memories wrapped around my heart and squeezed until I couldn't breathe. How many times would I have to say goodbye?

"Do you like it, Sivan?" Emily asked.

Her innocent, little smile calmed the ache between my ribs. "Yes, it's beautiful."

Emily wrapped her arms around my legs and held on tight. The heaviness lifted and I concentrated on regular breaths.

A girl, about my age, entered the kitchen. "Sorry, Betty. They got ahead of me." Wow. She was kinda perfect. Super-blonde hair that didn't look fake. Long eyelashes fluttered over big, green eyes. Tall and model-like. Not usually aware of people's looks, I tried not to stare.

Her large, green eyes locked on mine, "Oh. I heard you'd be here." She scanned me from head to foot. There it was. *That* look. The one filled with disapproval. I knew it well. Judging. This should be interesting.

The expression cleared quickly, replaced with what appeared to be fake excitement. *Super, a budding actress.*

"I've been so excited to meet you!" she squealed.

That was quick. Maybe even Oscar-worthy.

"Sivan, this is Regina. She helps me out around the house and with the girls every so often."

I tried to smile in a polite way, but girls like Regina were aliens to me.

"Siv-an." She raised perfectly plucked brows. "You're so . . . pretty." Was she still smiling, or was that a sneer?

"Um, it's pronounced Sivon. You know, like when a light bulb goes *on*." I struggled to keep my eyes from rolling while I smoothed my wrinkled shirt. Of course, Regina wore stylish designer clothes.

Regina flipped back her hair and said, "Whatever." Her smile was still in place, but the hard look in her eyes gave her away. It was the same look I'd seen replayed from high school to high school. The I'm-better-than-you-so-stay-out-of-my-way look. I returned her look with my own I-don't-give-a-flying-crap-what-you-think.

Betty's head moved back and forth between us and she said, "Thanks again, Regina. I'll give you a call tomorrow," ending our very awkward meeting.

Betty must be a mind-reader. I bit back a smile.

Needle-like pain spiked up my leg. Where was that pressure on my left side coming from? Still drowsy from sleep, I cracked open an eye. A small bit of sunlight squeezed through the wooden slats from my bedroom window revealing a mop of dark, wavy hair. Emily had latched onto me, hot and sweaty from sleep. I tried to move so I wouldn't wake her. A couple stretches of my foot, and the tingling stopped.

In her sleep, she whispered, "Momma?"

My heart seized. Poor little Emily. She reminded me of a pint-sized me. The way I used to be. Innocent and unafraid of the world. The past six years had shown me every evil imaginable. I prayed she would never see that side of life or human nature. I didn't want her to become like me, detached and afraid to feel. Like someone had shot a double dose of Novocain in my heart.

Betty won't let that happen.

I watched Emily's peaceful face while she slept. Emily and Alice wouldn't be alone again. The muscles around my shoulders relaxed when I realized they wouldn't feel the horrible, bone-crushing emptiness and complete loneliness like I had. They had Betty now.

Betty's here for me, too.

Not if she reads my file. If she did, the pity-filled expressions and forced conversations would begin. "How are you doing, Sivan? I mean, *really*, how are you holding up?"

I'd enjoy the reprieve before she found out the truth. It was nice she didn't treat me like I would break, or worse, as though I couldn't be trusted.

For now, Betty treated me like an equal, including me in all her daily routines. After we made breakfast for the girls and they were off at school, we'd walk the same loop outside around the barn and pastures, enjoying the fresh air and changing season. Betty would tell me stories about her adopted community and how much she loved living with people who were down-to-earth and honest. She'd also made sure I came with her on every errand, grocery, hardware, and even to her hair salon, never missing the opportunity to introduce me around. She'd loop her arm around my shoulder like we belonged together.

How'd she do that? Make things feel natural? Since the day my family had died, that type of warmth and kindness were MIA. But she pulled it off in her Betty-sort-of-way that felt comfortable.

I smiled to myself remembering how she slapped a list of chores in front of me and said, "Get these done, or else," while ruffling my hair on her way out.

I laughed and answered, "Hey, I'm not five!"

Her answer? "We're all five, honey."

In eight more months, I'd no longer be a ward of the state. Eighteen. I'd been looking forward to it for a long time. But now? Not at all. I'd no longer have any ties to Betty or the girls.

I smoothed back some of the curls from Emily's sleeping face. When awake, she was a wide-eyed spark of energy. She'd be okay. Her story was different than mine. She had Alice.

"Their parents died in a tragic accident. The system planned to split them up, and I couldn't have that happen," Betty had told me.

"What happened?"

"Small plane crash. They were celebrating their anniversary." She shook her head.

"Life is hard sometimes."

She had that right.

A look at the clock confirmed I was awake too early. 6:30 a.m. Might as well get up and start feeding the animals. I carefully removed the sheets and blankets from my legs. If I was going to do this early rising thing, I'd need reinforcements. First up. Coffee.

I tucked the blankets around Emily and padded my way into the kitchen, careful not to make any noise. No Betty in sight. Good, she was sleeping in. The coffee maker tucked next to the toaster on the other side of the kitchen was my sole focus.

Three steps in, I froze. A large shadow blocked the morning sun from the kitchen table. I held my breath and turned slowly, fear deep in my gut. Slouched over, a man's head rested on the table. I scanned his appearance. A black eye, messy hair, ripped clothing . . . and was he snoring? Holy crap, a drug addict or homeless man had broken in.

My adrenaline kicked into high gear. Betty. The girls. Protection mode shoved out the remaining fuzziness. I knew exactly what needed to be done. The fire extinguisher. I'd spray him first then knock him over the head.

Chapter Five

Jax

IT'S HIM! GET HIM!

Not again. Silver braces, curly red hair, and freckles. Her eyes wild with frenzied excitement as she came at me. This time, I wasn't running. I stood tall and put my fists up. Yes, I'd punch her if she made a move. She stopped, opened her mouth, and began to scream. I covered my ears. The sound pierced through my skull, then it became a screech, breaking into syllables, kind of like . . . a rooster?

I rolled over and landed with a thump on the hardwood floor.

The screeching sound repeated.

Where am I?

Sweat covered my forehead. Wait. The lavender smell. That's right. Aunt Betty.

I'm on the farm from hell.

It wasn't even light outside yet. The screeching sound repeated. No, not a girl screaming. A rooster. Barbequed chicken flashed in my head. That sucker had crowed his last cock-a-doodle-do.

My first day, and I already planned the death of one of her animals. Not good.

I grabbed the edge of the bed, pulled myself up, lost momentum, and flopped back onto the mattress.

Ugh. A bad dream, a rooster, and hunger made my stomach feel like someone had spilled a can of acid in there. I glanced at the clock. Four a.m. *Really?*

Irritation moved to frustration and morphed into anger. I needed sleep. Damn.

The little bit of hope I'd been hanging on to evaporated. I shouldn't be here. I should be home. I groaned and threw my feet back onto the floor. After blinking a few times, I could make out the furniture and the door leading to the hallway.

I needed food, then back to sleep for at least a day. I stood and stretched. My muscles protested, objecting to being stuck in a flying tin can off and on for twenty-four hours.

I'd grab whatever cereal they had from the kitchen and head back. Five minutes tops. I opened the door and peeked out. Good. Quiet and empty. If I were back at home, I wouldn't have to sneak around like this. Bitterness bubbled, like slow-moving lava. I looked down at my clothes. Worse than I remembered. Add wrinkled to the ripped and torn fabric. Yeah, avoid meeting anyone at all costs.

The tiniest bit of light filtered in through the large window at the end of the hall. I paused, letting my eyes adjust a little more before I crept forward, toward the stairs. Once I made it to the landing, the downstairs lights made it easier.

I'd forgotten how massive this house was. The foyer branched out in three different directions. I picked one and followed it down a hall and to a door leading to a garage. On autopilot, I retraced my steps. Lack of sleep was starting to win over my hunger pangs. A vision of the comfortable bed flashed. I rubbed my eyes, ignoring the temptation to flop back into it, and chose the next hallway. Success. I flicked the light switch, and the entire room lit up.

Cereal. Cereal. Cereal.

A total inspection of every cupboard came up with nothing but organic, vegan, gluten-free Goldfish. What the hell? The refrigerator contents were a little better. But nothing already cooked. Too tired to make eggs, I sat at the long table, settling for the crackers, which turned out to taste like little pieces of cardboard. Defeated, I laid my head on the table.

Back in the water, but this time I was drowning. The red-headed, curly-haired she-devil pushes my head under the waves. Out in the ocean, miles from the shore, I was sure of my impending death. Groaning, I push up.

I opened my eyes, the dream falling away, but the water continued to assault me. Wait, it wasn't water. It was some type of foam. The chemical smell reminded me of science class. I stood, but it didn't stop.

What the hell?

The foam was smothering me. I kept my eyes covered and shouted, "Stop!"

But the spraying continued. I staggered a few steps back,

wiping it from my face and eyes. Damn, that stung.

Black hair and fierce blue eyes.

Adrenaline shot through my veins. “You!” I pointed. “You stop that shit right now or I’ll call the police!”

A mirthless chuckle. “You’ll call the police? You’re the one who broke in here. You make a move and I’ll squirt you again and then hit you with this.” She held up the fire extinguisher. Her eyes shifted to the butcher block. “Or I’ll take a knife to you. I can hit an apple from fifty yards.”

Great. Assaulted by a psycho chick. I was almost tempted to let her do her worst. But the floodgates opened instead.

“Do you think I’m afraid of some deranged, whacked-out Goth-Girl? This is my aunt’s house. Go ahead and call the police. I think jail would be better than this place. Do you think I need this crap? I don’t know who you are, but I can guarantee you haven’t been through the shit I have.” I moved farther away in case she had any more aggressive moves planned.

I should stop my rant. But the need to vent was strong. What did it matter anyway? This girl apparently was as crazy as I felt.

“I’m—” she started.

I held up my hand. “No, you stop right there. I’m talking.” I knew I was being rude, but I kept going. “My life has turned to hell. That’s right, hell. My own family exiled me to this place, I’m attacked everywhere I go, no friends, and now some girl who looks like she’s going to a funeral decides to coat me in this chemical shit. God, it’s probably poison.”

She tilted her head. “I’m not goth.”

“Okay. Emo-Girl.”

“Join the new century. I’m not emo, either.”

“Whatever. I—”

"What in the world?" Betty stood at the entrance to the kitchen, wide-eyed with her hand over her mouth.

"Aunt Betty. Who's this insane girl in your house?"

Betty's eyes crinkled. Was she trying not to laugh? This was not funny.

"Sivan, this is my nephew, Jax. Jax, Sivan."

Sivan lowered the fire extinguisher, her eyes still wary. I released a pent-up breath.

"I found out he was coming for a visit after you'd gone to bed," she told the girl. Betty pressed her lips together. Now I was sure she stifled a smile. "I guess you've already said your hellos."

"Who is she?" I pointed at my attacker, Sivan, or whatever her name was. "An over-achieving security guard?" I'd left Ray at home for this very reason.

A little humor flitted across Sivan's eyes. Her eyes. The bluest I'd ever seen. No matter. She was nuts and would probably turn out to be some fifth cousin or something.

"No, silly. She's one of my foster children."

The brain fog gave way to clarity. I'd just told a foster girl to basically shut up because my life was much harder than hers.

Yep. I was an ass.

"My mom didn't tell me. She said you had two little girls." I'd been flown across the country to avoid this very thing. I glanced at the black-haired attacker. Maybe not a fan though. She might even hate me by the look of things. Her smirk had vanished, and her eyes shot daggers my way.

"Your mom and I haven't had a chance to catch up. She finally reached me late last night." She smiled warmly at the girl. "Sivan's been here three weeks now."

That's right. Aunt Betty didn't have voicemail. Mom complained about it all the time.

"Yeah. That's great." I looked at my wet clothing then back up to Betty.

Betty met Sivan's eyes and burst out laughing, "Oh, Jax. I'm sorry, I shouldn't laugh." Her eyes traveled up and down. "What happened to you? Your clothes, oh, and you have a black eye. Sivan, did you do that?"

Sivan bit her lip and shook her head. A small laugh escaped, and she turned away.

"Breakfast!" Two small girls shouted as they ran into the kitchen. Their eyes widened when they spotted me by the table.

"Is it a snowman?" the younger one asked. Both girls looked back and forth from Sivan to Betty. The older of the two crossed the room and latched on to Sivan's leg.

Sivan answered the younger one. "No, Alice. He's trying to win the title of Most Arrogant Man in the World."

Betty snorted and covered her mouth.

The older girl asked, "What's an arogent?"

"It means he tells people not to talk because his voice is more important," Sivan answered. "It's also called an inflated ego," she added with a glare in my direction.

"Like a balloon?" the girl asked.

"Yes. All puffed up and expecting the world to revolve around him."

This must be a bad dream. No, a horror movie. "I'm standing right here."

"Unfortunately."

Betty clapped her hands together. "Okay, everyone. We're going to do this over. Jax, go upstairs and take a shower. I'll put some of Henry's old clothes on your bed. Sivan, can you get the girls breakfast before Regina takes them to school?"

She nodded.

Aunt Betty turned back to me. "Your mom called a few minutes ago. They've located your suitcases and will deliver them around noon today." She walked over and placed her hands on my cheeks. "I'm so glad you're here. You've gotten so tall. And handsome. I'll give you a proper hug and kiss after your shower. Now, go." She gave me a shove.

Yeah. I wanted to go. Straight out the door and to anywhere else. But I said, "Okay," and left for my room.

Women.

I was outnumbered. I never thought I'd miss the belching and taunting from my brothers.

I overheard Sivan say, "I'm sorry, Betty. He's just so . . ." as I left the room. I didn't stay to hear the rest. I might've said some stupid things, but that girl looked like the type to hold a grudge until the end of time, I was sure.

At least I didn't have to worry about her fan-girling over me.

I stood in the shower and let the warm water wash away the I-hate-my-life disappointment and leftover sodium bicarbonate. Thanks, Mr. Lacasse, for the 4–1-1 on fire extinguishers in tenth-grade chemistry.

The clothes, as promised, were folded and placed side-by-side on the bed. Socks, pants, a t-shirt, and . . . a velvet jacket? Not happening. I put on the pants, and they came right above my ankles. The shirt was tight, but the socks fit. Great.

The smell of eggs and bacon drifted up into the room, and my stomach growled again. Had to get the survival things, food and sleep, out of the way before I had a long talk with Mom. I needed to get out of here.

Time to head back into enemy territory.

The two little girls sat at the kitchen island while Sivan leaned over to get their empty plates. One of the girls, Emily, I thought, said something, and Sivan laughed and touched her cheek.

The world froze, and I stopped breathing. Sivan. She was . . . whoa, a knock-out. Her natural smile was different, surprising, and changed everything. Warmth replaced the frigid glare she'd given me earlier. The sunlight made her hair shine. Her pale skin looked so soft. And her eyes. God, those eyes were a brilliant shade of crystal blue. I'd never seen anything close to that color. Ever. Was I sweating? Yes. And staring. I was definitely staring.

She looked up, our eyes locked, and the warmth in hers disappeared. Back to the ice queen. Okay, so she still hated me. Fine. I could live with it. No problem.

I crossed my arms. "Where's my aunt?"

"Don't know." She turned her back to put plates into the dishwasher.

Focus on the food. I found the dish with eggs and bacon on the stove, snagged it, and started toward the kitchen table, a healthy distance from Sivan.

Before I could sit, the back door flung open, and a blonde walked in. "Emily and Alice, I'm here!" Her eyes landed on Sivan. "Oh, it's you."

Holy hell. What was it about girls in Iowa? This one could have just walked off the Miss America stage. Tall, blonde, and gorgeous.

"Good to see you too, Regina." Sivan rolled her eyes.

Ignoring Sivan, she picked up two backpacks. "I'll carry these to the car." She grabbed a piece of toast off the island with her free hand and started toward the door. "Hurry girls, or we'll be late."

She turned back around and finally noticed me standing in the middle of the room. Her eyes went wide. Not good. She dropped both backpacks and the toast. "Wait. You're—" Her face flushed, and she opened and closed her mouth a few times.

Here we go again.

Sivan's eyes widened. "What's going on? Regina, are you okay?" She looked back at me.

I shrugged, too tired for explanations.

Quick as lightning, Sivan grabbed Regina from behind, placed her fist against her stomach and pushed in.

Regina coughed and sputtered, "What the hell are you doing?" as she shoved her away.

"I thought you were choking." Sivan placed her hands on her hips.

"Do you have any idea who that is?" Regina pointed to me.

I returned their stares with a blank look. Not helping this along. She probably thought I was my brother.

"Yeah. He's an as—I mean, Betty's nephew. Why?"

I sat at the table and started to shovel food in my mouth. As long as they didn't form a mob, I might as well enjoy watching them puzzle it out.

"You know who he is. You're obviously lying. Is that why you attacked me?" Regina shouted.

"What? I was trying to save you. I thought there was toast stuck in your throat."

"Yeah. She attacked me earlier, too. She's a fiery one," I said. And, just for fun, I gave Sivan a wink.

CHAPTER Six

Sivan

COULD CHOKING SOMEONE BE CONSIDERED manslaughter instead of murder? A reduced stint in jail might be worth wiping the smug expression off his face. That cocky, self-important jerk. So what if he was good-looking? Lots of people were. Well, maybe not as hot as Jax, but still.

His dark, wavy hair and green eyes, a chiseled jaw and high cheekbones were actually annoying. And his lips? Why did they have to look so soft and full—

Stop it.

It didn't change the fact he thought the world should revolve around him.

Probably just your typical pampered, rich kid. He didn't

have the clothes, but his attitude screamed spoiled brat.

"I thought you were homeless or some drug addict." There. That should bring him down a few notches.

"What?" His overconfident smile faltered.

"Yep."

"Oh, so that's how you treat a possible homeless person?" He raised an eyebrow.

Ugh. His irritating smile returned.

"No. Only the homeless who break and enter. Who knew what you were up to? And don't forget about the drug addict part. Yeah, I think you look more like someone coming down from a meth high." I folded my arms across my chest.

Zing.

"Um. Look, Sivan." Regina glared at me. "You may have lived in a cave or something before you came to Betty's, but you can't talk to him like that."

I'd almost forgotten she was in the room. "Of course I can talk to him that way. Why would you care anyway? Do you know him?"

"Duh. Everyone knows him. He's, like, uber-famous." She rolled her eyes.

Oh, great, worse than I imagined. A spoiled, rich, pampered, and *famous* jerk.

"I'm not famous. You've mistaken me for my brother." His lips turned down into a frown.

Regina smiled like she'd just won a spelling bee. "Oh, I know who you are. You have the little scar above your right eyebrow. You're Jax."

Jax ran his hand through his hair and muttered, "I need sleep."

"I can help you with that!" Regina blurted.

Jax raised an eyebrow.

"I mean, I can turn down the bed or something." Her face flushed.

She'd turned into a tween. *Who is this guy?* An actor or some other type of entertainer?

Betty swooped into the room. "Oh good, you're still here. Regina, I have a document for you to sign."

"Me?"

"It's an NDA. The Jayne's attorney just faxed it over. We'll need your signature if you continue to work here."

"You want me to sign a non-disclosure?" Her eyes blinked slowly.

"It's standard in these situations." Betty placed the sheets of paper in front of her. "Read it over carefully. This is a legal document."

"But . . . but . . . what about Sivan? Doesn't she have to sign one, too?" Regina's eyes widened, and she fixed her stare on me.

Betty ignored her question. "You can take this home tonight and have your parents' attorney look it over if you want. I'm asking you not to tell anyone that Jax is here, not a soul. If it gets out, he'll have to leave."

Betty's last three words would guarantee her silence. I chuckled to myself. Betty was a sly one.

"I won't tell anyone. I promise." She turned her eyes to Jax. "It will be our secret."

He smiled and shook his head a little. "Thanks, um . . . Regina?"

"Yes! Regina. That's my name."

I wanted to stuff cotton in my ears and keep my eyes shut until Regina left the room. So what if he was famous? Regina falling all over him made me want to gag.

Betty gave Regina a pat on her back. “Okay, it’s time for the girls to get to school.”

I’d never seen Emily and Alice so quiet. They sat on their stools, watching, and maybe waiting for Regina to make a bigger fool of herself. Even children knew when a train wreck was unfolding.

“Okay. Sure. Yes. I’ll get their backpacks.” She picked them up off the floor and turned toward Jax. “Will you be here when I drop them off this afternoon?”

She stood as still as a statue. Was she holding her breath?

“I’ll be in bed. I mean, I’ll be sleeping.” He rubbed the back of his neck. “No. Sorry. I need to catch up on my sleep.”

“There’ll be plenty of time to get to know each other.” Betty started to herd Emily and Alice to the door.

“I’ll see you later?” Regina’s green eyes had a puppy-dog look to them.

“Yeah. Bye.” He gave a little wave.

Regina left the room, her feet dragging with the two girls behind her. As soon as the door closed, Betty looked at me, her eyes crinkling. I sucked in a deep breath, but it couldn’t be stopped. We broke out into fits of laughter.

“Oh dear Lord, does that happen often?” Betty asked Jax.

Jax groaned, and his eyes drifted toward mine. I tried to stifle my giggles, but Regina’s performance was comical.

“You two think this is funny?”

“Yes!” I answered, which made Betty laugh harder.

He narrowed his eyes, crossed his arms, and tapped his foot.

Betty regained her composure and cleared her throat. “We aren’t laughing at you, Jax. I hope you know that. It’s just, I’ve never seen Regina act that way before. You’ve got to admit, she lost her marbles over you a bit.”

A bit?

Jax continued to tap his foot, but his stare appeared vacant. Was he asleep standing up?

“Jax, sweetie. Let’s get you to bed. You look like you’re about to drop.”

He nodded once, turned, and walked to the back door. He would go outside if Betty didn’t stop him.

“This way, Jax.” Betty guided him by his arms in the right direction.

Maybe his poor-little-me complain-fest was due to lack of sleep?

No. He had that whiny outburst locked and loaded.

A few minutes later, Betty came back into the kitchen. I’d finished loading the breakfast dishes and had the counters sparkling.

“Whew. Got Jax all tucked in. That boy is exhausted. Hopefully, after some sleep he’ll feel better about things. I don’t believe he has a very good impression of us so far. What do you think?”

Well, I had a horrible impression of him. But I’d keep that to myself.

“It could’ve gone better.” I smiled.

“My sister will worry about him if he doesn’t want to stay. We have to do something.” She scrunched her nose. “I know. How about that pudding pie you made the girls last week? You know, win him over by way of his stomach.”

"You'll bend your rules about sugar?"

"For this, yes. Consider the once a month sugar rule lifted until further notice."

"Emily and Alice will be thrilled."

"But keep it organic, okay?"

"Done."

"How about we move to the porch for a little talk."

My stomach went *splat* on the floor.

"I know you're not a big fan of these types of chats, but it's important I get your input." She motioned me to follow her.

I could rebel and not follow. I paused for a second, but my feet disobeyed and started the trek down the hall toward the porch. Why couldn't I be like the typical, angst-filled, teenage foster child I read about in my psychology books?

Betty. She's making me weak. Or maybe she's helping to make me stronger?

She snagged a blanket from the couch on our way out and threw it to me. "Here, it's a little chilly today."

"Thanks. What about you?"

She waved her hand in the air. "It's balmy for me. Wait for the winter to hit." Betty opened the door and paused so I could go first.

"Let's sit on the swing. It's relaxing."

A chat where I needed to be relaxed. Only one problem; I was strung tighter than a bow.

Breathe, Sivan. Nothing bad will ever come from Betty.

We both sat, and Betty gave a little push with her feet. The swing started a slow, rocking motion. "That's better." She leaned toward me. "First, the most important question is—are you okay?"

"It's been a bit of a hectic day, but I'm good." Well, not really.

"You've already told me about the trigger." She reached for my hand. "Is that for all ages, or does Jax—"

"It's okay, Betty. The trigger is for older men living in the same house. I'm fine with guys my age. I've dated a little." I shrugged.

"I'm sorry you didn't get a warning first." A small smile began to form at the corner of her lips. "But we would have missed the epic spray-down."

"About that . . . I'm sorry. I thought—"

"I know what you thought. I don't blame you. I would've done the same."

"Really?"

"Of course. A strange man in our home? I might've hit him over the head."

"That was my plan." I laughed.

"I know he came off rather . . ."

"Like a jerk?" I put a hand over my mouth and cringed. "Oops. Kinda slipped."

Betty smiled and put her head back against the cushion. "He's a good kid. This past year's been rough for him. Charley, my sister, told me he might arrive a little irritable."

"She was right. He was rude and—" I decided to let it stop there. He was her nephew after all.

"I'm not sure what he said or did, but Charley told me he was attacked at the airport and they had to divert him to Boise. It took almost twenty-four hours to get here." Betty held up her hand. "It isn't an excuse for rudeness. But I think he was a little sleep deprived."

"He was attacked? What happened?" I guess that explained his black eye and ripped clothing.

"His fans got a little excited, and he didn't have enough security." She shook her head.

"Is that why he's here? Hiding out?"

"Exactly. If he's willing to stay . . ." she paused, " . . . he'll be here for the rest of the school year."

It was early October. *Oh hell. That long?*

"Does his presence here make you uncomfortable in any way?"

Yeah, but not for the reason she thought. I just didn't like snobby people. He'd look down his nose and judge me like the others. Or worse, pity me.

"No, it'll be fine. I'll be fine. And, Betty?"

"Yes, honey?"

"If you want to have a boyfriend, please don't let me stop you. I trust your judgment. I know you put the girls first and wouldn't bring around anyone who wasn't . . ."

She rubbed my arm. "Thank you, Sivan. It means a lot to me." Her gaze drifted out onto the pastures. "I won't ever date."

"You're still so young," I blurted.

"You girls, my animals, the food bank. It's enough for me."

I nodded. She'd included me in with Emily and Alice. My chest warmed.

Breathe, Sivan. She just meant for now.

"Let's go walk the fence."

The fence encircled the area for about a mile around the pastures. I loved walking the loop in the morning. The remaining dew, the smell of hay coming from the barn, wildflowers left over from summer, and, more than anything, the feeling of the farm on my skin. It was heavenly.

"You'll both be homeschooled this year."

Jax around twenty-four-seven? No, thank you.

Think. There must be a way to get rid of him at least for part of the day.

"Really? Won't he go to the high school? I'm sure the kids around here won't bother him. It's a small town." Not such a great argument. Regina was in her first year of college, with a four-point-oh grade point average, and I was sure she'd lost half her brains cells in a matter of minutes.

We passed the barn with the familiar smell of horses. I took a deep breath as we turned toward the east fence. A clear day, so I could see the pastures stretch out for miles.

"His mom is concerned for him. Not just about the social environment. His studies last year didn't go well. His junior year was a disaster."

"Drugs?

"Oh, no. The band."

Not an actor, a musician.

Universe, are you there? Why are you torturing me?

I'd found the perfect place with Betty and the girls. I'd felt safe for the first time in forever. My stomach twisted. *Music.* Jax would ruin everything.

"The band?" I managed to squeak out.

"Yes. See?" She pointed to her shirt.

What? I took a closer look. "Why is Jax on your shirt?"

"No, it's his twin brother, Gage."

"Oh."

"Charley has four boys, and the three oldest formed a band. Have you heard of The Jaynes?"

I shook my head.

Betty smiled. "I didn't think so. I remember you don't like boy bands."

My cheeks burned. "No offense to your nephews. I'm sure they're talented." I'd insulted her family without even knowing it.

She chuckled. "None taken. Anyway, Jax decided he didn't want any part of it. The type of music he prefers is a little different than his brothers. Indie rock. Are you familiar with that type of music?"

"Yes." It was the only music I found at least a little tolerable.

We'd reached the halfway point of our walk. The northeast corner had all the prettiest wildflowers. "Can I pick a few for the house?"

"Of course. These flowers won't last much longer. The chill has already set in."

After collecting an armful of every conceivable color and size, I asked, "Why was Jax attacked in the airport? Did the fans of The Jaynes mistake him for his twin brother?"

"We all thought the same thing when this first started. But, as it turns out, he has a following of his own."

"Why? Has he released any of his own songs?"

"No. The opposite. He's refused to play since last May. His mom is quite concerned."

He's shut out music just like me.

"So, this following of his is because . . . ?"

Betty shrugged. "Your guess is as good as mine. All I know is, Jax doesn't like it."

Oh. Now I understood a little about his rant.

Didn't mean I would ever like him. Nope. Not going to happen. Someone needed to convince him, or Betty, or his parents, that he was better off back where he came from.

CHAPTER Seven

JAX

SHE HATES ME. HARD.

First, it was the botched "famous" pudding pie she served me. Who mixes up sugar with salt? Sure, they're both white, but Sivan was supposed to be this great cook. Her wide-eyed expression and apologies with hand over heart didn't fool me. The mischievous gleam in her eye gave her away.

Then it was the chicken eggs that mysteriously found their way into my outdoor boots. I shoved one foot in before discovering the broken shell and slimy goo. Sivan's face held the same innocent expression when she suggested perhaps the dog had dropped them in. Only if the dog's name was Sivan would I believe that one.

It would've been kinda funny because I loved a good prank,

but the fact she really wanted me gone gnawed at me.

"Would you just stop it!" Sivan's voice cut through my distracted thoughts.

"What?"

Her eyes darted to Betty and the girls. She lowered her voice, "The pacing. I think you've walked five indoor miles today. What's the deal? Why don't you go outside?"

Outside? What would I do out there?

I hadn't realized I was bothering her until she shouted at me. The family room was the biggest room in the house, perfect for stretching my legs and letting off steam.

On the farm for ten days, and I was going out of my mind. The rules about technology, basically no Internet except for homework, had started to get old. Aunt Betty's television wasn't hooked up to cable. The evening entertainment consisted of watching movies like *Frozen* from an old DVD player. Not on my "must see" list.

Aunt Betty looked up from her book. "Takes time for the mind to slow. Give it another week." She glanced at Sivan. "Maybe we could start him in on the farm chores?"

Sivan shook her head. "No need. I've got the animals covered."

Wait. "Animals?"

Sivan rolled her eyes. "In the barn. You know, like a five-minute walk from the house?"

"Are you talking about the rooster?" I still had plans for him.

"The rooster, hens, pigs, goats, and horses."

"Aunt Betty? Last time I was here you didn't have animals."

She shrugged and wiped the corner of her eye. "Lots of things changed after . . ."

Damn. Uncle Henry.

"I love animals!" I about yelled.

Sivan's head popped up, and her eyes narrowed for a moment. "Great. I think we should start him on cleaning out the pen." Her smile was soft and sweet, but the glint in her eye—pure mischief. "The pigpen."

Why did I come out of my room?

Betty chuckled. "We have the farmhand, Mark, who does the pens. How about brushing down the horses? That should be a good start."

I turned back to Sivan and gave her my best you-don't-scare-me look. "I can do the pens. That's not a problem."

Sivan cocked her head. "Good. I'll get you the shovel."

"You know what," Betty said as she got out of her chair. "I think you have a fantastic idea, Sivan. Let's give Mark a break."

Fun times ahead.

"And we have two shovels, one for each of you. Isn't that great?" She raised an eyebrow and smiled.

Sivan shook her head.

Busted. Aunt Betty knew what she was up to. She motioned for us both to follow. We trailed behind her, and I tried not to laugh at Sivan's latest plot to trip me up. She gave me a death glare.

"This is your fault," I whispered.

"Ugh!" She stomped as she followed.

Betty led us out of the house toward the huge barn. A small tool shed was tucked along the backside. She opened the door and reached in for the two shovels and work gloves.

Smiling, Betty held them out for each of us to take. Sivan

muttered, "Thanks," while she put on the gloves and grabbed a shovel. I did the same with a smile.

Pigpen? No problem. This wouldn't be so bad. I liked seeing the tables turn on Sivan for once.

Aunt Betty started her trek back to the house. About halfway, she turned and said, "You might as well do the horse stalls while you're at it. Thanks!" With a wave, she left.

"I think you may have fallen off Aunt Betty's most favorite list." I chuckled.

"What do you mean by that?" Her cheeks flushed pink.

"She's having you clean out pig and horse shit with me."

"No. I mean the most-favorite comment. I'm not her favorite."

"Are you kidding? I've never seen two people get along so well. It's like you're twins separated at birth."

A line creased between her brows.

"Not in the physical sense. You know, simpatico, in-sync, on the same page. That sorta thing."

"Betty gets along with everyone."

Didn't she see it? Aunt Betty loved Sivan. I could tell. It was the same way my Mom treated me. A twist of guilt squeezed my stomach. I hadn't called my parents in three days.

"Yeah—never mind. Do you want to get this over with?" I motioned toward the pen.

She blew out a breath. "Yes. Let's do it." She threw her shoulders back and trudged to the pen behind the barn. "I've seen Mark do this a couple times. It shouldn't be too hard. We just need to get in, scoop up the wet hay and pieces of . . ." She paused and bit her lip.

"Shit?"

"I was going to say excrement."

"Aren't you proper. No swearing?" I laughed. Why did I enjoy irritating her? Probably because she always seemed to have a tight hold on her emotions; it made me want to break through.

"I don't need to use swear words. They're so cliché."

Damn. Darn. *No, damn.*

She tilted her head and studied me. "You're swearing in your head right now, aren't you?"

Smart-ass.

"Yes." I smiled, and we locked eyes.

For a split second, her eyes softened. She blinked a few times and rubbed her hand over her neck. "I guess we'd better get started." She motioned to the pen.

My heart pounded. Why did she have to be so damn beautiful? She was fiery, yet seemed vulnerable when she didn't have her guard up. It made me want to pull her to me and . . . ugh.

Try to remember she hates you.

"I'll do it. You can go back to the house."

She turned sharply toward me. "What?"

"It's okay. I don't mind. I really do love animals." Well, except for the rooster.

"Loving animals and cleaning up after them are two different things." She laughed and paused for a moment. "Are you trying to trick me into thinking you're a nice guy?"

Well, that was insulting. "I am a good guy."

"I'm not saying you're bad or anything. Maybe just a little self-centered?"

"You've known me for ten days. Already made up your mind?"

"I'm a pretty good judge of character. And . . ." She glanced back toward the house.

"I'm not the person you met on the first day. Well, maybe a little bit. I haven't been myself since my brothers formed their band. But I plan to change that." I took a deep breath. "Even though I've only been here for a short time, I can already feel the difference."

"But you still want to go back home, right?" Her eyes lit up, and she leaned forward. "You seem restless."

"No. That's just me working things out in my head. I like to pace when I'm thinking."

Her shoulders slumped a little.

"I get it. You want me gone."

She pursed her lips, and I watched in fascination as one emotion after another crossed her face. Denial. Defensiveness. Anger. After expelling a deep breath came . . . resignation. And the last expression appeared to be pity. Great. An all new low for me.

"Not gone from the planet or anything. Just the farm." She let out a little laugh.

Whenever she smiled, which wasn't often around me, was like a punch to the gut. Why did she fascinate me so much? Why did I want to be around her all the time? My physical reaction to her confused me. The girls I dated before had always been the same. Blonde hair, green eyes. They were easy to figure out. Simple. Sivan was the opposite.

She's not my type.

I rubbed my chest, willing my heart to slow.

"Okay. So, you don't wish me dead. We're moving in the right direction."

She chuckled, shook her head, and pointed to the pen. "I got you into this. So, let's get it done."

"Are you sure? I'm willing to let you off the hook, you know. You can go back to the house. I can do this on my own."

"Yeah, yeah." She ignored me and opened the gate.

The smell inside the pen was horrible, but not horrible at the same time. It had an earthiness mixed with cedar shavings. I took a deep breath and let my shoulders relax. This is all I needed to do? Come join the pigs?

"Ewww." Sivan's face scrunched, and she put her hand over her mouth. "Gross!"

I laughed. "This isn't so bad. Look, there're only a few pieces of sh—I mean, excrement."

She shook her head again and went right to work with one hand over her nose the entire time.

"It'll go faster if you use two hands."

"You think?" She wiped her forehead.

"My offer still stands. I'll finish up."

Sivan's eyes narrowed. "I'm not a quitter. Even when I want to."

Had to respect that. I nodded.

After we were done, I pointed to the full wheelbarrow. "Where do we dump this?"

"Over there." She motioned to a large receptacle about twenty yards away. "I think they recycle it into fertilizer."

We finished the rest within ten minutes. "That was easy."

"Speak for yourself. That was disgusting."

"So, you won't be staying on with Aunt Betty, living the life of a farmer?"

I knew I'd made a mistake when her face fell into an expression I could only describe as lost.

"No, umm. I turn eighteen in May, and then I'll be on my own. I haven't decided what I'll do yet."

"I want to be a vet," I blurted. Where the hell did that come from? I hadn't told a soul about it yet.

Her eyebrow arched. "You?"

"Is that so hard to believe?"

She studied me for a moment. "You're just full of surprises, aren't you?"

"I believe the word you're looking for is mysterious."

"Oh God. You're back to being full of yourself. Were you joking about the vet thing?"

"Nope. I've applied to a couple pre-vet schools for next fall." What the hell? Why did I keep talking? "But I haven't said anything to anyone. So, if you could maybe not mention it?"

She smiled again. But this time, her eyes crinkled, and it was genuine. When her face transformed like that, my body, God, it went into full meltdown. She was striking and smoking hot. I glimpsed at her lips for a split second and imagined kissing her.

You idiot. She hates you. Snap out of it.

"I knew a vet once, a long time ago. He really loved it." She just about glowed. "You really do love animals?"

"Yeah." Except for that damn rooster. "I think my mom would blow a gasket if she knew though. I think she's still holding out hope for a music career for me."

"Really?" She cocked her head.

"You haven't met my family yet. It's all about the music. Growing up, we were either taking lessons, playing, or writing lyrics. It's been the same since the day I was born." I sighed. "Don't get me wrong. I love it. Or at least I did. I just don't know anymore."

She didn't answer right away, instead staring out at the pasture beyond the barn. "I think all moms just want their kids to be happy. She'll be okay."

Sometimes Sivan acted young, like her age, but, other times, she seemed much older. A complete contrast to her stubborn, bratty side.

"I think there will definitely be a period of unhappiness before that happens." I wanted to steer the conversation away from any talk about my mom. I sounded like a big jerk complaining when she had lost her parents. "Where are the horse stalls?"

"This way. George and Bailey are the best. Follow me." She opened one of the large barn doors, and I followed her inside the entrance. The light was dim, so it took a minute before our eyes could adjust.

Again, the sweet smell of hay acted as a calming agent. "George and Bailey?" Why did those names sound familiar?

"Betty named them after her favorite character. You know, from *It's a Wonderful Life*?"

A light bulb went on. "Oh yeah. My mom makes us watch that movie every year. I can't believe I didn't recognize it right off."

"Betty had us watch it twice already, and it's only October." Sivan rolled her eyes.

"Sounds like my mom."

"Are they close? Your mom and Betty?"

"They're different, but yes, very close. That's why I was shipped out here. She's the only one my mom trusts."

She nodded slowly, not meeting my eyes. I motioned toward the stalls. "So, George and Bailey?"

"Oh, right." She snapped out of whatever had her in deep thought.

"Bailey is in foal. We'll need to be careful around her. She's been a little skittish. I think she's pretty close—maybe a week or two."

"Sure, no problem." Could I handle another skittish female?

"We'll need to take them out of their stall first and into an empty one. Have you been around horses before?"

"A few times." Like, never.

"Okay, we'll move Bailey first. She should still have her bridle on." She slowly opened the stall door. "Oh no." Her face went sheet white.

"What? What's wrong?" Just past her shoulder in one of the stalls, a huge black horse on its side thrashed around. A large wet area surrounded her lower half. That couldn't be good. "That's Bailey?"

"I think she might be ready to deliver. Look, her water has broken. But I don't think this is normal. Can you go get Betty? I'll see if I can get her settled down."

I was out the barn door in seconds. I rushed to the house and burst through the back kitchen door.

Aunt Betty jumped and dropped an oven mitt on the floor. "Jax! You scared me. Don't barge into the house like that. I about had a—"

"Sorry. It's Bailey. The horse. Sivan thinks she might be about to deliver. You should come," I spit out.

She turned toward the family room. “Emily, Alice. Get your boots, we’re going to the barn.” She grabbed a coat from the hook. “Don’t panic. I’ll call Dr. Petrie. I’m sure he can get over here in a few minutes.”

I wasn’t panicking, not quite yet, but close.

She gathered the girls together and began to put on their coats and hats.

“We should probably hurry.” My breathing increased. Would the horse be okay?

A quick glance my way and she moved into action. She threw the coats into the girls’ arms and started out the door. “Come on, girls. We’ll finish putting your coats on when we get to the barn.”

“But I’m cold,” Emily complained.

We’d been outside for about two seconds. “Here.” I took the coat and held it out for her. Aunt Betty gave me a nod and continued to the barn without us.

“Thanks, Jax,” Emily said as she wrapped her little arms around my leg.

“No problem, squirt.” I rubbed her head. “Let’s go see if Bailey needs us.”

“Bailey is going to have a baby! Will it be tonight?” Emily asked.

I hoped not.

“Maybe. Betty will call the vet and we’ll see.”

“Yay!” Alice clapped her little hands.

I’d forgotten what it was like, being so young and innocent. No worries, except maybe where they’d lost their Barbie. All I could think about right now were a hundred ways things could go south with Bailey.

Back at the barn, the first thing I noticed was Sivan's worried face. She wrung her hands. "Betty said Dr. Petrie can't come. He's out of state, and the on-call vet is in the hospital with a possible heart attack." Betty had her back to us, clutching the phone in one hand and gesturing with the other.

I would have a heart attack if someone didn't get here soon. Didn't most horses need intervention when they birthed? "What should we do?" I looked back into the stall, and Bailey was still lying down. She seemed a little calmer, but her breathing sounded labored.

Betty shouted from the phone, "Jax! You're the strongest and have the longest arms. You're going to deliver this foal."

No. No way. Hell no. Not gonna happen. I'd rather—

"It looks like you're going to get a chance to practice being a vet," Sivan whispered.

"I was talking about the domestic-type veterinarian practice. You know, like dogs and cats. Or maybe a gerbil now and then."

"Oh. Well, it looks like you're going to work your way down to that."

Kill me now.

Chapter Eight

Sivan

JAX CROSSED HIS ARMS AND shook his head as Betty told us how things would go down.

"Dr. Petrie will talk us through it." Betty turned to me. "Can you walk Emily and Alice out? The neighbors are going to take them for a few hours."

"Sure. Come on, girls." Thank goodness. I didn't want Emily and Alice around if anything went wrong.

Relax, Sivan. Things don't always go bad.

"Can we see the baby horse when we get back?" Emily's big, hopeful eyes made my stomach sink.

Please, don't let the foal die. No. Don't pray. Almost forgot;

prayers didn't work.

Even when an eleven-year-old girl prayed her heart out for her family.

Either God didn't care or forgot I existed. I bit my lip as sadness surged through me.

"The baby horse might need to go to the vet. We'll have to wait and see." Might as well prepare them now, just in case.

Emily, seemingly unaffected, threw a piece of hay into the air. "Can we give her a carrot when we get back?"

I shrugged. "I'm not sure the foal can eat so soon. But how about you'll be the first carrot-giver?"

"Okay!" She took her sister's hand. "Come on, Alice, let's go. Mrs. Thompson has cookies."

Well, that was easy.

I loaded the girls into the Thompson's car and hurried back to the stall.

"The water has broken, so we have only twenty or thirty minutes at the most. Get going!" Betty had stretched the phone cord and positioned herself just outside the stall.

Jax came out of his trance. "Okay." He swallowed. "Okay." Sweat glistened on his forehead, and the color drained from his face.

I stepped in the stall next to Jax. "I'll help you." I offered. Why did I say that? I knew nothing about this stuff.

"Thanks. I have no idea what I'm doing." He reached over to take my hand.

"Don't." I pulled away.

"Sorry. I thought, uh . . ." He ran his hand through his hair "I don't know what I was thinking. Sorry."

"Let's just get this done, all right?" I needed to keep distance between us. Tingles and a rapid heartbeat kicked in whenever he was around. Attraction? No, couldn't be. If Jax found out I had mixed feelings, his ego would probably burst.

"Jax!" Betty shouted.

"I got it," he yelled back.

We both entered the stall slowly, trying not to spook Bailey. "I'll talk to her while you see how things are going." I pointed to where it looked like a foot was starting to stick out.

Jax's eyes widened. He took a deep breath and squatted down next to her. "I can see two feet," he called to Betty.

"Two feet are showing," she said to Dr. Petrie. She nodded. "Jax, are the soles pointing down or up?

His brows scrunched together as he examined the two feet poking out. "Up," he answered.

"He said up," Betty told the doctor. Her face transformed from her usual calm to worry. "Are you sure? Dystocia?" She frowned. "Jax, you're going to need to reposition the foal."

Jax's wide eyes met mine. His head swerved back to Betty. "Aunt Betty, I've never been around a horse before. How the hell am I going to reposition?"

Sweat poured down his face. He shook out his hands.

"I'll try to calm Bailey while you do whatever you need to." I wiped my palms on my jeans before pointing to where the feet were sticking out. I didn't envy him. I moved closer to Bailey's head. "Hey, girl. It's okay. We've got you," I said in my most soothing voice, but it trembled.

She thrashed violently and rolled to her other side. Whoa. I jumped out of the way. *Well, that didn't work.*

Jax focused solely on Bailey as he approached her, his voice low. "Don't worry. I'll take care of you." He pushed up his sleeves and inhaled deeply. With a steady, low-pitched voice, he continued to talk, and Bailey finally calmed back down.

"What are you, a horse whisperer or something?" I asked, slightly insulted his voice calmed her when mine didn't.

A slight lift of his lips didn't waver his concentration. "Okay, Aunt Betty. Give it to me. What's next?"

She pointed to the sink. "Okay, first you'll need to wash your hands and arms up to your shoulders in that sink over there." She continued to nod into the phone, stopping to ask, "Really?" She glanced back at Jax. "You're going to reach up and turn the foal so the soles are pointed down.

He finished washing his hands and asked, "All the way up?"

"Yes, all the way up and in." She grimaced. "But you'll need to wait and do it between her contractions. Once you've turned the foal, make sure the legs are slightly staggered. That will help when they go through the birth canal."

This was where his long arms would come in handy.

"Oh God." He walked back into the stall and sat down next to Bailey. "Uh, Betty?"

"Yes?"

"What's a contraction?" His voice rose a little.

Betty held up a finger and turned away for a moment. I heard her whisper to the doctor, "He doesn't know what a contraction is. Should we switch?" She nodded into the phone a few times and finally said, "Okay."

I kneeled back down by Bailey's head, hoping my familiar presence would comfort her.

Betty turned back around. "Jax, I'm going to walk you through this step by step. Don't worry. With your arms and strength, Dr. Petrie thinks you're the best one to do this."

Jax positioned himself, took another deep breath, and said, "I'm ready."

"Put your hand on her belly and wait until it tightens. That's a contraction."

My heart froze, then pounded as I watched Jax go to work. He waited for her contraction to end then reached in. Bailey groaned, and Jax's breathing became labored, almost like Bailey's, as he strained to reposition the foal.

Go, Jax. You can do this.

After a few minutes of grunting and groaning from both, Jax wiped his brow with the back of his sleeve. "I think I've done it. What now?"

"Yes, doctor," she said into the phone. Her eyes locked onto Jax. "Now you're going to pull that sucker out."

"Just pull? On both legs?"

"Yes. We don't have much time. Pull!"

Jax pulled and grunted and tugged some more. Finally, one shoulder appeared then another, followed by a nose, and the rest of the foal plopped out.

Jax stared at the foal with bulging eyes. "Oh my God. It's out!"

"You did it!" I clapped.

Please, please, let it be alive.

The foal was covered in a white sac-like substance. Was that normal?

"What do I do with this?" Jax asked Betty, pointing at the whitish material covering the foal.

"You puncture and rip away the amniotic membrane. Hurry,

Jax. We need to make sure the foal gets oxygen." She checked her watch.

He wiped his brow and reached down to an opening by one of the feet and started to peel back the stretchy, white sac. It was kinda disgusting, but I couldn't take my eyes off them. "It's breathing. Aunt Betty, it's alive!"

Emotion took over and tears immediately formed. I swallowed a few times in an effort not to fall apart.

Betty put her hand over her heart. "Thank God." Her eyes shined bright.

Jax smiled that charming smile of his. The innocent, boyish one. And was that a dimple in his cheek? Warmth flooded my body, and my nerve endings tingled. That smile was dangerously attractive, especially now.

"Do we cut the cord or something?" he asked Betty.

How was he not freaking out?

Betty conferred with the doctor.

"No. Dr. Petrie said it will detach naturally. We need to give them both time to recuperate. They should start moving around in about ten minutes."

Ten minutes turned into fifteen, and we all watched the mother and foal like expectant parents. Jax paced, I wrung my hands together, and Betty would say, "Come on, girl. Get up," every few minutes.

My pulse was galloping appropriately. Jax finally stopped pacing, and instead stared at the pair as if he willed them to get up. His stance stayed rigid, with hands on each hip, those full lips pulled in, and his intense eyes locked on both, unwavering.

On shaky legs, the foal stood. Soon after, Bailey gave one last groan and got up.

Thank you, God.

Betty whooped and gave each of us a high five. "Excellent job, you two. We make a great team."

I held my hands up. "This was all Jax."

Her smiling eyes shifted to Jax. "I'm so proud of you. A natural if I've ever seen one!"

Jax just shrugged her off, but I saw him hide a smile.

"Okay, you two, I'm headed out. I'm sure Emily and Alice are climbing the walls by now, driving poor Mrs. Thompson crazy." Betty grabbed her sweater. "I'll be back in a few."

"See you when you get back." I waved.

Jax turned to me. "Will you be okay for about ten minutes while I go take a quick shower?" He laughed and held out his arms.

The excitement distracted me, so I hadn't noticed he was covered in slime and goo. "Yes. Get out of here." I smiled, and gave him the *shoo* motion.

"Give me a call on the intercom if anything happens. They look pretty good, don't you think?" His eyes went soft as he glanced over at Bailey and her foal.

"They're great. Nice work, Doctor Jayne."

He smiled and winked before he left.

Why did that make my stomach do all sorts of flip flops? I smoothed my hair back, straightened my shoulders, and stood outside the stall to watch over Bailey and her new foal.

The birth was the coolest thing I'd ever seen. Jax blew me away. Betty was right, a natural.

Relax, Sivan. You can ignore Jax and those stupid feelings.

I wouldn't let him get to me. I had willpower. So what if he was handsome and somewhat charming? He also wanted to be a vet and was good with animals. Ugh. I wished I could banish that last part from my brain.

A vet.

A comfortable warmth began to start before I could stop it.

No, he'd probably change his mind and join his brothers in the band. With his looks and personality, he'd be certain to be a big hit. He already was according to Regina, so the easy way would be to follow along in his brothers' footsteps.

A follower? Not him. He was as stubborn as a glob of sticky gum in hair. That guy would not take no for an answer. I'd already seen him in action with Betty. He'd been able to get her to relax her sugar ban, something I never thought would happen. She didn't know it, but he had her wrapped around his finger. He could sell beef patties to a vegetarian, I was sure.

"Hey."

I jumped back a foot and rammed my elbow into the wood enclosure. "Ouch. Don't sneak up on me."

Jax held both hands up and laughed. "I didn't. You seemed like you were in a different world. What were you thinking about?"

You. "Nothing."

He pointed to Bailey and her newborn. "That was spectacular, right?"

"Yeah." The best thing I'd ever seen.

"I've never felt so, I don't know . . . alive." His eyes danced, and he grinned like he was the happiest person on earth. He took both my shoulders. "Wasn't that amazing? Don't you feel awesome?"

"Yes." My breath left me. "I feel pretty great."

He stopped suddenly. His gaze intense. "You know what would make this day perfect?"

"Hmm?" My emotions swirled in a pleasant haze.

His hands tightened on my shoulders. He glanced down at my lips.

What was he thinking?

He moved closer, his clean and woodsy body wash filled my senses. A fluttery, nervous sensation hit my stomach.

Danger! Alert!

His eyes had me locked in his gaze. So intense. I couldn't look away. For the first time, I noticed his piercing green eyes had little flecks of grey and gold. Such beautiful—

Don't look!

I moved back a foot. He moved forward and reached to touch a lock of my hair. "So soft."

The big fat wall I'd built started to crumble a bit. I *wanted* to kiss him. I'd been staring at his lips since he arrived. It wouldn't hurt, would it? Just one?

He leaned in, his lips just a breath away. "Say yes."

I closed my eyes for a second.

Mistake.

The memory of Ronald Kent—"Daddy"—flashed before me, and my breath caught. A deep revulsion swept through my body, ice cold. I went into autopilot, and my knee went up. Jax buckled forward, and I spun around and landed a roundhouse kick, leaving him curled up on the floor.

"We're back!" shouted Emily as the trio entered the barn.

Oh God. I just used Tae Kwon Do against Jax. I'd been wrong when I thought he would ruin everything. I just destroyed any chances of staying here. Wrote myself a one-way ticket out by assaulting Betty's nephew. Nausea formed in the pit of my stomach, and heat flushed through my body.

What have I done?

Betty's head veered back and forth between Jax and me, her eyes wide and questioning.

"I'm so—"

"I have a cramp!" Jax shouted.

He moved his hand from his crotch and placed it on his leg.

A cramp? I just kicked him—oh. My heart took a little tumble when I realized what he was doing.

"Yeah. Sivan was just going to the house to get me the heating pad. Right, Sivan?" He stayed curled up, but seemed to be coming out of the worst of it. My tense muscles relaxed a little.

Think, brain. "Heating pad. Right. I'm getting that now. I'll be back." I turned and ran from the barn.

After finding the pad and placing it in the microwave, I sat at the island and put my head in my hands.

I'd been trying to make Jax's life miserable since he arrived. He had the perfect chance to get rid of me. Why didn't he take it?

Wait. He wanted to kiss me. Probably riding an adrenaline high. I was just in the line of fire. I rubbed my hands over my face. That must be it. Spontaneous insanity.

Who was more insane, Jax for trying to kiss me, or me for wanting it to happen? Why? I didn't like him. Not even a little.

Maybe a little.

I tapped the counter, waiting for the timer to go off. Perhaps I did like a few things about Jax. When he wasn't all whiny, he was kinda funny in a sarcastic, dry humor sort of way. He never got angry with me for my little pranks. He'd tease me a little, but that was it.

Maybe he wasn't the person I thought he was. Maybe I just wanted him to be spoiled and entitled. If he were a total jerk, I could convince myself it was nothing. A crazy anomaly.

But Jax isn't a complete jerk.

Great. These feelings might be real.

An overwhelming fear gripped me right in the center of my chest. I doubled over and put my head on the counter. Worst case scenario? I'd do something stupid, like fall for him. He'd go off and live his life once he graduated, or he'd—

Stop thinking about it.

Where had my defenses gone? Jax had distracted me, and I'd let my guard down.

I'd go back to numb. Numb was safe.

CHAPTER Nine

JAX

THREE WEEKS LATER, AND I was still pissed.

Rejection. I hated it. Physically, I'd recovered. It took a few days, but eventually I could walk without a limp.

In the library, Sivan sat across from me, staring at her laptop while tapping her pencil against her lips. Like I needed anything more to draw my eyes there.

Aunt Betty had pushed two desks together, and our chairs were pointed toward each other. Surrounded by overstuffed furniture, and floor-to-ceiling bookcases, the room should have been chill. But my stomach was in knots. Was Sivan tense, too?

I studied her for the millionth time. Our mandatory two-hour study sessions were driving me insane. Aunt Betty, in another attempt to shun technology, refused to have a wireless router installed. Instead, Sivan and I had to come into the library between nine and eleven in the morning to use the dial-up Internet. Our afternoons were for writing essays and math, usually in our separate rooms.

I shot Sivan another quick glance. Biting her lip, she wore a slight frown as she continued to peer at her laptop.

Damn.

Why couldn't I shake off this attraction? Her feelings toward me seemed to bounce from dislike to indifference. Sometimes she had a look of confusion—those were the good days. Mostly, it appeared she wanted to be anywhere else. She'd barely spoken to me since the birth of the foal.

The library door flung open, and Aunt Betty approached the desks. She wore her usual colorful clothing, but her smile was a little off. "Okay, you two. I got your recent test scores back."

Sivan's eyebrows rose.

"Okay," I answered.

"Jax, you scored seventy-nine percent on your last calculus test. Sivan's was a hundred percent." She glanced at me first, and then at Sivan. "Sivan, you scored eighty-one percent in chemistry and Jax scored ninety-eight."

The last sentence made Sivan's scowl deepen.

"You know what that means," Aunt Betty said.

"We need to study harder?" Sivan asked.

She chuckled. "No."

"We get more time on the Internet?" I asked, even though I knew the direction this was going.

"Nope. You two are going to mentor each other until both scores come up." A smile lit her face, and she clapped her hands together. “It’s the perfect solution. You’ll help each other for an hour a day.” She started toward the door. “I have to go check the muffins in the oven before they burn. We need to talk about something else when I get back.” She turned and left the room.

“Oh God,” Sivan mumbled. She let her head drop down to her desk, paused, and repeated the action.

“You’re actually banging your head on the desk? Is an hour a day that bad?” After the words left my mouth, I regretted them. I had also been playing indifferent these past three weeks, and I just let it slip.

Her eyes widened. “No . . . Um . . . No . . . I, uh. Well.”

“Never mind.” Now I felt pathetic. “We can tell Betty we’re helping each other. I’ll spend my time on the Internet going over exponential functions. Don’t worry about it, I’ll figure it out.”

Sivan’s face turned a deep shade of red, and her lips pressed tight.

What the hell?

“I’m having a little issue with being around you,” she blurted, and then winced.

“That’s pretty obvious.” Heat flushed through my system. I didn’t need her to spell it out. I unplugged my laptop and started toward the door.

“Wait.” She bit her lip.

I stopped. Was she trying to torture me?

“Let’s do it. I can help you. And I, uh, could use some help with chemistry.” She shook out her hands. A small smattering of blood made a dot-like pattern on the English essay laying on her desk. Her eyes widened. She caught my eye and placed her sweater over the paper. She cleared her throat. “How about it?”

Nothing about Sivan escaped me, and I'd already caught on to her habit of rubbing her thumb over her forefinger. It was worse when she concentrated or was agitated. Sometimes she'd wear a beige rubber band and play with it instead. She probably hoped no one would notice, but I did. I couldn't help it. I never mentioned it, because it was obvious she didn't want to talk about it.

"If you're sure. I can be a little bossy, as you know," I said, trying to lighten the mood.

A slight smile curved her lips, and she nodded.

The door flung open again, and Regina charged in.

"Jax! You're here."

I tried not to roll my eyes at Regina stating the obvious.

"Betty said you need to get out of the house, and there's a football game tonight." She had her hands clasped in front of her, and she bounced from foot to foot.

I was tempted to ask her if she needed to use the bathroom just to see her face. Nah, too rude, even though it would be fun. "Thanks, Regina, but, you know, I'm in hiding and all that." Had she forgotten the NDA she had to sign?

She held up a finger. "Wait right here." She turned with a flip of her hair and disappeared back out the door.

Sivan cocked her head. "This should be interesting."

I sat back down and chuckled. "Can't be good, right?"

She shrugged and shook her head.

"I'm back." Regina held a small bag to her chest. "You're going to love this."

I don't think so.

She began taking out makeup and hair supplies from the bag, placing them on the desk.

I crossed my arms. "I've tried disguises before. They don't work."

"Listen. Betty told me about your disguises, if you can call them that. A hat and t-shirt? Really? I could spot you a mile away." She pointed to her stash of goodies. "Once I get done with you, no one will ever guess."

"Yeah, but won't your friends ask who I am, even if I look different?"

Her smiled faded. "Yeah. That's what Betty said. She suggested you go with Sivan." She frowned. "I think she's probably right. Jax Jayne would never be seen with . . ."

Oh no she didn't.

I narrowed my eyes.

"I, I . . . meant to say you'd never be in this area." Regina nodded and shot Sivan a quick glance.

A nice save, but I didn't believe her.

"I can't go anyway," Sivan said.

"Why not?" The words didn't come out as casual as I would've liked.

She laughed. "Okay. I'll rephrase. I don't want to go."

Aunt Betty spoke from the doorway, "I heard that. I need to talk to both of you." She turned to Regina. "Can you give us a few minutes?"

Regina's shoulders slumped. "Sure."

Aunt Betty closed the door behind Regina and pulled a chair up next to our desks. "I asked Regina to get the disguise."

Huh. I wasn't expecting that. I assumed this was another way for Regina to rope me in to spending time with her. Every couple of days, she'd find excuses to find me. Did I have any shirts that needed to go to the cleaners? Would I like a batch of cookies she'd made? The last time, she asked if I wanted to go to the mall. No thanks. Not with her anyway.

Aunt Betty paused, her gaze going between Sivan and me. "You're out of balance."

"What does that mean?" I asked.

"I agreed to the homeschooling for both of you, because, for different reasons, it made sense. But I've been watching you, and you've barely spoken to each other for weeks, and I worry that you'll become reclusive. Once you get into that kind of mode, it's hard to break out of it."

"Is that why you want us to study together?" Sivan asked.

She chuckled. "No. That really was to bring your test scores up. This, though, is me interfering."

I glanced at Sivan, but she averted her gaze.

"Go have a hotdog and cheer on the team. You need to get out of this house. You're both off to college next year, and I'm worried if you get too comfortable here, it's going to be a rough transition."

I crossed my arms over my chest. "I'll go if Sivan goes."

Sivan's head jerked up, and her eyes shot daggers at me.

Aunt Betty's smile widened. "Wonderful." She turned to Sivan. "You in?"

Sivan squirmed a little. "You know, I think Jax should go with Regina. They can pretend to be on a date or something."

Betty shook her head. "If he went with Regina, there'd be too many questions. Regina has friends from twenty counties around here. You and Jax can pose as brother and sister."

I leaned back in my chair, a small smile on my lips. Well, this was getting interesting. Although, not a fan of the brother/sister thing.

"How many people go to these games? We're out in the boonies." Oops. "I meant to say, we're in the country."

Aunt Betty waved me off. "This is Iowa. Football is a religion here. There will be thousands in attendance. With the disguise I had Regina purchase, you'll blend right in. I wouldn't ask if I didn't think you'd be safe."

"All it takes is one person to recognize me." The mall and airport memories flashed for a moment, making my stomach take a dive.

"Listen. It's not healthy to stay on the farm all day, every day. I get it. You've had some bad experiences; that's why I haven't said anything until now. I had hoped you and Sivan would have decided to go do things on your own by now. So, I'm giving you a little push. Call it homework. Go, get out of this house, and enjoy the game."

Sivan placed her elbows on her desk and rubbed her face. "Okay. I'll do it."

I blinked. *What?*

She laughed when she noticed my expression. "I love football. I went to every game when I was a cheer—" She stopped abruptly.

"No way. You were not about to say you were a cheerleader." If she said she'd murdered someone I'd be less surprised.

She tucked a black lock of hair behind one ear. "We all do stupid things when we're young."

Aunt Betty leaned over and said, "Pssh. You're still young." They locked eyes, and it seemed like they were communicating without speaking. Sivan's usually guarded expression softened.

She smiled at Betty and nodded. "Yes, I guess I am."

Betty took her hand, and they continued grinning at each

other.

"How long ago? You know, the cheerleader thing." I tried to keep my face blank so she'd spill.

Her eyes narrowed. "Why does it matter?"

I shrugged. "It doesn't. Just curious." Watching her squirm was my enjoyment for the day.

"Let's just leave it at young."

I studied her for a moment, realizing I always viewed her the same. Dark hair, dark clothes, dark expression. Was there a time when she laughed and wasn't closed off? I'd seen glimpses of it, but not very often.

She crossed her arms and narrowed her eyes. "What?"

"What do you mean, what?"

"You're staring. Knock it off."

"Can't help it. You've just shattered everything I thought I knew about you."

She huffed, and I laughed.

"If you want me to be your fake sister tonight, you'll let this drop and never speak of it again." Her arms remained crossed, and she added a tapping foot to the mix.

"Okay, okay. Hey, I'll tell you one of my secrets so we're even."

"Do I want to know one of your secrets?" A small smile began to form.

"This one is good. You ready?"

She nodded.

I grinned. "Not everyone likes me."

"Oh, really? Tell me something I don't know," she muttered

as she walked to the door.

"Hey, I heard that," I said to her retreating back.

"Betty, I'm about to make lunch. Do you want anything?" Sivan completely ignored me.

"No thanks, honey. I've already had lunch, and I'd like to talk to Jax a little before I head to the barn."

"Okay, I'll see you later." She rolled her eyes in my direction before leaving the room.

Betty folded her hands on the desk. "You like her."

Wait. What?

"Um. She's okay, I guess." My hands began to sweat, and I shifted in my chair.

"Jax, I've seen that look before. She isn't just *okay* to you." She paused, then sighed. "That girl's been through a lot. I'm not sure what yet, so it puts me at a disadvantage."

"What do you mean?"

"Sivan is strong, but she's also fragile. We're in the building trust phase, and until I know more, I don't think it's a good idea to start any type of romantic relationship. You understand?"

"Not really." I tried to calm my beating heart. "Why don't you know about her background?" Didn't make sense. Aunt Betty seemed to know everything about everyone.

"I decided not to look at her file. The moment we met, I knew she needed her privacy; therefore, I need to be careful with her."

I rubbed my face. Sivan's past was a mystery to me, but it was unsettling that Betty didn't know her background either. "Can you find out more?"

"I have her file tucked away in the case of an emergency, but I feel confident I won't need it. She's told me a few things, and we're working on the rest."

"What did she tell you?"

She tilted her head. "You know I won't tell you that."

"I thought I'd give it a try." I laughed. "I'll agree to your terms. But I have a question. It seems like you were putting us together? First, having us study together, and now the football game . . ."

"I had hoped for more of a brother/sister type of relationship between you two. But then I saw that look . . ."

"Did Sivan have the same 'look' as you call it?" Hope stirred. My breath stilled.

She chuckled. "No, sorry. It appears it's one-sided for now. Let's keep it that way, okay?"

Damn.

Chapter Ten

Sivan

THE NIGHT WAS COLD AND crisp, a perfect fall day. The smell of hotdogs and popcorn mixed with the scent of dirt and grass as we passed the concession stand. The crowd roared as one of the teams kicked off the ball.

"Harold, don't you just love football games?" I asked Jax.

His eyes widened, and he whispered, "Harold? God, call me anything except that."

"Too late." I pressed my lips together to hide my smile. "We've already worked it out with Betty. If Regina sees you tonight, that's what she'll call you."

"I thought the plan was for Regina to act like she didn't know me."

"She asked Betty if she could pretend you went to middle school together or something. Who knows with Regina? I'd be prepared for anything tonight." I'd never met anyone as calculating as her.

"Let's sit over there." He pointed to a few empty spots midway up on the crowded bleachers.

"Who are we rooting for anyway?" I asked as I tried to get comfortable on the cold metal bench.

"The Jaguars. Aunt Betty told me they're wearing blue and gold." He shifted. "I'm gonna freeze on these seats. Is it always this cold in November? Aren't you freezing?"

"No. You're from the West Coast. Give it a few months and you'll adjust." *Maybe.*

He rubbed at his upper lip. "And this mustache is scratchy."

"Are you going to complain the entire night?" I chuckled.

"Maybe." He smiled, and my heart stopped for a few beats.

"You're giving up a little comfort for a great disguise." I hated to admit it, but Regina had done a great job with his get-up. I barely recognized him with his plaid shirt, puffy coat, and boots.

"I guess."

"Oh, there you are!" Regina's high-pitched voice broke through the crowd. "Harold!" She threw her arms around his neck and hugged him like they were long-lost friends.

Here we go.

"Um, hi." Jax pulled away from her.

Regina blinked a few times and flipped her hair over her shoulder. Next to her stood two girls wearing heels and miniskirts. Really? Someone needed to tell those two this wasn't a dance.

She motioned to them. "Harold, these are my friends Mia and Amber. Girls, this is Harold. We went to middle school together."

Both girls stared at Jax like he was an ice cream sundae. I didn't see recognition in their expressions, but even with his disguise, he couldn't hide those dark lashes that contrasted his intense green eyes. Nothing could douse that flame. I turned my head away. Ugh, I needed to quit looking. I didn't want to turn into Regina.

Jax nodded. "Hey."

Regina sat and scooted closer to Jax, putting her hand on his leg. Mia and Amber remained on the steps right beside us. "We were very close in middle school. Very."

Jax edged closer to me. "This is Sivan, my—"

"Almost forgot. That's Sivan, Harold's sister," Regina chimed in. "Isn't she sweet in her black flannel?"

"I decided against hypothermia tonight." I tried to smile, but I think it might have looked more like I was baring my teeth.

Regina kept her hand on Jax's leg and placed her head on his shoulder. He stiffened beside me.

He glanced down at his leg and said under his breath, "Not that close."

His eyes darted around the crowd and finally landed on my hand. He pressed his lips together and reached for it, linking his fingers with mine. Raising my hand to his lips, he kissed it softly.

My body froze. *Why did he do that?*

It wasn't a brotherly kiss, either. Not with the way he lingered. Heat started where his lips touched my skin and sparked, leaving a path of fire. My heart rate kicked into triple time, and I had to concentrate to keep my breathing regular.

All this from just a kiss on the hand?

Trouble. I was in deep trouble.

Mia and Amber's eyes about bugged out. One said, "Yuk," while the other said, "Ick," and both looked at Regina as if she'd lost her mind.

"My sister is beautiful, don't you think?" Jax said as he rubbed my hand against the stubble on his cheek. He continued to kiss and caress my hand while the three girls stared with their mouths open.

Holy hell. I was on fire.

"We're outta here. Where'd you go to school, in the back mountains?" Mia—or was it Amber?—asked as they left.

Regina stood and glared at me like it was my fault.

I shrugged.

She stomped her foot, huffed, and left.

Jax still held my hand. Our eyes locked, he squeezed tighter and lowered his gaze to my lips. I thought I'd be safe with him at a football game with thousands of people. I wasn't safe at all. His lips looked so—

"Oh shit. I forgot." He dropped my hand like a grenade about to explode, then tucked his hand under his armpit.

I swallowed a few times before I could speak. "What did you forget?"

"That you, uh, don't like stuff like that. Sorry." He looked down.

Reality hit me like a cold bucket of water.

I unclenched my teeth. "I knew what you were doing. Just faking it so Regina would back off." My chest tightened. Feelings I didn't want, butterflies . . . attraction, started to creep in. Not good.

"Yes. Faking it. That's what I was doing." He nodded a few times.

"I know. That's what I said."

He rubbed his face and took a deep breath. "Sivan."

"Yeah?"

He stared at me for a few seconds and said, "Nothing."

"Are you trying to drive me crazy?" I held my breath and waited.

"If I were, we'd be even."

"Why is that?" My pulse increased.

He sighed. "Never mind."

I thought about trying to get him to spill, but his face was set in stone. "Okay, let's just watch the game."

North Iowa High School ended up not needing our support. The Jaguars crushed the poor Bulldogs, fifty-eight to three.

"What do you think about bringing Emily and Alice next time?" Jax asked as we filtered through the crowds toward Betty's old truck.

"Maybe." Nice of him to think of the girls.

"They'd love the energy of the crowd, the players tackling each other. It was fun, don't you think?" He cocked his head, waiting for my answer.

"Yeah. It was good to get out. I hadn't even noticed we'd become hermits until Betty brought it up." I sighed.

"Here we are." He opened the passenger door for me. The loud creak made me jump back a little.

"I'm capable of opening my own door." It came out a little bitchier than planned.

He laughed. "I know that all too well."

I guess he was referring to the Tae Kwon Do kick that flattened him to the ground.

"Get in the truck, *sister*. Can you at least let me pretend to be a gentleman?" He raised an eyebrow.

"If your ego needs it, okay." I lifted myself in.

Jax shook his head as he closed the passenger door. He looped around the front of the truck. I couldn't help but notice him. Everything about him, how he looked and moved was so, so . . . I closed my eyes and groaned. *Stop it. Stop looking.*

After taking a deep breath, I prepared myself for the ride home. Just a little while longer, and I could go hide out in my room and get my head straight. No more thinking about things that couldn't happen. Concentrated social time with Jax was a mistake.

"I want to do this again," Jax blurted once he sat behind the steering wheel.

Oh hell. I shifted my eyes his way to see if he was joking. He stared back at me with those piercing eyes of his.

"Even though I had to wear a disguise, I felt normal for the first time in forever." He let his head fall back and closed his eyes. "It was good."

Guilt wrapped around my chest, making it feel tight. All this time, I thought he was moaning and complaining about things most boys his age would want. Bounced across the country with people he barely knew, he spent all his time either doing homework or staring out the window. And how did I treat him? First by trying to convince him to go home, then ignoring him.

I turned toward him. "I'm sorry. I don't think I realized until just now how awful moving away from your family has been for you."

"Some parts are good." His eyes remained closed and he smiled.

"What parts?" I whispered before I could get my mouth to shut up.

Jax turned his head slowly toward me. Our eyes locked, and he glanced at my lips. Every time he did that, it was like he'd lit a match to my clothes.

He winced, and said, "The animals."

Oh.

"And also Aunt Betty and the girls. Of course, my new sister isn't too bad." His teasing grin was back.

"Yeah, yeah." I tried to hide my smile.

"Really, though. Do you think we could be friends? Maybe go out and do stuff?"

An excited flutter took hold before I could stomp it down. "What type of stuff?"

"I don't know. Normal things like going to a movie and the mall?" He shifted in his seat and tapped his fingers on the dash.

Those were dating activities, but they could also be considered friend-type dates.

"Maybe." Could I handle it? "But I'd bet Regina would go." My brain to mouth filter had shorted out.

"Oh God. Regina." He shook his head and scrunched up his nose.

I tried to hide my laugh behind my hand. "But she's so, well, just so pretty."

He shrugged. "If you like that sorta thing."

"Most people do."

"I want the people I hang with to have some depth. Maybe

have something more to talk about besides their next party or salon visit." He heaved a sigh and looked out the window.

A small part of me was relieved. The thought of Jax and Regina made my stomach twist. "Can't argue with that."

Jax put the keys in the ignition but stopped. "We're gonna be stuck in this lot for a while." Traffic was backed up, trapping us in our parking space.

"I guess next time we'll need to leave before the end of the fourth quarter."

"You're saying there will be a next time?" He raised his brow, and a slow smile formed.

"Perhaps."

"Good. It's settled."

"But—"

"Let's kill some time by asking each other questions. I really don't know much about you. I'll go first." He looked up and tapped his finger against his lips.

"No." Not going there.

"Nothing too personal. No deep dark secrets or anything. Just general crap. Like, you know, the usual what's-your-favorite-color type questions."

Hmm. "You're not trying to lull me in?"

"That will be the hardest one, I promise."

"Okay. My favorite color is green. My turn." I drummed my fingers on the dashboard. "When did you first decide you wanted to become a vet?"

"That's a little personal." He winked.

I raised an eyebrow. "I didn't make the same deal."

"If I answer your question, you have to answer a similar one from me." He tilted his head and waited.

"But I don't want to be a vet." I pursed my lips together so I wouldn't smile.

"Smart-ass," he said under his breath. "Okay, I'll tell you. It was a bird."

"Did he whisper in your ear?" I tried to stifle my laugh, but it came out as a snort.

His eyes danced. "Kinda. He fell out of a tree first."

"Aww. And you saved him? How old were you?"

"Twelve. And it was a big deal. I was the hero in our neighborhood for two whole weeks." A smile lurked around his lips. "I loved that neighborhood. Anyway, I kept him in a shoebox and fed him worms."

I cringed. "I'm afraid to ask. Where'd you get the worms?"

He chuckled. "I was twelve. Where do you think?"

"At the corner drug store?" I hoped.

"I dug them."

A shudder ran through me. "Gross."

"I loved that feeling. I knew Cheep wouldn't have survived if I hadn't been there that day." He ran a hand through his wavy hair. "That's when I first thought of it. Now it's your turn. What do you want to study in college?"

A laughed escaped me. "Cheep?"

"I repeat. I was twelve. Now answer the question."

"I can't."

A frown creased his brows. "No fair."

"No, it's because I don't know yet. I haven't quite figured things out." Survival had been my focus until I came to Betty's.

I tucked a strand of hair behind my ear.

"That makes sense. Most people haven't figured it out before they get into college. Do you know where you'll be headed?" His body leaned a little closer.

"Betty is helping me. I guess there are all sorts of scholarships out there. I'll probably just pick the best one." The thought of it made my stomach twist.

"Betty was a high school guidance counselor, you know."

"Yeah. She's great at the whole college application process." We'd spent hours poring over the different choices. The indecision had started to wear on me. *Why couldn't I decide?*

"Maybe we can figure this out. What do you like to do?" He leaned closer still.

"Math?"

He pointed and chuckled. "You're sick, maybe even evil."

I punched him lightly on the shoulder. "Look who's talking, Mr. Chemistry Whiz."

"Really, though. How do you do it?"

I shrugged. "I see the equations in my head. Sometimes I even dream the solutions."

"Do you have a photographic memory?" His eyebrows raised.

"For some things like math and—well, a few other things." Almost slipped. "But not chemistry, unfortunately." I crossed my arms, willing him not to ask any more questions about it.

"That's what I'm here for." He grinned. "What else do you like?"

Thank goodness. "I like to eat."

"A food critic?"

"Ahh. Good one."

"What else?"

"Um, I like kids."

"A teacher?"

"I know." A smile played on my lips. "I can teach kids to critique food."

Jax paused and slowly shook his head. "You're avoiding the question."

My smile faded, and I turned to stare out the window. "Yeah, I guess I am." Six years spent focusing solely on turning eighteen and getting out of the foster care system were coming to an end this spring. For the first time, the thought of my birthday filled me with dread.

"New plan. Let's go with three rounds of Would You Rather," Jax suggested.

"I think I played this game in middle school." At least we could stay away from the past and future. My shoulders relaxed a little.

"I'll go first. Would you rather live in one town for your entire life or travel the world? But, you'd have to move once a month."

"That's easy. One town."

"Really? But you'd never see anything except for that one place."

"Look around."

His head veered from side to side. "I see a lot of damn cars blocking us in."

"Take a closer look." I wanted him to notice the beauty and simplicity all around us.

"All I see is a huge traffic jam."

I crossed my legs and sat up straighter. "It's the bigger picture. Notice the field, the lights, the energy of the people." My hands motioned to the football field. "The reason everyone had such a good time tonight was because they're part of something—a group that shares a common bond. It's all about the people. If you traveled around, sure, you'd see a lot of beautiful things. But if you slow down and look around where you are, you'd uncover all there is to see. You know, like a new foal brought into the world on a small farm, being with people you trust." I pressed my fingers to my lips. "Sorry, got a little carried away."

He put his hand on his chest. "You, Sivan, are a romantic."

I laughed. "No way. I'm a realist."

"Okay. Whatever you say." He shook his head. "It's your turn."

"How about this one. Would you rather look old, but feel young, or look young, but feel old all the time?"

"Like tired kind of old?" he asked

"Yep."

"And I'd lose this handsome face?" He smoothed his mustache.

"The handsome face would still be there, but just old."

"You think I'm handsome?" His eyes crinkled from his huge grin.

Busted. A flush of warmth crossed my cheeks.

"Answer the question."

"Okay, okay." He continued to chuckle. "I'll go with looking old, but I don't like it."

"Good choice."

"My turn. Would you rather marry a guy who was your best friend or someone you were attracted to?"

"Someone I was attracted to," I blurted.

"That was quick."

I laughed. "I think that needs to come first. The best friend part can come later."

"Yeah, my parents are like that. They met and married within six months. They have that best friend, madly in love type of thing going on. It's kinda disgusting." He shook his head.

"My parents were exactly—" I snapped my mouth closed and gripped the edge of the seat.

Where did that come from? What was wrong with me? I never, ever talked about my parents. A stabbing pain hit me smack in the middle of my chest. I rubbed it and tried to calm my beating heart.

He cleared his throat. "You can talk to me about stuff. You know, as a friend."

"Thanks. Maybe another time."

Like, never.

Time to change the subject. "Would you rather stay stuck here in the parking lot all night or finally hit the road?" I pointed to an opening in the line of cars and faked a smile.

His eyes softened, and a small smile appeared. "The parking lot."

CHAPTER Eleven

JAX

WHAT A LIAR.

All that friend talk . . . pure bullshit. I wanted more. Much more. Did she know? Had she guessed? Damn, my slip. I shouldn't have told her I'd rather stay in the parking lot all night. It was the truth, but I didn't want her to get spooked.

Sivan was different from any girl I'd ever met. Fiery, yes. But I liked that about her. She'd been through something. Grief and loneliness peeked from behind those eyes. And strength, she just didn't know it yet. She also had a vulnerability that made me want to protect her—from everything, past and present.

She didn't even know how beautiful she was, hiding behind her black hair and clothes. But that wasn't the best part of her. She was genuine. Real.

Funny, smart, and honest.

I was a goner. But I couldn't do anything about it. Would she even be interested in me? Didn't matter, because the promise I'd made to Aunt Betty meant I couldn't even try. I wanted to grab her and—

"What are you thinking about?" Sivan asked from behind the counter.

We had moved our Saturday study session to the kitchen table so we could get breakfast.

"Nothing." I kept my eyes on her so she wouldn't suspect I was lying.

"You totally spaced out." She smiled. "Here you go." She set a plate down in front of me.

I sat a little straighter. "Grilled cheese and pickles. My favorite breakfast. You remembered."

She rolled her eyes. "Like I could forget with you reminding me every day."

True.

I examined the sandwich. "What did you put on the cheese? It looks like mold." The incident with the salted pudding pie from a little over a month ago was still fresh on my taste buds.

"Those little green specks are rosemary. It'll give it some added flavor."

"Are you feeding me those plant things?" I motioned to the pots on the windowsill. Not sure if I liked the idea.

"Yes. Those are called herbs." She laughed and shook her head. "Are we going to get back to work?"

I took a bite of the sandwich. Delicious. "Mmmm. This is the best grilled cheese I've ever had."

She tried to hide her smile. "Whatever."

With a full mouth, I asked, "What's next?"

She sighed. "An hour of chemistry."

"Okay, we'll continue with the attack strategy. Tackle and conquer. You're good at that."

She crossed her arms and glared. Why did I enjoy irritating her so much? Her cheeks had turned pink, and fire lit her eyes. *That's why.* She looked hot whenever I annoyed her. I swallowed and wiped moisture from the back of my neck.

"You want me to attack again? I'd be happy to accommodate," she threatened.

"Who's going to attack?" Regina asked, appearing in the doorway.

Sivan went from flustered and adorable to stiff and quiet.

My jaw clenched. Regina was back to ruin the fun. How to get her to leave? "We're attacking chemistry. Atomic theory, chemical bonding, polarity. You know, the usual."

Regina's face brightened. "Chemistry. Oh, my favorite subject." She plopped down on the seat next to mine. "Don't you find the quantum-mechanical model of the atom fascinating?"

I heard a gagging noise coming from across the table, but when I looked up, Sivan wore an innocent expression. *Good cover.*

"Yeah. It's great," I answered.

My spontaneous strategy to get rid of Regina, a big fail.

"Sivan, do you think the model is based on probability or certainty?" Regina's huge smile could only be described as fake.

"We're *probably* going to be late if we don't head out and get this done." Thought I'd throw her a hint. "Right, Sivan? Do you want to move to the library?"

"The model is based on probability." Her eyes had gone from fierce to gentle. She wasn't smiling, but her face appeared softer. "I would have known that even without the hint, Jax."

"See? I'm a great teacher."

"It's always about you," she muttered under her breath, her smile returning.

"Let's go hit it, Sivan." I started to gather our books. "We'll see you later," I said to Regina.

Something about Regina didn't sit right with me. Always smiling and polite, but it appeared she had another side to her that wanted to bring Sivan down, making me want to defend her. I knew Sivan was strong, but I sensed something brewing beneath the surface. I still didn't know what had happened to her or how she'd lost her family, but I sensed sadness and possibly trauma. Maybe because she never brought them up and steered away from any conversation about the past. She was good at it, but I noticed.

"Wait." Regina stood.

"Yeah?" I glanced at her.

"Well." She folded her hands in front of her. "Betty asked me to take the girls to the Harvest Fair today at twelve. She also mentioned I'd need help because, well, you know the girls. They like to go off in different directions, and it'll take two people. Can you come, Jax?"

Oh, hell no. Emily and Alice were fun, full of energy, and made me laugh, but the cost was too high. Spend the day with her? Not gonna happen. "I hate fairs. Sorry, Regina. Maybe Sivan could help out." I kinda threw her under the bus, but maybe if they spent some time together they could work out their differences, and I'd be off the hook. Win-win.

A glance at Sivan's darkened expression confirmed my suggestion didn't go over well. No, more like an impossibility.

"I'm also not a fan of fairs. I'm sure one of your friends would love to go with the girls. Mia or Amber?" Sivan's innocent look was back, but this time it held an edge.

I had to bite my tongue not to burst out laughing. Mia and Amber both looked like the type of girls who'd enjoy a kegger at a frat party—not a day at the fair with kids.

Regina placed both hands on her hips. "They're busy today."

Probably with a hangover.

"I'm sure you'll work it out. Sivan, you ready?"

She grabbed her books and notepad and was out the door in a flash.

Regina moved in front of the doorway, blocking my exit. "Jax, I don't think we got off to a very good start."

An understatement. Now, how to shake her loose?

"I'm sorry if I seem pushy. I don't have a lot of guy friends, and that's what I hoped we could be. Friends. How about it? I'd love to spend the day getting to know you better."

The first time I met her, she seemed desperate. Shortly after, she'd morphed into her superior act. Now she acted almost normal. Another act?

"I'm also friends with Sivan. You're not very nice to her. Maybe you should spend the day getting to know her better."

"Sivan? She couldn't care less. Betty favors her over everyone. Haven't you noticed? I don't get how you can be around—"

"What?"

"She's just so, so . . ."

“Go on.” My heart rate doubled, and my hands fisted. She’d better choose her words carefully. I was dangerously close to telling her what I really thought of her.

“Dark.”

A coldness hit my core. “That’s it? You don’t like her because she wears dark clothes?” Ridiculous.

“No, I meant everything about her is dark. What do we really know about her? She doesn’t even have a family, that’s got to mess a person up.”

“A lot of people don’t have a family. I don’t get why you think that’s a problem.”

Her eyes narrowed. “Have you ever seen her face when people talk about their family? There’s something bad going on there.”

“I think that’d be a normal reaction if you’d lost people you love.”

“I’m a psychology major, and I’m telling you, there’s some big trauma there. Who knows when it’ll all come bubbling out? Betty trusts her with the girls, but who knows—”

“Stop right there.” I stepped closer and lowered my voice. “Listen to me. Whatever Sivan went through is her business. It’s not for you to speculate during your first-year psychology studies. She’s not your case study.”

She crossed her arms and frowned. “But—”

“No, let me finish.” I took a deep breath. “She’s normal and grounded, especially with what she’s probably been through in her life. She’s amazing, and I won’t have you stand here and cast doubts about her mental health. Betty is a great judge of character, and she’d never trust Sivan with the girls unless she was one hundred percent confident in her abilities. Are you jealous because you think she’s replaced you?”

"She hasn't replaced me." Her bottom lip popped out into a pout.

"She *will* replace you if you keep up with this. If Aunt Betty feels like you're going after Sivan, you'll be gone in a flash. Why don't you take some time and try to get to know her?"

"She wears black fingernail polish! Doesn't that tell you anything?"

"Yes. It tells me she likes to wear black polish."

"Ugh. She's expressing something scary about her personality."

"Are we back to your first-year psychology studies? Quit analyzing her. She is who she is." Anger propelled me forward, and I pointed my finger at her. "If I had to pick someone scary, it'd be you."

Her face flushed, and she took a few quick breaths. Oh hell. I shouldn't have said that.

Don't bring out the tears.

"You think I'm scary?" Her lips trembled.

I raked a hand through my hair. "Okay, maybe not scary."

"Really?" She blinked rapidly.

"I just think you could make more of an effort. You know, try to understand where Sivan is coming from."

"Okay. I can do that." She morphed right out of her tears, smiled, and gave me a hug. "I'm sorry I made you mad."

I gave her a little pat on her back. "Just try to be—"

"Oh, sorry. I didn't mean to interrupt." Sivan had reentered the kitchen. Like a deer in headlights, she stood still for a moment. I tried to pry Regina's hands from my back, but she didn't budge.

"There it is. Forgot my pencil." In a flash, she grabbed it from the table and was out of the room.

Shit.

Regina finally let go and started to wipe her eyes like nothing had happened. "Thanks, Jax. I'm glad you're not angry with me." She grabbed her purse off the counter. "See you later!" Before I could say anything, she left.

What just happened?

Damn. She did that on purpose. Now Sivan probably thought Regina and I were together.

No way in hell.

Did it matter though? I couldn't have her. Aunt Betty was firm. No messing around. But I had real feelings for her. Could I talk to Aunt Betty and explain?

What would I say? *Aunt Betty, I think I'm falling for Sivan. I know we live in the same house with children, but we'll be good.* Or, *Aunt Betty, you remember what it's like to be in love?*

Wait.

Not love. No way. But the feeling of Sivan's hand on my cheek when I held it at the football game haunted me. Small, delicate fingers that smelled of lavender. I'd never wanted to kiss anyone so bad in my life. Her lips, so soft and inviting. The look in her eyes. I held back, but it about killed me. That wasn't love, right? Of course not. Physical attraction, that was it.

Relief pushed out the panic, but an unwelcome voice crept in.

You've never felt this way about anyone. Ever.

I wiped moisture from my forehead. It didn't matter. She didn't like me anyway. She barely tolerated me. Now it had probably shifted to hate.

"Hey, you coming? I don't have all day."

I looked up to see Sivan's smiling face. She didn't appear pissed. She seemed . . . relieved?

"That wasn't what it looked like. You know, with Regina."

"No worries. I'm not judging. She's your type. I get it."

"Sivan!" I about yelled. My pulse kicked into high gear.

She jumped back a little. "Why are you shouting?"

"I'm not. I want to make myself clear. Regina was crying, so I gave her a pat on the back, and that was it."

Her expression was blank. "Okaaay."

"I know you don't care either way, but I didn't want you to think I'd go for someone like that."

"I don't judge people. I mean, there must be *something* good about her, or Betty wouldn't have her helping with the girls." She laughed a little. "I just haven't seen it yet." Holding up her hand, she said, "But I'm not judging."

I had to laugh along. "Believe me, she's not my type. She's a little too, I don't know, fluffy."

"Fluffy? Is that a thing?" she asked, still laughing.

"Yes. It means she doesn't have substance. I want someone who's real. Maybe a little darker." I glanced at her hair, and then let my eyes rest on her lips.

She stepped back. "You shouldn't want dark. Dark is bad. It can hurt you."

"There are different shades of dark. Some shades can be complex, but they're more real than anything light and meaningless. Dark isn't always bad. It can be a transition, kinda like moving from one stage to another."

"Some people are stuck; they can stay dark their entire life." She glanced down at her fingernail polish.

"Some people may look dark, but they're full of light. It can be deceiving." I paused, and our eyes locked.

Aunt Betty entered the kitchen, interrupting us. "I have a favor to ask you two."

"Sure," Sivan offered right away. She let out a huge breath.

I almost told her to speak for herself, but then I noticed Aunt Betty's eyes looked tired. And red?

"Is everything okay?" I asked her.

"Yes, I'm fine. Just didn't sleep well last night." She rubbed her eyes. "I can't take the girls to the November Harvest Fair this afternoon and Regina backed out."

Sivan blurted, "Of course we'll take the girls. Right, Jax?"

"I love the fair," I said without thinking.

"Thanks. I really appreciate it." She glanced around the kitchen and paused. "I can't remember why I came in here." Her eyes squinted, and she looked up toward the ceiling.

"Betty?" Sivan said softly and touched her arm.

"Hmm?" She turned and smiled at Sivan. But it wasn't her normal, happy smile.

"Can I do anything else to help?"

"No, dear. I need to make it through today, and I'll be okay." She inhaled. "It takes a lot off my mind to know the girls won't be disappointed. They've been looking forward to this fair for weeks. I'll give you all the details later." She wandered back out of the room.

"What the hell was that?" I asked Sivan.

"I don't know, but I'm going to find out."

Chapter Twelve

Sivan

I'D NEVER SEEN BETTY SO distracted. Maybe even sad?

"The girls are watching a movie in the family room. Can you go and keep them company while I go talk to Betty? Or would you like to talk to her?" I didn't want to barge into family business.

Jax paled. "Me? No, no. You're much better at doing the girl talk thing. I wouldn't know where to start."

Probably true. "Okay. I'll report back."

The hallway seemed longer as I steered myself to Betty's office. I rapped on the door and waited for an answer.

"Come in." Betty's tired voice filtered through.

I opened the door. "Hi." I lingered a bit before entering. Should I just ask if anything was wrong?

"Good, you're here. I have the directions printed out. Do you think Jax would mind driving the Buick?" She sat behind her desk and rubbed at the dark circles under her eyes.

"Um. No." I was pretty sure I saw him caressing the dashboard. He had some major bonding going on with the old classic.

"Good. You should be all set. Could you leave a little before lunchtime?"

"Sure. Uh, Betty? Are you all right?"

She paused and took a deep breath. "And I thought I was doing an okay job covering up." She motioned me in. "Come, sit down."

I plopped down on one of the chairs in front of her desk.

"Here, take my hand." She reached out for me.

I wasn't a hand-holding type of person, so I hesitated.

"It's okay. I have a story I want to tell you, but I'll need to hold your hand for a minute."

I reached across the table, and she gently squeezed it. It wasn't so bad.

"You know how when you're young you do stupid things?" she asked.

I laughed. "Do I?"

She tilted her head. "I don't know if you're aware of this, but we're very similar."

Huh. "We are?"

"We both have big losses in our life, and we both don't talk about them."

Oh, yeah. There was that. I shifted in my seat.

"Don't worry, I won't ask. Anyway, back to my story. My Henry, he loved his birthday." She smiled a little. "Every year, we'd plan a new adventure. We traveled to Spain one year, another year it was Australia." She shook her head and laughed softly. "But one of my favorite years was when we stayed in town and ordered Chinese food and watched a movie. He loved action adventures." She wiped the corner of her eye.

My eyes filled with tears. The pain on her face made my heart twist. "Betty, if this is too hard—"

"No, I need to talk about it. Are you okay listening?"

"Sure." Was I?

"Henry was so excited about getting married. You should have seen him. He'd tell anyone within listening distance that we were getting hitched. We decided . . . we decided . . ." She stopped and took a breath. "To get married on his birthday."

It hit me. I closed my eyes and squeezed her hand. *Oh no.* Today was Henry's birthday *and* their wedding anniversary. I blinked back tears. Betty, beautiful, strong Betty, was suffering.

"Betty," I choked out.

"We never thought about dying. Not really. We believed we'd be together forever." She got up from the desk and came around the table. I stood, and she hugged me. Through the tears, she said, "It was worth it. Every minute I miss him, every bit of the pain I feel now, and still, I wouldn't change a thing. One thing's for sure. My love for him never died."

I grabbed on to her and nodded into her shoulder. She held me tight, and I couldn't stop the flow of tears. We understood each other. We both knew pain and loss too well. By the end, I wasn't sure who was comforting whom.

"My dear, sweet Sivan." She smoothed the hair back from my face. "Don't be sad for me. I was lucky. I had the one great love of my life. I wanted to grow old with Henry, but I'd take a few hours of wonderful over a lifetime of okay. Does that make sense?"

I grabbed three or four pieces of tissues off her desk, handing her one. "Yes. I understand."

"I hope you meet someone like Henry one day, have that type of love." She placed her hands on my face, staring straight into my eyes like she could see into my soul. "I don't want you to hold back because of fear. That's not living."

She was right. Part of the reason I didn't want a boyfriend was because of fear. I couldn't deal with one more loss. My heart wouldn't survive.

You're cursed, Sivan. Everyone you love will die young. Sue, my new foster stepsister at the time, felt it was important to give me that information a few weeks after my family had died.

"Maybe, but I'm not ready yet." I looked away so she couldn't see the truth in my eyes. I didn't want to love anyone. If it happened again, I wouldn't survive this time.

"I know. But please keep your heart open to the possibility." She gave my shoulders a gentle shake. "Look at me."

I lifted my eyes slowly.

"It was worth it, worth this horrible day. Because, you know what? No matter how bad the days, there are so many good that follow." She smiled through the tears in her eyes.

"I haven't had many good." This was Betty's day. Not about me. *Shut up, shut it down!*

"I know. You've had to do so much on your own since you lost your family."

I nodded and pressed my lips together. Not going there. The wall protecting me firmly in place.

She tucked a lock of her colorful hair behind her ear. It was the first time I'd ever seen her mood not match her hair.

Betty smiled again. "We'll be okay. We're tough." She hugged me again.

A heaviness lifted from my chest.

She let go and straightened, her expression softened, and she smiled. Betty was back to her old self. "Emily's booster and Alice's car seat are already installed and ready to go."

"Great. We'll leave as soon as I can get the girls ready."

"Sivan?"

"Yes?"

"Thanks for today. I appreciate you coming in to make sure I was okay. It means a lot to me. You've become a special member of this family. I want you to know that." When she smiled, warmth covered me like a cozy blanket.

I almost couldn't speak from the tightness in my throat. "Thanks," I managed to get out.

"Now go, have fun. I'll be fine." I knew this was true.

"Do you want us to bring you anything back? Like some deep-fried butter or something?"

She put her hand on her throat. "Don't make me sick. Please don't feed that to the girls. I can't fathom the thought."

"Maybe we'll go for the deep-fried cheese?"

She winced. "The lesser of two evils, I guess." She waved her hand in front of her face. "Just don't tell me. I don't want to know."

"I'll try to steer them away from the really bad stuff. But we might not be able to pass the cotton candy booth without them noticing."

"Do you know about the dyes they use for that poison?"

"Yes, you've told me."

She put her hands over her face. "Good. Please detour around that."

I probably shouldn't tell her about the deep-fried Butterfingers or Reese's Peanut Butter Cups. "We'll bring them back in one piece and try to avoid the sugar coma."

She walked me to the door. "Have fun, and thanks again."

Another hug, and I was out the door. I found Jax and the girls wrestling in the family room. Both girls were sweaty and giggly.

"Hey, grab your coats. We're off to the fair," I shouted to the girls. Screams of delight echoed as they ran to their rooms to get ready.

"I guess we're taking the Buick," I told Jax.

"No way." His mouth dropped open, and his eyes glazed over. Geez, it wasn't the lottery.

"Yes way. The car seats are all ready to go." I laughed watching his expression change from shock to ecstasy.

"This might be the best day of my life." He placed his hand over his heart.

I shook my head. "I'm going to help the girls get ready. Meet you at the car in ten minutes? Is that enough time to get your disguise ready?"

"I'm going now." He took off like a cannon shot.

Ten minutes and two outfit changes later, Emily, Alice, and I left the house and started toward the garage. No need though, because Jax had parked the car directly in front of the large porch. He stood outside the car, cleaning a smudge on the window with the edge of his shirt.

"You need a moment?" I asked.

"Do you realize this is a 1953 Buick Roadmaster Skylark? I probably won't get another chance like this again in my lifetime."

I'd put money down he was wrong.

We buckled the girls in the back seat and headed to the Hundred Acre Fairgrounds. Thankfully, the drive only took thirty-five minutes, but I was sure I saw disappointment flash across Jax's face when we pulled into a parking spot. I chuckled to myself. Guys and cars. What was with that?

We paid admission and entered through the Blue Gate. I scanned the huge fairgrounds. Barns, rides, food booths, and games. The smells of hay, animals, and fried food were oddly pleasing.

"What do you girls want to do first?" I asked.

"Let's go on the Ferris wheel," Emily squealed.

"Um . . . no, we should see the animals first. I think they'll be taking a nap soon. We don't want to miss it." Jax motioned to the barns.

"Napping animals?" I asked.

"Yes." His posture was stiff. "They nap. We should do that first."

Hmm. What was that all about?

"Emily and Alice, do you want to see some cows and pigs?"

"Yay!" They both clapped and jumped in excitement.

After walking what felt like a hundred miles through barn after barn, I stopped and asked Jax, "Did you need to pet every animal?"

He smirked and said, “Yep.”

I rolled my eyes. “What do you want to do next?” I asked the group.

“Let’s go on the rides!” the girls shouted.

Jax shook his head. “Nah. It’s time for lunch. Aren’t you hungry?”

I leaned over and said quietly, “Maybe we should do the rides first. You know, in case they get sick. We don’t want them to hurl, if you know what I mean.”

Emily overheard and asked, “What does hurl mean?”

Hmm. What to say? “Ah, we’ll just need to make sure we go on rides that don’t spin you around right after you eat. Are you hungry?”

“Yes! Yes!”

I chuckled. They’d say yes to just about anything. “They have a crepe restaurant over by the Ferris wheel. Do you want to try that?” Betty would approve of the non-fried version of lunch.

We sat inside the café and enjoyed probably the only vegetarian dish at the fairgrounds.

“Let’s go play a few of the games and head back home. It’s getting late.” Jax pointed to the arcade.

“What about the rides?” I asked.

“They’re overrated.” He looked away, avoiding my eyes.

“What’s over rabid?” Alice asked.

“They aren’t all that fun,” Jax answered.

“Jax, do you have something against rides?” I asked in a low voice.

“I don’t think they’re very safe,” he whispered.

"Betty checked them out. You know how she is with this kinda thing. She's given the all-clear for the rides. They've been looking forward to the Ferris wheel."

Emily grabbed Jax's hand. "Let's go on the Ferris wheel!"

His face paled.

"You're not scared of the Ferris wheel, are you?" I kept my laughter to myself. But I was giggling like a ten-year-old inside.

"Of course not," he answered.

But his tense shoulders and the way his eyes darted around screamed he wanted to be anywhere but here.

"Okay. Let's get the tickets." Once we got into the line, Jax stood rigid while he rubbed the back of his neck.

I leaned closer. "It's okay, you know. Lots of people have a fear of the Ferris wheel," I said, fighting to keep a straight face.

His eyes narrowed.

I added, "And I'll protect you if any clowns show up." This time, a little giggle escaped.

This opportunity was too good to let pass.

He groaned and crossed his arms.

When it was time to get on, Jax paused for a moment. Emily grabbed his hand and gave a tug. He followed and slowly sat next to me. Alice and Emily sat on the other side, giggling with excitement. He looked off into the distance, his eyes unfocused.

"You can get off, Jax. Really. Your face is a little pale." Poor guy.

"No. I'm doing this."

Now I felt bad. Maybe this was a real fear.

"If you're sure."

He gave me a curt nod, and his fists tightened.

Uh oh.

Emily and Alice squirmed and laughed as it started its incline. Once in motion, the fabric on my shirt moved, and I looked down to see Jax had a white-knuckled hold on the hem.

Oh, Jax.

I put my hand over his and gave a little squeeze. He leaned his head back and closed his eyes. A slight smile formed on his lips, and his body relaxed a little.

Something cracked and opened inside my chest.

No. Not happening.

He looped his pinky up over mine. That darn heat returned, starting at my finger and shooting out into every molecule of my body. The sparks were intense, but I couldn't move my finger away.

Five rotations lasted an eternity. We finally came to a stop. The ride attendant opened the door, and I helped Emily and Alice from the passenger car. We walked a few feet before I noticed Jax hadn't exited yet.

"You coming?" I asked.

A slow smile formed on his lips. "I'm in no hurry."

"Show off," I muttered to myself.

He laughed and jumped out of the cage. "That wasn't so bad."

I raised an eyebrow.

"Okay, I may have died a few deaths and injured your finger. How is it, by the way?"

I stretched it out a few times. "Circulation has been restored."

"Ugh. That's humiliating."

"Why'd you go on?"

"Wanted to conquer my fear. Isn't that what life's all about?" He smiled and tilted his head.

"I guess." I just hadn't figured that part out yet.

"Let's do some games!" Emily distracted me by yanking us toward the arcade.

The ring toss and milk jugs were tough, but Jax wouldn't stop until he won Emily a stuffed giraffe and Alice a stuffed elephant. The girls jumped up and down and giggled the entire time. They were in heaven.

On the way back to the car, Jax leaned toward me and said, "Thanks for today. It was one of the best days I've ever had."

"Really?" I was shocked.

"Yeah. Felt like I was ten again. Even though you made me go on the Ferris wheel."

I laughed. "I only pushed a little."

He said softly, "Thanks."

My heart fluttered a little before I could rein it in.

Jax opened the back door and helped the girls get buckled into their car seats. I hopped in the front seat and turned to watch for a moment. He was so gentle and sweet while he clicked the seat belts in place, making sure their hair was smoothed out of the way. The girls smiled sweetly as they held their new stuffed animal friends.

By the time we arrived home, both girls had completely passed out. A snack and an early bedtime sounded good as we lifted them out of the car and started up the stairs. Betty opened the door, took one look at us and laughed.

"I don't know who looks the most tired among the four of

you!" Her usual Betty smile shined through.

Thank goodness.

"Guess who's coming next month for Christmas?" Betty's face glowed, and she clapped her hands.

Chapter Thirteen

Jax

"WHERE IS HE? WHERE IS he?" My mom's voice echoed down the hall.

"I'm right here, Mom." I rounded the corner and got my first glimpse of her in almost three months. It was good to see her.

"Jax! You've grown. Sam, don't you think he's taller?" she asked Dad. Her purse dropped to the floor as she ran toward me.

I braced for the freight train that was Mom. She reached me and threw her arms around my neck, squeezing hard.

"Mom, I can't breathe."

"I haven't seen you in forever." Then the waterworks started. Not surprised. I just thought she might hold out longer than ten seconds after entering the house.

"It's okay, Mom. I'm good. Everything's great."

She took my head in both hands. "I missed seeing your face so much."

"Charley, you'll need to let him go so I can get a hug in," Dad said.

"Not yet. You wait your turn."

"Where's everyone else?" I asked, noticing there wasn't another car out front.

"Your brothers took a different taxi. They'll be here soon," Dad answered. He turned to greet Aunt Betty, who came dashing in the room. "Hey, Betty. How are you?"

"What? Where is she?" Mom asked and let go of me.

"Betty!"

"Charley!"

The two sisters hugged it out while Dad and I gave each other an eye roll. We'd be ignored for the rest of the visit, I was sure.

Dad slung his arm around my neck. "I forgot where the kitchen is in this monstrous house. Lead the way before the caffeine withdrawal hits."

I led him down the hallway and into the kitchen. Time to give him the bad news. "Dad, I have some news."

"Uh oh. No coffee?"

"It's worse. Betty only eats organic since she started fostering the girls, so no sugar or junk food in the house."

His eyes widened. "No Pepsi?"

"Banned."

He frowned. “How about pizza or nachos?”

“You’re in luck. Betty makes a really good pizza with a homemade crust, and she uses organic blue corn tortillas with cheese from the farmer’s market for the nachos. They’re both really good.”

He took me by the shoulders. “What have you done with my son? Tell me, and I won’t kill you.”

“Very funny.” I hadn’t realized how much I missed my parents.

He paused and checked me over. “You do seem different. But in a good way. You’re more relaxed and happier.”

Happy? I hadn’t given it much thought. Before coming to the farm, I’d go from one thing to another, not stopping to consider how I felt about stuff. But thinking on the last three months, it was true. I was happy.

“I guess I am. The farm is great, and Aunt Betty is a lot of fun.”

“I love hearing the stories about the girls.” He looked around. “Where are they?”

“They’ll be back in a few hours. Do you remember how we’d all wrestle when we were younger?”

“How could I forget?” he chuckled.

“Turns out these girls like to do the same thing. They live for our wrestling matches.”

His eyebrow rose. “And the older one, does she like to wrestle?”

“Ha ha. No wrestling going on there. Actually, nothing is going on at all. Aunt Betty gave me the hands-off lecture, and Sivan just wants to be friends.” I shrugged.

His head tilted. “And you’re okay with that?”

I want to pull her close and kiss her until she admits she has feelings for me.

"I'm cool with it." Expert liar right here.

A slight smile formed on his lips. "Okay, whatever you say."

Mom burst into the kitchen. "Don't think you can get away from me so fast!"

"I thought you and Aunt Betty would be in a huddle for at least another hour," I joked.

"No, I broke away to get another hug from my youngest." She came at me again. This time the squeeze was even tighter.

"Ugh. Mom . . ."

She began crying into my shoulder.

"I'm going off to college next year, so you're gonna have to get used to it."

Wrong thing to say, because the crying notched up. I looked over to my dad for help, but he gave me a smile that said, "What are you going to do?"

"I feel like I'm losing my last year with you," she sobbed.

Before, I would have probably told her it'd been her choice. She'd forced me to come here. But I didn't feel that way now, not anymore. Actually, I was grateful.

"It was a good decision coming here. Thanks for the nudge." Her sobs quieted, and she looked up. "Really? You're not just saying that?"

"Yes, really. I love it."

"You love it here?"

"Yep."

"I thought you were just telling me that when I called, to make me feel better." She studied me. "You don't feel isolated?'

"Nope. A few months ago, Sivan and I started hanging out, doing stuff I used to like before the band got popular. You know, things I did before. Movies, the mall; we even took the girls to the fair last month. The disguise Betty arranged for me to wear in public is genius. No one has figured out it's me."

Mom nodded.

"I feel free here. If that makes sense."

She wiped away more tears that fell down her face. "I know you needed this break, but I'm sorry I couldn't have done more so you wouldn't have had to leave."

"No more guilt, okay, Mom? I know it's only been a short amount of time, but it's like I'm another person. Someone better." I shrugged.

She studied me for a moment. "Yes. I can see it."

"We'd better get something to eat before Ray and the boys get here," Dad broke in.

"Ray is coming?"

"Of course. He's like family. You know that."

Ray had spent the past couple Christmas holidays with us. I'd assumed it was out of convenience, because of his bodyguard duties.

Huh. He flew across the country to spend Christmas with us? Here? Poor guy would be bored silly.

"Also, Betty doesn't have gated security. We'll need him if word gets out."

"You'll need an army." I laughed.

"Don't worry. He has backup agents in the area if needed. He's prepared for all scenarios."

"Sounds good." Even without gated security, I felt safe in Aunt Betty's house.

The chime from the doorbell sounded.

"That must be Ray. The boys would just barge in. I'll get it." Mom started toward the hall.

"No need. I've got it," Betty said as she whisked by down the hall.

We followed her out to greet everyone.

Betty flung open the door. "Welcome!"

Ray stood on the porch. He took one look at Betty, and his eyes widened. "You're, you're . . ."

She laughed. "I'm Betty. You must be Ray?"

He nodded and didn't take his eyes off her. "You're so . . . uh, I meant to say, you look like your sister."

I blinked. Ray flustered? What the hell?

"When we were younger, people would get us mixed up. But now, with my hair," she smoothed it back, "it hasn't happened since."

"It's beautiful. I mean, I like all the colors."

And then the impossible happened. Ray blushed. Had the world stopped spinning?

Aunt Betty waved him in. "Thank you. Come on in. It's freezing out there."

Ray moved slowly inside, never taking his eyes off Aunt Betty. I shot my mom a glance. She nodded, giving me a knowing smile. Dad was oblivious.

"Where are the boys?" Dad asked.

Ray came out of his trance. "They're unpacking the rental car. I hope you have room for all their suitcases." His eyes scanned the large foyer and huge connecting rooms. "Never mind." He laughed.

"The house has ten bedrooms, so no one has to share," Dad told him.

"Gorgeous," Ray said, staring right at Betty.

I was pretty sure his secret crush on my mom had just been transferred to Aunt Betty.

Aunt Betty, who hadn't noticed Ray's strange behavior, asked, "What's taking those boys so long?"

She didn't need to ask, because, not two seconds later, they came barreling in the door, all at the same time, their voices blending together.

"How does anyone live like this? It's freezing!"

"Quit being such a baby. It's not going to kill you."

"I can't feel my fingers, and my toes are . . ."

"This place is out in the middle of nowhere. We drove for an hour without seeing a mall. Are there any girls around here?"

"Oh, hi, Aunt Betty. Thanks for having us." Milo bowed to her.

"I'm so glad you could all come. We've been so excited to see you all again." Aunt Betty swung the door wide open, hugging each of my brothers as they walked in.

"Hey, Jaxster. How's it hanging?"

"Milo, cut it out. This is the first thing you ask your brother?" Mom put her hands on her hips and sent him a glare.

The oldest of our pack, Milo had always been held to a higher standard, expected to set an example.

"Things are hanging just fine." I smiled at Mom to loosen the tension.

She put a hand to her forehead and groaned.

"We thought you'd be wasting away out here in exile, but you look good." Dylan punched me on the arm.

"Yeah, we were expecting you to be in a corner sucking your thumb or something," Gage said, and punched my other arm.

I missed my brothers, but wasn't quite sure I was up to two weeks of arm punching. "Cut it out, you guys. I've been working out, and I don't think you'll like the return punch."

"God, he's right. Look at those guns. We can't mess with little bro anymore." Dylan laughed.

The three of them stared at my biceps. I hadn't meant to call attention to them, but I wanted to make sure they knew I wouldn't be their punching bag for the next two weeks. It had never been mean spirited, but they did pack a mean jab.

I took a closer look at them as they stood there in the foyer, and, for the first time, realized what all the fuss was about. They looked the part. Rock stars with their messy hair, ripped clothes, and tattoos. No wonder the girls couldn't keep their hands off them. Of course, I'd never tell them that.

"Okay, boys. I'm going to take you to your rooms. You only have a few hours before our welcome party begins," Aunt Betty announced.

My three brothers froze in place and looked over at Ray.

Ray waved them off. "They've all been cleared and signed NDAs. We shouldn't have any breaches of security. If we do, I have an exit plan in place. But I don't think we'll need it."

I leaned over to Milo, "There's a girl coming you'll love. She's beautiful and just your type." He was the player in our group, always with some blonde girl hanging on his arm. Regina was perfect for him.

He waggled his eyebrows. "Can't wait. I'll need something to occupy me while I'm here."

Regina would be thrilled to occupy his time. Maybe I should

warn Milo? Regina wasn't the type to let go easily. I opened my mouth but shut it again. Nah. Milo could handle her.

"How about the girl who lives here with you? What's her name—Silver?" Milo asked.

For some reason, it irritated me that he'd messed up her name. I growled out, "No. Sivan."

He cocked an eyebrow. "You got a thing for her or something?"

Another flash of annoyance. "No, she's a nice girl. Not your type. She's like a sister to me."

Why did I lie . . . again?

Mom took hold of my arm. "I need to talk to you for a few minutes. Can we go somewhere private?"

My stomach dropped. "Yeah. Anything wrong?"

"No, no. Don't worry. Everything's fine. Can we go into the library?"

"Sure."

Once seated on the reading couch, she blurted, "I'm sorry."

"What? Why?"

"I should have figured out a way to make things more normal for you at home. This past year has been so crazy. I feel like I've let you down." She stopped and raised her hand to keep me from speaking. "I've done a lot of thinking and planning. What do you think about coming home with us after Christmas?"

Leave the farm?

Leave Sivan?

The feelings I'd been trying desperately to shove away bubbled to the surface. "I've also done some thinking. The situation back home was out of control. It is what it is." I shrugged. "All the planning in the world wouldn't change it. Seattle is the group's hometown. The media is crazy for The Jaynes, and that's not gonna change. I'm okay with it. I don't blame you or anyone." I met her eyes. "I want to finish out the school year here on the farm." Relieved I could finally put words to what I'd been feeling.

She nodded and folded her hands in her lap.

"It's not that I don't miss you or Dad. Or even the guys. I miss all of you. But I've learned some things about myself and what I want from life."

Should I tell her about my pre-vet school application?

Her eyes narrowed a little. "Go on." Her mom radar must be on full alert.

"Well, I haven't changed my mind about the music business."

She winced.

"I've applied to NYU. They have a Bachelor of Veterinary Science program. I want to be a vet."

There. Let the shouting and screaming begin.

She looked straight into my eyes and whispered, "Oh, that's wonderful."

What?

"You've always been so gentle with animals. If your dad didn't have allergies, we probably would've had a houseful. I saw that nurturing side when you were very young. Oh, I'm thrilled!" She clapped her hands.

Her words didn't register at first. "You aren't upset I'm not following in my brothers' footsteps? No music?"

"You'll always have music, Jax. It's a part of you. But

whether you do it as a profession like your brothers is no concern of mine. I want you to be happy. That's the most important thing. Is that how you feel? Happy?"

I chuckled. "Yeah. I feel great."

She took a deep breath. "I could tell there was something different."

"I can come back for the summer before I head out for school. That okay with you?"

"Six more months?"

I nodded.

A soft smile formed. "That sounds like a good plan."

I leaned over to hug her. "Thanks, Mom. Thanks for understanding."

She stood up to leave. "And here I thought a household of girls would drive you nuts. Betty said you're really good with the girls, Emily and Alice."

"Yeah. They're a lot of fun."

"I FaceTime with them every week. They're a hoot. I'd try to steal them away if Betty wasn't so attached. Ah, to have some girls to balance things out." She sighed.

"You'd definitely get your girl-fix with them. They love everything pink and frilly."

"And Sivan, is she pink and frilly?"

"You haven't seen her?"

"No, I think she's a little camera shy. She always seems to be off doing things when I'm FaceTiming Betty." She shrugged.

"She's . . . different."

Her eyebrows rose. "What do you—"

Dad poked his head in the door. “Hey, Charley. Betty needs you in the kitchen. She said something about an appetizer disaster.”

“We’ll talk later. I’m happy you’re doing so well.” She touched my cheek.

“I have you to thank for that.”

She put her hand over her heart. “Aw, Jax. What a nice thing to say. You’ve really grown up, haven’t you?”

I smiled and shrugged.

“Come on, Charley. I left Ray and Betty alone. He looks hungry, but not for food, if you know what I mean.” Dad had apparently figured it out.

I shook my head. “Poor Ray. He doesn’t have a chance with Betty.” For the first time, my mom’s face went slack.

Her shoulders slumped. “I know. I just wish . . .” She sighed.

Sivan had told me she didn’t think Betty would ever get over Uncle Henry. It looked like Mom thought the same thing. But I still held out hope for Ray. He annoyed the hell out of me most times, but women considered him the manly, handsome type.

So . . . let the games begin.

I laughed to myself as I left the library and headed to the shower. Tonight should be interesting.

“Oh my God. You were right, Jax. She’s beautiful. No, she’s stunning. I’ve never seen anyone like her.” Milo stood staring, his eyes bulging. “I think I’m in love. That’s a woman who could take me to church.”

Wow. I knew he’d like Regina, but I didn’t think he’d be so

enthusiastic. The party was in full swing when I came down from my room. All Betty's neighbors and close friends had been invited, but I hadn't seen Regina yet. I could only imagine the type of dress she'd be wearing.

Milo's breathing came out labored. Was he sweating?

"Geez. Settle down, boy. She's pretty, but not that—"

I followed his gaze, and ice formed in my veins. Wearing a deep blue velvet dress, standing off to the side talking to my dad, was Sivan.

Oh, hell no.

CHAPTER Fourteen

Sivan

THE FAMILY ROOM WAS DECKED out with sparkling lights, a ten-foot Christmas tree, ribbons, bows, and candles. Round tables covered with beautiful pale linens were accented by vases that held pink and red roses with baby's breath. Silver, china, and crystal gave the tables an elegant feel.

Betty had prepared all the food herself, spending the last week making appetizers that were organic and GMO-free. Delicate finger sandwiches, deviled eggs, and an assortment of fruits and vegetables were set up along a long buffet table.

I had to hand it to Betty. She'd assembled a large, trusted group to welcome her sister's family. A crowd of about forty filled up the family room and kitchen. The entire house was filled with delicious smells and laughter.

Emily and Alice were beside themselves. They'd never seen such a party. Decked out in their best party dresses, they did twirls for the guests, for which they received ooohs and admiration.

Betty approached from my right. "What do you think?"

"Oh, Betty, you've done a beautiful job. It looks fantastic. I was just headed to the punch bowl, and then I'll make my move to the appetizers. That is if there are any left." The guests buzzed around the tables like bees.

"Eat up. I have backups in the kitchen." She placed her hands gently on my shoulders. "Sivan, you look beautiful. That dress . . . I'm speechless."

I smoothed the dress Betty had insisted I wear. An antique she'd worn ten years earlier to another party. Pretty, but it fit a little tight around my hips.

"I'm worried it's a little short?" I tugged on the hem.

"No, it's perfect." Her face glowed.

"Good evening," a ruggedly handsome man greeted. He came to a stop right next to Betty, but his eyes traveled around the room.

"Sivan, this is Ray, The Jaynes' Head of Security."

I'd heard Jax talk about him, but only that he was his former bodyguard. "Nice to meet you. Jax has told me about you."

"Thank you. Have you seen him yet? I need to go over a few things with him." Ray's eyes kept moving.

"He's most likely going to get a lecture about security like I did." Betty laughed.

Ray smiled at Betty. "I'll have everything in place before we leave. We still on for coffee in the morning?"

Betty's cheeks flushed a little. "Yes, we can talk security

tomorrow."

Was this Ray guy making a move on Betty? I gave him a closer look. Brown cropped hair with a strong jawline. Tall, with friendly eyes. He had my stamp of approval for now. Mental note: Ask Jax if he's good enough.

"I better go check on the last batch of phyllo puffs." Betty turned toward the hall.

"I'll go with you and help." Ray stilled and waited for her answer.

Betty sighed. "Sure."

Left alone at the punchbowl. Where was Jax?

"You must be Sivan," an older man asked. No mistaking those green eyes with flecks of grey and gold. Jax's dad.

I offered my hand. "Mr. Jayne, nice to meet you."

"None of that. Call me Sam." He ignored my hand and gave me a hug.

"Oh, thanks." I stiffened a little. *Relax, he's Jax's dad.*

"Have you met my other sons?"

"Not yet. I just got here."

"Here, let's get some punch, and I'll point them out."

He picked up the ladle, filled a crystal glass, and handed it to me.

"Thank you."

"Okay, so over by the door is my oldest, Milo."

Good Lord. He looked like a combination of the hottest Hollywood actor mixed with bad boy rock star. Long, brownish hair, with high cheekbones and a perfect jawline, he belonged in the movies.

"And my next born, Dylan, is attacking the last batch of lobster rolls right over there."

He had the same good looks, but was blond and a little taller.

"And Gage, he's ten minutes older than Jax."

Identical. But I could see the differences. Gage had darker eyes and hair. Their facial features were alike, but Gage seemed a little quieter. He stayed on the outskirts of the room, observing.

"Nice genes," I said, then caught myself. "Oops. My filter seems to be off."

Sam tipped his head back and laughed. "No, I like your honesty."

"Dad." Milo moved in front of his father. "I'd like to meet Regina." He faced me with a huge grin.

"Wait, Milo." Jax approached and tugged his arm. "Why'd you take off. I was—"

"Talking too much?" He shot Jax a look. "I wanted to meet the girl you think is so beautiful and just right for me." He turned his dangerous, rock star smile on me.

"That isn't Regina. That's Sivan," Jax said, scrubbing his hand over his face.

"Sivan? The girl you said was like your sister?" He looked me up and down, hesitating on my legs for a second too long.

I tugged down the hem of my dress. *I knew this was too short.*

"Are you blind? She is not sister material." Milo continued to stare at me, still smiling.

Ugh. Jax was back to the sister talk. "Yeah. He's referred to me as his sister before." I tried to laugh, but it sounded more like a cough.

Milo leaned closer to Jax and whispered, "Are you crazy?"

But I heard him.

Jax hissed, "You don't know what's been going on, so just shut up."

Oh no. Would he tell Milo about my kicking him?

"You must be Regina," asked an attractive older woman while giving me a hug.

What's with the Regina assumptions?

Sam put his arm around her shoulder. "Honey, why does everyone think Sivan is Regina?"

That's what I'd like to know.

Charley's eyes grew large. "You aren't Regina?"

"Um, no. My name is Sivan."

"Sivan? The same Sivan who's been living in this house with Jax for the past three months?"

I shifted, wanting to disappear. "Yes."

Her wide eyes turned to her husband. He shrugged. "He said she's like his sister."

No, disappearance wasn't good enough. Now I wanted a black hole to suck me in.

"Oh, how nice. I'm so glad to finally meet you." Jax's mom had a smile almost like Betty's.

"Thank you. I'm happy to meet you, too."

Milo took a step closer. "So . . . if Jax thinks of you as his sister, does that mean I might have a chance?" He turned his high-voltage grin up a few notches. "Sivan, are you dating anyone?"

"No." I swallowed and willed my cheeks not to blush.

"I know this is sudden since we've known each other for about two minutes, but can I take you out for dinner?"

Oh, he was smooth. I glanced at Jax. He stood rigid and looked like he wanted to say something.

I needed a stall tactic so I could think about it. "Oh, gosh. I have one condition."

"I'll do anything." He raised his hand to his chest, a sweet smile on his face.

"It's tradition. First, you have to beat me at a game of chess. I can't go out with anyone who doesn't know what to do with their queen."

Charley burst out laughing. "Oh, I love you! Betty was right. You are one in a million. It's going to be fun to see the three boys fight for your attention."

Now that would be even more awkward. I smiled at Jax, but froze when I noticed his face had turned beet red, and his hands were squeezed into white-knuckled fists.

Was he jealous? No, it couldn't be. He would have told his brothers to keep their distance. Instead, he told them I was like a sister to him. A green light if I'd ever seen one.

"I take your challenge," Milo countered.

I couldn't believe he actually agreed. But, no worries. He'd never win. I'd been playing since I could walk. When I got bored with my competitive partners, I'd hit the online games.

"Sure, if you think you're up for it," I teased.

"I'm up for it all right." He exaggerated a wink.

Which earned him an elbow in his ribs from Jax.

"I just meant it will be my pleasure. Would you like to meet at dawn?"

I had to admit, he was charming, but I'd never fall for it.

"How about eleven? I'm sure everyone wants to sleep in."

"Oh, you want everyone to watch me whip your . . . I mean, capture your king?" He cocked an eyebrow.

"I'm not after an audience. I just need a few hours of sleep." I yawned. Up since dawn helping Betty prepare had finally hit me.

"Yeah. I want to be awake for that. I'd love to see someone beat Milo. Been waiting for years." Sam chuckled.

Uh oh. Jax seemed off. His normal skin color had returned, but he still scowled.

"What's the matter?" I asked Jax in a low voice.

He took my arm and moved us a few feet away. "You have to win tomorrow. Milo isn't . . . I mean, he's not good for you. People call him The Shark." He looked to the group to make sure no one was listening. "He dives in, charms his latest conquest, takes what he wants, and leaves with few pieces left. He'll rip out your heart, Sivan. Don't go out with him."

Ugh. I pulled my arm free from his grasp. "First of all, I can take care of myself. If I do lose the game, which I doubt, there won't be any heart ripping." I'd need to have a heart for it to be ripped out. All I had was a numb space where it should have been.

"Just don't lose. I've seen him in action before."

"Do you think I'm the type of girl who meets a guy and falls in love in a matter of weeks? That can't happen."

"Of course it can happen. It happened to—I mean, it's happened to almost every girl he's dated. I'm not kidding. This has been going on even before they became famous. You can Google it."

"I'm not looking him up online. You need to let this go. He's just having a little fun with me."

Jax crossed his arms and tapped his foot. A crease formed between his eyebrows.

"Jax."

He wouldn't make eye contact.

"Hey."

He slowly turned toward me again.

"Thanks. I appreciate the warning."

His expression softened.

"You'll be careful? You won't, uh, fall for him?"

I wanted to tell him if I were going to fall for anyone, it'd be a different brother. The same brother who thought of me like a sister. What an idiot I was.

"Well, hello." Regina stood between our two groups with a wide grin. She wore a white, form-fitting dress with a neckline that plunged almost to her belly button. "Jax, will you introduce me to your brother?" She eyed Milo like he was dessert.

"Oh, yeah. Milo, this is Regina." Jax gave a lackluster wave between them.

"Hey, Milo. I'm a huge fan." She fluttered her fake eyelashes at him. At first I thought maybe an eyelash had gotten loose, but no.

Milo gave a half-smile and said, "Hey."

She stared at him with a here-I-am-come-and-get-me look.

Milo turned to me and said, "Tomorrow at eleven? Don't stand me up, or you'll break my heart." He clutched his chest in mock pain.

Jax pursed his lips.

"I'll be in the library, ready to go." I loved a challenge. Even if I lost, spending time with Milo would be fun. Even if Jax didn't like it. He'd just have to deal.

Milo grinned and said, "Can't wait." He continued to stare until another guest pulled his arm in another direction.

"Oh. My. God. Really?" Regina's smile had faded, and she spoke through clenched teeth.

"What?"

"Both? The oldest and the youngest? Ugh!" She stomped off in a huff of white lace.

I turned back to Jax. "What is she talking about?"

He shrugged and said, "No idea," before he wandered away, too.

I took in a calming breath. The library smelled of lemon polish, aftershave, perfume, and old books. Milo and I sat across from each other at one of the small wooden reading tables. Betty had pulled out an old chess set that had been gathering dust in the corner.

Everyone had come out to watch the competition. Even Emily and Alice stayed perfectly quiet.

An hour passed.

The clock ticked an impatient beat.

Milo wiped his brow.

"Double check and checkmate," I said to Milo, hiding my smile.

"No way. No freaking way." Milo stared at the chessboard like it had grown wings. "How . . . What . . . How?"

Jax chuckled. "I warned you."

"I had your knight pinned and was about to attack your F7 square." Milo shook his head like he couldn't believe his strategy had failed him.

"Yeah, I noticed that. I decided to use deflection and the skewer and pin." I let myself enjoy the hard-fought victory.

"Damn." His shoulders slumped, and his frown was pitiful. "Does that mean you won't go out with me?"

What to do? It was harmless.

"Sure, we can still go out. You didn't lose your queen, so there's that."

Milo's handsome face exploded into a huge smile.

"No!" Jax shouted.

I about jumped out of my seat.

Milo crossed his arms and said under his breath, "Damn, I knew it."

"You knew what?" I asked, looking back and forth between them.

He paused and shot Jax a glance. "Jax wanted me to see that new action movie tonight. Isn't that right?" He cocked his head, and his smile came back.

Jax's shoulders relaxed, and he raked his fingers through his hair. "Yeah. I'd be bummed if we couldn't see it together."

"That's what I thought." He turned to me. "Bros before—I mean, brothers first."

I shook my head and laughed.

CHAPTER Fifteen

JAX

THE BED DIPPED DOWN AND back up again. "Jax, wake up! Wake up! Santa came! Come on, we get to open presents!" Emily and Alice both jumped in unison, a jumble of flailing arms, footie pajamas, and flushed faces.

"What time is it?" I rubbed my face.

"Time to get up! It's time, it's time!" Giggles added to the general pandemonium.

I shifted and looked out the shuttered blinds. "It's still dark. Go back to bed."

"Betty said it's time." Emily's bottom lip quivered.

Oh hell.

"Okay, squirt. Let's go check it out."

Squeals and more giggles followed as I struggled to get out of bed.

Emily took Alice's hand once we reached the hallway. "Let's go get Sivan!" They dashed off in a different direction.

Good luck with that.

I shook my head and started toward the kitchen for a much-needed cup of coffee. It would take more than a few jolts of caffeine to get me going.

Mom, Dad, Aunt Betty, Ray, Milo, Dylan, Gage, and Sivan sat at the long wooden kitchen table. "Wow. I wasn't the first? What'd I miss?"

Dad answered, "About ten minutes. Those girls are on a rampage."

I glanced over at Sivan. Man, she was gorgeous with her messy hair, sleepy eyes, smeared makeup, and ratty nightgown. My heart stalled in my chest.

I had it bad.

I met her eyes. "They were headed your way."

She laughed. "I heard them in your room. I knew I was next, so I snuck down the back stairs." She covered her face. "I know, I know, I'm a Grinch."

I smiled. "You're a smart Grinch. I was jumped, pulled, and drooled on. Not the best way to wake up."

We smiled at each other until Mom cleared her throat. "Let's all move into the family room. Once the girls find out Sivan jumped ship, they'll be down." She winked at Sivan.

Everyone gathered their cups of coffee and headed out, except for me and Sivan. I crossed the room, praying they hadn't emptied the entire pot of coffee already. I grabbed the handle and, ugh, only half a cup. I needed more.

"Here, let me start another." Sivan took the pot over to the sink and started to fill it.

"Thanks." I didn't think my brain function had roused enough to remember all the steps.

Once she had it set and ready to go, she said, "I have a present for you, but I didn't want to give it to you while anyone was around."

I leaned in. "That sounds promising." She smelled like lavender again. My favorite.

She laughed and pushed my shoulder. "It's not what you're thinking." She went over to the large hutch and opened the bottom cupboard.

"That's the hiding spot Betty uses for all her super-secret stuff." I waggled my eyebrows.

"It is?" She examined it closer.

"Yeah. I was looking for some extra glasses for the Christmas party and was digging around in there, and I thought she was going to have a heart attack. I had very clear instructions not to look in there again." I tried to look over her shoulder. "What do you think she's got hidden in there?"

Sivan glanced at a small file cabinet tucked into the back corner. Her face lost its color. "Oh, probably important documents. Things we shouldn't look at." She hurriedly pulled out a wrapped gift. "Here it is." She stood and handed it to me while biting her lip.

"Hmm. Looks like a book."

She rolled her eyes. "Okay, Einstein."

I ripped open the paper and found three small books. *The Making of a Veterinarian, Bite-Me, The Tell-All Tales of a Veterinarian,* and *Veterinary Anatomy*, a coloring book with a set of Crayola crayons sitting on the top.

"Two of them are for fun, but the first one might be helpful."

I caught a glimpse of her rubbing her thumb against her forefinger. My throat constricted, and warmth circulated throughout my body. Something light released from inside me. This gift was so perfect, so right, I couldn't put words to it.

"Thank you," I whispered, staring at the books in my hands which were so much more than paper and binding. Validation.

By the time I looked up, Sivan's face had gone soft, and tears welled in her eyes. She knew exactly what this gift meant to me.

"You'll have to hide it for a while, you know, until you tell your parents."

I snapped out of my trance. "I haven't had a chance to tell you. I told my mom, and she was okay with it. I guess you were right; she just wants me to be happy."

Her face lit up. "Oh, Jax. That's the best news ever."

I took a step closer. She glowed, and I wanted—no, I needed to get closer. "Merry Christmas," I said as I smoothed a messy lock of hair away from her face. I kept my hand on her face, my heart beating triple time. We stood frozen for a few moments. "Sivan, I—"

She blinked rapidly and shook her head. "I have to go. The coffee's almost done."

"Wait." *Please don't go.*

"I can't. I just . . . no." She turned and almost ran from the room.

My heart sank. Why did she always run off? I knew she had feelings for me. It showed in her eyes almost every time we were together.

After an inward groan, I poured myself some coffee and added extra sugar.

I should give up. That would be the easiest route. For whatever reason, Sivan didn't want a relationship with me.

Ray entered the room. "You had to pick the one girl on the planet who doesn't like you."

I was in no mood for him.

I leaned back against the counter. "Ray. Nice to see you."

He crossed the room and grabbed the coffee pot. "Thank goodness there's a fresh pot."

"You can thank Sivan for that."

"Seriously, how're you doing?" Ray leaned against the counter and took a gulp from his mug.

"Good. I love it here."

He cocked his head. "I'm the observer, remember? Something isn't right."

"The only thing I'd change is Sivan. But you already guessed that."

He chuckled. "I never would've believed it."

"What?"

"I'd think she'd be falling all over you like the rest. Your ego okay?" He laughed and playfully jabbed my arm.

"Smart-ass." Time for payback. "You're no better. I've seen you around Aunt Betty. My observation skills are also—"

"Oh shit." His smile dropped. "Am I that—"

My turn to tease. I snorted. "Yep."

He moved closer and lowered his voice. "What's her story? Your mom told me she's a widow. She doesn't date?"

"Not once since I've been here."

"Still grieving?"

"I don't think so. She always seems good." *Except for that one day.*

"I'm going to keep trying. I think you should also." He nodded like he was trying to convince himself.

"It's complicated."

He crossed his arms. "So? Life is complicated."

"Is everything black and white with you?"

He smirked. "Pretty much. If you want something, go after it. Simple."

"I wish." I had two things going against me. Aunt Betty's ban and Sivan.

Give up.

Don't give up.

"Let's go. Emily and Alice will be rabid about now." I pulled his arm. "I'm sure they're waiting on us."

We entered the family room, and, sure enough, surrounded by a mountain of gifts, the girls were almost hyperventilating.

Everyone had already formed a circle around them, some sitting on the floor, others lounging on chairs. All waiting for the madness to begin. The girls started ripping away, but Aunt Betty insisted they open one at a time.

Sivan sat in the background, watching with a sad smile on her face.

I snuck around to the back of the tree and grabbed her gift with sweaty palms. I circled around and plopped it in her lap.

Please don't hate it.

A smile curved her lips when she opened it. "Black?" She took the scarf from the box and put it on. "I thought you weren't a fan?"

"I wasn't. Until recently. Now I love black."

Her cheeks pinkened. Were those tears in her eyes? Nah. Probably just tired.

Milo pointed his finger at me. "If you don't tell her, I will."

No one else was in the kitchen as we sat at the table with our plates of eggs and hash browns.

"You don't understand. I have almost six months left with Sivan, and I don't want to risk it if Aunt Betty finds out. She made it clear. Hands off Sivan. If we got something started, she could send one of us packing, and I think it'd be me." I pushed the eggs around my plate.

His eyebrows furrowed. "Why is she so against it?"

"She's worried about Sivan. She doesn't want her hurt."

"Will you hurt her?" Milo shoveled a huge bite of hash browns in his mouth.

"Hell no."

"Then?"

"Aunt Betty doesn't know that for sure. All I have to do is wait until June, and then I can make my move."

"June?" He almost choked on his food. "You mean, right before you leave? That's stupid."

"Ugh. You're right." I rubbed my forehead. "But I can't risk losing these months together. She's become everything to me." The lump in my throat made it hard to swallow. I dropped my fork and scrubbed my hands over my face.

Milo raised an eyebrow. "I noticed. I'm surprised she's not clued in. You about jumped down my throat when you thought she was going out with me." He laughed. "But you did refer to her as a sister, so there's that."

"Shit. I'm sure that's been a romance killer."

Stupid. Stupid.

I got up to throw my half-eaten food in the garbage.

"Do you think you have a chance with her?" He tilted his head.

Ah, the dreaded question. My stomach sank, and I broke out into a sweat. "Honestly, I don't know. She's hard to read. Sometimes I think I have a chance, and we'll get a little closer, and then she'll retreat and become closed off." I took a sip of my coffee. "She seems, I don't know, like she's still recovering from some sort of trauma. Either Betty doesn't know what happened, or she's not telling me, so I'm going in blind. But I feel the chemistry between us, so it's hard to believe she doesn't feel it, too."

"Maybe she thinks you're a jerk?" Milo chuckled and continued to stuff food in his mouth.

"Very funny." I gave him an elbow, but got serious and asked, "Do you think it could be because she lost her family?"

"Wasn't it when she was younger?"

"She was about eleven, but that's all the information I have. If I knew a little more, maybe I could figure things out."

"Yeah, but you'll need to be patient with that. You never want to push someone before they're ready." His gaze was steady, unwavering.

"I got it. But what do you think I should do?"

"Tell her."

"I have too much at risk. I could scare her off and lose her for good. And there's also the issue of Aunt Betty."

"You have a lot at risk if you don't. Remember, I almost took her for mine."

"You that sure of yourself?"

"Of course." He exaggerated a wink.

"I would thank you, but you didn't have a chance." I shoved his arm.

"Whatever. That doesn't mean she won't meet someone else in the next six months. You think you can keep her isolated here on the farm?"

"I wish I could." Nah, it'd never work.

"Have you seen her?" His eyebrows shot up. "She's probably the most stunning girl I've ever seen. Those blue eyes." He looked off in the distance. "Beautiful."

"Cut it out." If he wasn't careful, the next punch would be to his nose.

"I'm just saying, if that girl is anywhere in public, she's going to get asked out. You don't want to wait."

"She'd never let anyone pick her up out in the mall or someplace like that. You don't know Sivan."

"Pretty sure of yourself?"

I thought about it and sighed. "No."

"Then do something about it."

An idea flashed. "Do you think Mom could get through to Aunt Betty?"

"Mom? She's even more protective than Aunt Betty. Maybe Dad?"

"Dad. Hmm." I scratched my chin. "You know, that's a good idea. He can usually get his way with Mom. You remember the sailboat?"

"The one sitting at Shilshole Marina?"

"Dad spent a year convincing Mom he had to have it. He won the battle, took it out twice, and now it sits."

"Bad call for Mom." He laughed.

"But in his defense, the reason he hasn't taken it out is because of your tour schedule."

He grimaced. "Yeah, that's true."

I got up from the table. "It's settled. I'll start with Dad."

Two hours later, I wasn't so sure of my decision.

I jumped into Dad's rental car right as he was pulling out of the driveway. I'd overheard Mom asking him if he could pick up more sparkling water, so I decided to make my move.

"I need you to talk to either Mom or Aunt Betty for me," I croaked out.

"What about?" He glanced at me, his head tilted.

"Well, see, it's like this." I cleared my throat. "Aunt Betty told me I can't date Sivan."

"Well, then don't date Sivan. That's easy." He put the car in reverse.

Damn, this wasn't going well.

"Dad. I want to date Sivan. Like, I really want to date her. If she wants me, that is."

He stopped the car only a few feet from our starting point. "Betty doesn't make these rules lightly, son. I'm sure she has a good reason for imposing that rule. I, for one, can think of a good one."

Here we go.

"It's tempting to want to take things a little too far when you live under the same roof."

Did not want to have *that* conversation, but it looked like I'd have to put things straight.

"Aunt Betty said it's because she thinks Sivan isn't ready for a relationship, not because she thought we'd have sex all over the house or something."

"Jax!"

"Well, it's true."

"You should let this go. You're living under Betty's roof. Her rules."

"Dad."

"What?" He frowned.

"I think I might kinda, sorta love her." Oh crap. Did I say that out loud?

Dad sighed and leaned back against the headrest.

Yes. Out loud.

"Jax. You can't throw something like that out there if you aren't serious."

"I am serious."

"You're only seventeen. You're too young."

"I turn eighteen next month. Didn't you meet Mom when you were eighteen?"

He looked up to the sky and asked, "Why me?"

"Because Mom would freak out, and you're good at convincing her to listen."

He turned back to me. "Are you ready for this to blow up in your face if you don't get the answer you want? Because your mom is itching to get you home."

I rubbed my hands over my face. "No. I'm not ready for that. That's why I need you. Please?"

"What you said earlier. The kinda, sorta part? You're way past that, aren't you?"

I'd pushed out the thought a million times. Did I love Sivan? *I wanted to be around her all the time. Check. She's smart and beautiful. Check. She makes me want to be a better person. Check. Just thinking about her makes me happy. Check. I don't want to imagine a life without her. Check.*

"Yeah." He had me figured out from the get-go.

"You kids have grown up way too quick."

"You'll help me?"

He reached over and messed up my hair. "Okay, but no guarantees."

"Thanks, Dad."

New Year's Eve, and I paced my room at 11:50 p.m. Should I go down and join the party? Would Sivan be there? Aunt Betty had invited the same crowd as before, and the laughter floated up the stairs, taunting me. I couldn't be around Sivan right now. My emotions were too exposed, too raw.

But boredom ate at me. There'd be a room full of guests to keep me in line. What could possibly happen? I could rein it in for a plate of food and maybe a few gulps of champagne. If Sivan was around, I'd give her a quick hello and head back up.

Good plan.

Milo greeted me at the bottom of the stairs. "Hey, man. I think the universe is working in your favor."

"What do you mean?"

"Sivan. It's almost twelve. She's standing under the doorframe with mistletoe. Oh, and look, Mrs. Thompson just left. She's alone." He gave me a shove.

I moved forward but stopped. Sivan. The breath knocked out of me. Drop-dead gorgeous. Her black hair was curled and pulled back with a few wisps floating down her neck, like a swirl of dark water. Her dress was white and silky, and I wanted to touch it. Her blue eyes glowed beneath her smoky makeup. The warmth of the room had left her cheeks flushed, her eyes bright.

Oh God. Stop me now.

My legs didn't obey. Excitement and dread warred inside as I crossed the room.

Determination replaced all other emotions as I approached her. The world could go to hell. I was going to kiss her.

"Happy New Year." My pulse lunged into high gear.

She smiled and looked at the clock. "There're sixty more seconds."

"Can you give me fifteen?"

"Huh?" Her head tilted.

"That's the average amount of time most people kiss on New Year's."

Her eyes widened, and she shook her head.

"Look." I pointed to the mistletoe. "It's fate."

She looked up, then her hypnotic, blue eyes locked on mine. The tension crackled between us.

"What can it hurt?" I asked, but winced inside, knowing it could lead to disaster.

She bit her bottom lip, and her eyes roamed my face. I moved into her space, noticing the pulse on her neck beat rapidly.

"Do you feel it? This? We owe it to ourselves to see what this is."

"And if it's ordinary?" Her voice trembled.

I leaned closer. "Do you really think what's between us is ordinary?"

God, she smelled good.

"People are around." Her eyes darted around the room.

"They won't notice in about . . ." I checked the clock, " . . . ten seconds. Everyone will be doing the same thing."

"Okay. Fifteen seconds." She licked her lips.

I moved closer, resting my hand on her lower back. So soft. I tilted her chin so her eyes met mine.

"Let it go. All of it."

She searched my eyes, her brow slightly furrowed. Then her face relaxed. She nodded once.

The crowd started shouting down the ten-second clock to midnight. I pulled her close and said, "You're all I think about, Sivan."

I placed my lips on hers, and the world dissolved away. Every sensation came alive,

almost knocking me off my feet. I gripped her tightly, my hands traveling up and down her back.

No one else was there. Just us.

When her tongue touched mine, a bolt shot through me so strong, every inch of my skin became electric.

Fire. Heat. Flames.

All the feelings I had tried to stomp down surged and took over.

Ordinary? Not even in the same universe.

Chapter Sixteen

Sivan

HE PICKED UP A LOOSE section of hair that had escaped out of my clip, twirling it around his finger. His eyes, oh those eyes, gazed into my soul as his lips brushed against mine, sending a shiver down my spine. The initial touch was feather soft, tender, but with that small contact, it was like a hundred fireworks let off a sparking sensation that traveled up and down my body.

My heart stuttered, stopped, and then fluttered back to life. Something inside unfurled, the noise from the party faded.

This was not ordinary like I'd hoped.

He drew back, and his eyes widened.

"Wow." I curled my fingers around his shirt and pulled him

back. This time, when his lips met mine, it wasn't soft. Oh no. It was frantic and passionate, like the world was ending.

"Sivan," he breathed.

"Don't stop." My hands had moved to his hair. So soft . . . heavenly.

"We have to leave," he whispered in my ear as he clutched me tight.

"Why?" I leaned back to study his expression.

"I'll tell you in a minute." His eyes darted around the room.

That's when I noticed the silence. How long had we been kissing? I closed my eyes for a moment and turned to face the crowd.

Earth, please swallow me whole.

All activity had stopped. Yep, we were definitely the center of attention. Jax's brothers, Ray, and Betty's friends all smiled. His dad, though, had his head tilted, a quizzical expression on his face. His mom's hand was next to her throat, and her mouth formed an O.

Jax met his dad's gaze, put his finger to his lips, and mouthed, "Okay?"

His dad nodded once. What was that all about?

He grabbed my hand. "Come on, let's get out of here."

My feet stumbled as he pulled me along, down the hall, and toward the back door. "Where are we going?"

"Outside. We'll grab your coat and boots from the mudroom."

"It's freezing out there!" I stopped in my tracks.

"Exactly. No one will think to look for us there. I need a few minutes alone to talk to you."

"Oh, all right." I had a full length down coat to put over my silky dress.

Once we reached the mudroom, Jax held out the coat for me. I bundled up, and he grabbed my boots.

"You aren't going to try to put on my boots?" I raised an eyebrow.

"Maybe." He eyed the door.

"I don't think so." I took the boots from his hands and slipped them on as he got ready.

The outside chill hit my face as he took my hand again and steered us toward the barn. That would be better than being in the freezing cold. Betty kept it at fifty-five degrees for the animals.

"We're going to the loft. It'll be warmer." Once we entered the barn, he motioned to the metal ladder propped against the edge. "You first." He grabbed two wool blankets hanging on a peg by the door.

I hugged my coat around me and started up. "If I fall, you'll catch me, right?" I laughed.

"If you fall for me, Sivan, I promise to catch you."

Butterflies took over my stomach, churning like a tornado.

Relax, Sivan. You can handle this.

I climbed the ladder and made room for Jax to lay down one of the wool blankets on a thick coat of hay. "Here, sit." I sat on one side, and he wrapped the second blanket over my legs.

Moonbeams streamed in from the triangle-shaped window in the back corner. He took a seat next to me and paused, searching my face. "I need you close when I tell you how I feel."

My heart thudded so fast, I was sure I'd faint. The butterflies and tornado were still at war in my stomach, and my breath seemed to speed up and stop at the same time. The cold around me forgotten.

"Sivan," he said, never breaking eye contact.

"Hmm?"

He scooted even closer and cupped my chin. "You probably know this, but . . . I've had feelings for you for a long time. Maybe even from that first day."

"You were a lot of things that first day." I bit my lip. I needed to quit talking.

"Yeah." A slow smile formed. He smoothed back a loose strand of my hair. "I came here angry at the world. I didn't know what I wanted or even who I was anymore. You changed that. You changed me."

He took my face in both his hands and covered my lips with soft kisses. He stopped and asked, "That okay?"

I nodded. The lump in my throat wouldn't go away no matter how many times I swallowed.

"I want you to give me a chance." He held perfectly still.

"I'm scared, Jax." More like terrified.

Jax smiled softly. "That's how you know it's real." He rubbed my back. "We'll need to go slow with this. Like a snail's pace. I can't go back to pretending. I want to move forward."

Could I?

"I'm pretty slow, like, maybe even slower than a snail." I took a deep breath and waited.

He smiled a crooked grin. "That's okay. We can kiss, right? Because that was . . . God, I can't even describe it."

My cheeks warmed. "Yeah. I'm good with that part." Time to tell him. "But I have stuff, you know, in my past. Maybe I'll never be able to move forward. Maybe I'll be stuck forever.

Emotionally, I mean."

"I'll take that risk." His eyes stayed glued to mine.

"I don't want to hurt you." I fidgeted with the zipper on my coat.

"Look at me."

I glanced back up and met his eyes.

"I need to talk to you about something." He rubbed the back of his neck.

"What?"

"It's Aunt Betty." He cleared his throat. "She asked me not to, uh, pursue you."

Huh. "She did?"

"She didn't want me to potentially hurt you. She thought you might have gone through a lot and didn't want me messing with you."

Warmth flooded through me. I wanted to hug her. Oh, Betty. She was looking out for me. "That's kinda sweet."

"The thing is, I'm worried she might decide to split us up." He took my hand and frowned.

The world stopped. "What?" I whispered. My body began to tremble.

"Yeah. We'll need to approach this carefully."

"I'll be the one to leave. You're her nephew." My nerves were raw, and tears began to build, making my throat tight.

"No. No way. She made it clear you're her priority." His grin seemed more like an effort to make me feel better than a genuine smile. "Don't worry. We'll work this out. Aunt Betty is cool about stuff."

My shoulders loosened a little.

"We'll need to go back and face the firing squad." He glanced over at the barn entrance. The big doors remained closed, with a narrow stream of light coming through. The horses nickered and moved around their stalls.

"Okay, but Jax?"

"Yes?"

"Before we move forward, I wanted you to know I may not ever be able to talk about my past. Can I trust you not to go there until I'm ready?" I held my breath, waiting for his answer.

He cupped my face in his hands. "You don't ever have to tell me. If you want to one day, fine. If not, that's okay with me. Sivan, it's your future I want, not your past."

I blinked back hot tears.

Jax tucked a lock of hair behind my ear and kissed me gently. "I promise to never push. I'll wait for you to trust me with it. Cross my heart." He made a crisscross motion over his chest.

"Now I have it in writing." I giggled, and a sudden lightness swept through me.

"Okay you two, I know you're up there. Come down right now!"

"Aunt Betty. I guess the firing squad's come to us." He sighed and squeezed his eyes shut for a moment.

I stiffened beside him. This could be a disaster.

"It'll be okay." The crease between his brow didn't match his words. We both quickly got to our feet and prepared to get back down the ladder. "I'll help you." Jax dropped down the first few rungs, and then helped me tuck my coat and dress around my legs. Once we were both down, we turned to face Betty.

She stood rigid with hands on hips. "How long has this been

going on?" She glanced back and forth between us

"What time is it?" Jax asked.

With an uncertain tone, she answered, "Twelve thirty-seven."

A mischievous smile spread across his face. "This has been going on for thirty-seven minutes."

Betty's shoulders relaxed, and she almost smiled. "I'm too tired to talk about this tonight. Tomorrow morning at nine, I want both of you in my office."

"Ten?" Jax was pushing his luck.

"Nine." The days of him charming Betty looked to be over.

He nodded. "Nine it is."

She followed us back to the house to make sure we went our separate ways. I avoided the party and took the back stairs to my room and tucked myself into bed.

Everything felt different. Everything *was* different. Walls had been cracked and hammered and chiseled down tonight. A warmth seeped through the holes. Was that happiness? I liked the feeling, so I hung on tight. Maybe I could do this. Maybe the fear didn't have to dictate my life. Maybe I could love people, and they wouldn't die. Maybe . . . was the last thought before I fell asleep.

"Sivan."

Someone took hold of my shoulder and shook me.

"Go away." I slapped at the hand and tried to turn over.

A familiar chuckle.

I bolted awake all at once. "What . . . what're you doing in my room?"

He sat on the edge of my bed. "Our appointment with Aunt Betty is in five minutes. I don't want her pissed off any more than she is."

"But, this is my room!" I clutched the blankets at my neck.

"Yes, and I hope to see a lot more of it." He waggled his eyebrows.

"Jax!" Was he joking?

"Just kidding. I know, I know. Nice and slow." He winked and grinned at me with a charming smile that made me forget to breathe.

"How can you be this chipper in the morning?" Sleep still fogged my brain.

"Because I haven't slept. I've been up all night, figuring out my plan of attack."

I frowned. "Attack?"

"Well, more like strategy. I need to make Aunt Betty see we can be together, take things slow. If I promise not to be a jerk and screw everything up, I think I can get her to agree."

I smiled and took a closer look. His hair was mussed, and he had a little stubble on his face. He must be tired, but the air crackled around him, and excitement danced in his beautiful eyes.

"That sounds like a great plan." My heart fluttered with nervous energy. This was happening.

He took my hand and pulled. "Let's do this thing."

I yanked it back. "Oh no you don't. I'm not meeting with Betty in my PJs." I kept the covers pulled up to my neck. "You can be in charge of coffee while I change."

"Don't I get to see?" His eyes twinkled with mischief.

"Maybe in about five years." I kept my expression blank.

His head dropped forward, and he heaved a heavy sigh.

I laughed and pushed his arm. "You said you were okay with waiting."

He shook his head. "I had that coming. Okay, I've got coffee duty. You get dressed, and we'll meet at Betty's office in four minutes."

When Jax left the room, I bounced out of bed and headed to the bathroom. I whipped off my t-shirt and sleep pants and put on a pair of jeans and a sweater. A quick comb through the hair, brushed my teeth, a swipe of mascara, and dab of lip gloss. Done.

I hurried down the stairs and skidded to a stop right outside Betty's door. Jax stood, holding two cups of coffee.

Fortification. "Thanks," I whispered. "Should we knock?"

He gave a light tap and opened the door slowly.

Betty sat behind the desk, her hands folded under her chin. She raised an eyebrow in Jax's direction and motioned to the two chairs in front of her desk.

"First, I want to say I'm sorry for last night." Jax waited for me to sit, and then plopped down in the chair next to me. He let out a long sigh. "I tried. I really did."

Betty remained quiet.

"You see, it's like this. I've never met anyone like Sivan." He glanced my way. "If she would've been like every other girl, I would've easily been able to respect your wishes to stay away." He shifted in the chair. "I've learned so much. Not only about life in general, but myself. I'm not the same person who came through your door almost four months ago. That guy wouldn't be good enough for Sivan. But I am good enough now. You can trust me. She can trust me. I'd rather cut off my right arm than hurt her."

Wow, oh wow. His words, so sincere. Heat radiated through my chest, and tears formed behind my eyes.

Relax, Sivan. Don't cry.

"I talked to your dad." Betty cocked her head and examined Jax.

His eyes widened.

"He seems to think you're ready. He believes the farm is a good place for you, that you've changed for the better."

Was this the part where she tells me I was the one leaving? I stared at Betty's face, willing her not to say the words.

"Sivan." She paused. "I have to ask you a question. I apologize, but I need an answer."

Fear constricted my throat, so I nodded.

"We made a deal when you came here, remember?"

"The file?" I almost choked on the words.

"Yes. I'm willing to keep our deal, but I need to know from you if you believe, or if you feel confident, you can handle this. I want the best for you, but, honestly, this situation is hard because I don't know the types of things you're dealing with. I want to make sure this isn't going to be too much." Her eyes studied me.

"You aren't sending me away?"

Her hand flew to her chest. "Sending you away? Why would you ever think that?"

"I thought, if you weren't sending Jax away, it'd be me."

"You're family now. Nothing you could do would ever make me send you away. You're stuck with us." She reached over the desk and squeezed my hand.

I whispered, "Okay," and blinked rapidly to hold back the tears.

"Sivan. If you tell me you're ready, I'll go along with this."

I stared into her eyes. "Yes. I am." I knew I was.

Jax straightened in his chair. "We're going slow, Aunt Betty. Like slug slow, or molasses slow—"

"I get it." She laughed. "But I do have some conditions."

"Anything," Jax said.

"No night visits to each other's rooms. I don't want Emily or Alice to catch wind of this for now."

Heat warmed my cheeks because he'd just been in my room.

"When you tell me you'll both go slow, I'm going to take you for your word. You're living under the same roof, and I can guarantee it'll be difficult at times." Her eyes glanced back and forth between us. "When you go off to college, you can do that other stuff. But not here. You got that?"

"Yeah. College isn't that far off." He turned and winked at me.

My face would be in a perpetual state of red if he kept this up.

"Jax," Betty warned.

"Got it. No sleeping around while we're here, and no jokes about sleeping around." That charming grin was back.

She narrowed her eyes. "I'll be watching. Don't make me regret making this decision."

"Okay. I'll be good. I promise. It's just that, I'm having a great day." His smile widened.

Betty glanced at the clock. "Okay. I have a phone conference in three minutes. I trust you two will abide by my rules." She tilted her head and examined Jax.

Jax jumped up. “No problem!” He grabbed my hand. “Let’s go.”

I hesitated and turned to Betty. “Thanks for trusting me. Well, both of us. It means a lot.”

Betty’s face softened, and her usual happy expression replaced her worried one.

We walked out the door, and Jax closed it quietly.

“We forgot our coffee.” I had at least a couple sips left.

He checked up and down the hall and stepped closer, linking our hands together. He walked forward, nudging me until my back hit the wall.

“It doesn’t matter.” His smile mischievous.

“What are you doing?” I looked back at Betty’s door only a few feet away.

“You’re mine now.” His grin widened as he pressed me against the wall. “All mine,” he muttered as he ran kisses along my neck. His hands slipped behind my back, rubbing up and down, making me completely insane. “Kiss me,” he whispered, his mouth brushing mine.

“Jax.” My breath came out in short rasps. “Not here.”

I wanted his warm lips against mine in the worst possible way.

“One? I’ll make it quick.” His lips were a breath away.

Before my brain could get the message to my body, I wrapped my arms around his neck and pulled him into me. The kiss . . . oh wow, chills ran up and down my spine. With lips and hands and bodies touching, exploring, I couldn’t get close enough.

Jax groaned a little and pulled back. “God, Sivan. It keeps

getting better."

I caught my breath and tried to smooth my hair. "We can't do that again in the open or we'll get caught. Where are your parents?"

"Around here somewhere. Remember, though, we've already put on a show for them." He chuckled. "They're heading out in a few hours, so I guess we should pull back a little. But kissing is on the approved list. It's everything else we have to avoid. But, damn, it's gonna be hard." He placed his hands on my face. "I just . . . I have all these feelings. I'm feeling a little out of control."

"Same here. But let's not mention that to Betty."

"Definitely not," he agreed. He stared into my eyes. "I'm happy."

"So am I."

Happiness. *Relax, Sivan. Don't freak out.*

"Let's stick to the plan no matter what. I don't want to fu—uh, mess this up."

CHAPTER Seventeen

JAX

FAT, PUFFY SNOWFLAKES FELL OUTSIDE. I got up from my desk and stretched. With my homework done, and Sivan and the girls out shopping with Aunt Betty, the house was quiet. Too quiet.

I threw a glance at my guitar as I walked to the window. How long had it been since I last played? A year? A pang hit me dead center. I closed my eyes for a moment, trying to remember how it felt when it was good, before I blamed music for my problems.

Before I was even aware, my guitar was in my hands as I plopped down on the bed. *Old friends.* My fingers explored the wood grain, the strings, neck, and frets. It hummed up my arms and throughout my body as I gripped it.

I smiled. The bitterness had evaporated. If it wasn't for my brothers and the need to escape, I wouldn't have met Sivan.

Sivan. The feel of her, warm and soft. I ran my fingers along the strings. Silky hair, husky laugh, sharp wit and . . . I closed my eyes and carelessly strummed. Sivan and music together. A warmth settled around my chest. She still hadn't trusted me with her past yet, but that was okay. We'd technically only been together for a month.

The best month of my life.

The possibility of enjoying music again shoved and kicked and pushed the walls of resentment I hid behind, crumbling them into rubble. I'd always loved it. Before Sivan, my negativity had smothered the desire to play, even to create music. Songwriting had always been my favorite, with three or four melodies usually bouncing around my brain. Lyrics had started to come back, but, this time all of them were about Sivan.

I strummed the guitar, this time harder. Wow. Out of tune. I spent the next few minutes twisting knobs and plucking strings, getting the tone just how I liked it.

What song reminded me of Sivan? *Think*. Like flipping pages, songs, old and new, flashed by.

Bingo. "Come On Get Higher" by Matt Nathanson. Perfect.

I positioned my guitar on my lap, like friends embracing after a long separation. I strummed slowly, closing my eyes, letting the words flow out with the rhythm of the music. God, this felt good.

The air around me seemed to still, and I looked up. Sivan stood in the doorframe with her hand covering her mouth.

I stopped.

"No, continue, Jax. That was amazing. I didn't know." She

wiped beneath her eye. “I had no idea you could sing like that.”

She smiled, and her face glowed, and I felt . . . proud.

I stood. “I picked up my guitar today, and it feels freaking fantastic. Is it okay?” I searched her face. “I know you’re sensitive to music.”

“How did you know?” She looked down, her cheeks turning a light shade of red.

“Betty told us to keep it toned down when you were around because—”

Her eyebrows furrowed. “Yeah. I did ask her that when I first came. But, you know, I’m getting better.” She smiled again. “That was really brave of you. I mean, obviously something was stopping you, and you pushed past it. You tackled it and won.”

Something about her words caught my attention.

“Is that what you’ve been doing? Avoiding music?”

“Yeah,” she whispered. “I loved it until . . . I didn’t.”

I crossed the room and took her by the shoulders. Her body trembled under my hands. “Did it have something to do with your parents?”

She nodded once. “Yes. I haven’t been able to play since they died.” She bit her lip, and a tear escaped.

Don’t push. I wrapped my arms around her and let her cry. Her tears about killed me, but I vowed to be strong for her.

She pulled away after a few minutes. Her eyes became clear and determined, her chin high. “If you can do it, I can. Wait right here.”

She turned and ran out of the room. Hmm. Wonder what that was all about? She came back a few minutes later holding a ragged blue cloth.

“What’s that?”

She rubbed it between her fingers and smiled. "I saved it. My mom would always let me polish the keys. Come on." She took me by the hand and tugged.

"You play the piano?" I asked as she pulled me down the hall.

"Yep."

We entered the music room, and she came to a halt. "I haven't been in this room yet." She took a few deep breaths.

"We can sit and not do anything today. Just get used to the room," I suggested. My heart raced and my stomach clenched at the same time. Would this be too much for her?

"If I don't do it now, I might not ever." Her eyes scanned the room. Still holding my hand, she sat on the upholstered bench tucked under the piano. She closed her eyes, nodded a few times, took a deep breath, and let go of my hand.

I stayed still, daring not to breathe.

She took the cloth and started dusting the keys left to right. With her index finger, she tapped one key. The sound echoed throughout the room. Her shoulders visibly relaxed.

A smile lit her face. "I did it."

"Yes, you did." Sometimes Sivan seemed older than her years. But here, at the piano, her bright eyes reminded me of someone much younger.

"I didn't fall apart." Her eyes widened.

"No, you didn't." I smiled.

She placed both hands on the keys and began to play. Whoa. *What the hell?* Her nimble fingers flew over the keys in a graceful arch, each note clear and bell-like. Her eyes were closed, her expression serene, but her body and fingers were a flurry of motion. She moved like water, fluid, with each change of tone. The music, the beauty of it, stole my breath. Good God, she wasn't just good; she was freaking great.

A hand looped through my arm. Aunt Betty. She must have heard the music.

"Fantastic," I mouthed to her.

She shook her head. "You have no idea."

The music stopped. Sivan took a deep breath and let it out. She rose to her feet and turned to us with tears streaming down her face. I held out my arms, and she ran into them. She hugged me, and then reached over and embraced Aunt Betty.

Aunt Betty wrapped her arms around her. "Shhh. It's okay."

"I missed it. I thought I didn't. I told myself I didn't, but I did." Sivan cried onto her shoulder.

"When is the last time you played, honey?" Aunt Betty rubbed her back.

"Six years, eight months, and three days." She wiped her eyes and laughed.

"How did you do that? I mean, play like that after all this time?" I asked.

A flush crept up her cheeks. "Well, I told you about my photographic memory for some things."

"You see music like you do math equations?" I held still, hoping she'd open up.

"It's different with music. The notes appear to me in shades of colors, each one represents a different emotion."

I tried to imagine it, but couldn't. "Like a rainbow?"

"More like a kaleidoscope with patterns. The shades are mixed up depending on the composition of the melody." She held out her arms and spun around the room. "It's like I just woke up. I see it all again and my fingers remembered everything."

I smiled and took her hand. Sivan had never been more beautiful than she was in that moment.

Aunt Betty asked, "Were your parents famous pianists?"

She shook her head. "No."

"Was the word prodigy ever bantered around when you were young?"

Her lips curved up into a slight smile and she blushed. "On occasion."

"You've kept this incredible gift bottled up. That must have been so painful for you." Aunt Betty squeezed her eyes shut for a moment.

"How did you know?" Sivan asked.

"A talent as big as yours must have been so hard to contain." She smoothed a piece of Sivan's hair back off her face. "You are so brave."

"No, it was Jax. He's the one who inspired me to play again."

Her eyebrow lifted. "Jax?"

I shrugged. "She caught me playing my guitar after your errands."

"You too? Well, this is a night to celebrate!" She hugged me and whispered, "Thank you," in my ear. "I'm going to make my famous peanut tofu for dinner!" she said and headed for the kitchen.

After she left, I pretended to gag.

Sivan swatted my arm. "Don't you ever tell her we don't like tofu. It'd crush her."

We laughed for a moment, and I pulled her close. "You think I'm brave, but I'm nothing like you. I didn't play, because I was pouting. I resented my entire family, and I turned my back on something I loved. It only hurt me." I kissed her soft lips. "Because of you, those feelings are gone. Now, I feel free. I can do whatever I want with my life. My choices won't be because I'm angry or resentful." I squeezed her tighter. "But you did something much greater than me today. You reconnected with your past. That's brave."

She swallowed hard. "I loved music, but I pushed it away because it hurt too much after."

I waited for a moment to see if she'd continue. "We both did the same, but for different reasons." I paused again then asked, "You know why we are able to reconnect with that side of ourselves?"

She tilted her head.

I took a deep breath. "Because we're both open to love now."

She stiffened. "But—"

I gently placed my finger on her lips. "I know we're not ready yet."

"Jax." Her voice choked with tears.

"Today was huge. We'll get into all that other stuff another time. Right now, let's go celebrate by pretending we love tofu." I winked, hoping to cut the tension a little.

She hugged me again, and we headed to the kitchen.

We held hands under the table. I squeezed hers and said, "Aunt Betty, this is the best tofu I've ever had."

Sivan kicked me and giggled quietly.

"So, Sivan . . ." Aunt Betty smiled warmly. "You know how we've been researching where you'll go next year for college?"

"Yes, and thanks for all your help."

"I have a new choice to add to your list."

"You do?"

"Juilliard."

"Juilliard?" she whispered.

"If this is too soon for me to bring up, I'll drop it."

"It's not that it's too soon. I just haven't played for so long."

"I haven't mentioned this because you weren't comfortable talking about music." She studied Sivan a moment before she continued. "But I went to Juilliard, and I know a thing or two about the piano."

"Really?" Sivan asked.

I had a fuzzy memory of Aunt Betty playing the piano when I was young. But I hadn't remembered the part about Juilliard.

"I was good. But not in the same stratosphere as you."

Sivan's cheeks pinkened, and she waved her off.

"Even with all those years not playing, you're better than anyone I've heard. Sivan, your talent takes my breath away."

"If I hadn't come here, I probably would have never played again. So, thank you."

Betty approached Sivan and placed her hands on her shoulders. "The fact this has been a placc of healing for you makes me happier than you'll ever know."

Emily and Alice bounded in, followed by Regina. *Ugh.*

"We got to see the penguins!" Alice shouted.

"And the gorillas!" Emily joined in.

"Okay, girls. Let's get you into the bathtub before dinner." Aunt Betty left with them as she shooed them out of the kitchen.

Regina examined Sivan's tear stained face. Under her

breath, she said, "Finally."

"What do you mean *finally*?" I was fed up with her passive-aggressive remarks and actions against Sivan. Enough. I was calling her on it.

She pursed her lips together. "I said *finally* because I can see there's been some sort of conflict here. Sivan acts like she's so perfect all the time. Perfect student, perfect foster child." She paused and glared at Sivan. "Perfect girlfriend. No one is that good all the time. It's an act."

I gritted my teeth. "Compared to you, she *is* perfect. And you know what else—"

Sivan touched my arm. "Jax, it's okay. Just let it drop. It's been a good day. Let's not ruin it."

I scowled at Regina. "You're right. She's not worth it."

Regina flipped her hair back over her shoulder and left toward the bathroom with a, "Whatever."

My hands tightened into fists. "I'm talking to Aunt Betty. I want her gone."

"It's okay, Jax. Don't say anything yet. I think there's something else going on with her."

"Besides being a royal bitch?"

Sivan burst out laughing. "Yeah, something like that."

I shook my head. "One more chance. Okay? Then I talk to Aunt Betty."

"Deal." She reached out to shake my hand, but I pulled her in for a kiss instead.

Aunt Betty came back into the kitchen. "Okay, I'm just going to come out with it."

Sivan jumped back and smoothed her clothes like we hadn't just been kissing. I bit my lip to keep from laughing. We were so busted.

Betty waved us off. "For goodness' sake, I know you kiss. Quit looking so guilty."

Sivan covered her mouth and laughed. "We're trying to keep it low-key, you know, like you asked."

"Yes, about that. I thought it would be a good idea not to let the girls know you were in a full-fledged relationship with you both living under the same roof." She shook her head. "The best-laid plans . . ."

"What do you mean?" I asked.

"Emily asked me yesterday when the two of you were getting married."

A coughing sound erupted next to me. I gave Sivan a few pats on the back. "The thought has you all choked up, huh?"

Her face turned bright red. "Um, no."

"Apparently, even a five-year-old can pick up on what's going on between you. The smiles, the looks." She chuckled. "The holding hands under the table."

Sivan covered her face. "Oops."

"Pssh." She waved her off. "That's not why I'm here."

"Oh?" Sivan stilled beside me.

"I talked to my old friend, Rebecca, from Juilliard."

Sivan's foot started to tap on the floor.

"They're wrapping up auditions. They want to see you. But we'd have to be quick about it. There's a flight leaving tomorrow morning. I have Mrs. Thompson on backup to watch the girls. No pressure." She laughed.

Sivan straightened. "But, Betty, I haven't had any time to practice."

"I've explained your situation. Well, a little. I said circumstances prevented you from playing for six years. They were very understanding and excited to meet you after I told them about your talent."

Sivan searched my face. "What do you think?"

"I think I need to get out my mustache and take a trip to New York."

She grabbed my hand. "Okay, I'll do it."

CHAPTER Eighteen

Sivan

WHY DID I AGREE TO *this?*

The plane started its taxi down the runway. Too late. "What if I crash and burn?" I asked Jax.

He squeezed my hand. "They say it's safer to fly than to ride in a car."

"No, not the plane. My audition." I tried taking a deep, cleansing breath, but it didn't work.

"Oh." He laughed. "I thought it was your fear of flying."

"I'm not afraid of flying." *I might be a liar.*

He looked down to our clasped hands. My white-knuckle hold gave me away. "Then would you like to explain why I no longer have circulation in my fingers?"

I loosened my hold a little. "Okay, well, maybe it's been a while since I've been on a plane."

Jax chuckled. "I have the perfect solution."

"What? Get off the plane, go back home and sit in front of the fire?" Yeah, that sounded good right now.

Jax leaned in. "Kiss me," he said as he brushed his lips over mine.

Oh, yes. "That's working a little, I think." A smile pulled at my lips, even though fear and anxiety still had an iron grip on the rest of me.

He held my face in his hands, and we locked eyes. "More?"

"Yeah. I think I'll need more, you know, fear therapy." I shot a glance around the plane. Everyone was occupied, getting ready for takeoff, and Betty didn't have a line of vision to our seats. "We're safe. No one's looking."

"Good." He kissed my lips again. "Because I'm not going to stop until you feel better."

"Okay."

He placed his hand on my face and stared directly into my eyes. "I'm going to be there for you. You can lean on me when you're scared, or lonely, or just whenever you need me."

Tears formed, and I blinked them back. "I'm scared right now." But it wasn't a fear of flying. My feelings for him overwhelmed me. Could I handle it if something happened to him? If he left me?

"Let's get started then."

His smile turned mischievous as he placed his lips back on mine. This time, he kissed me like he was making up for all the months of denial and tension. The intensity knocked every thought from my head.

We broke apart, breathless. “I think I’m better now.”

“I’m not. I think a little bit more, and I’ll be over *my* fear.” Jax grinned.

I tilted my head. “Wait. You aren’t afraid of flying.”

“I developed a fear just today.” He nuzzled my neck.

“That tickles.” I laughed and tried to move away. Jax’s disguise included a scratchy mustache.

“Not a fan of the mustache?” He pretended to twirl it.

“Not so much. But you need it so your fans won’t recognize you.”

Jax groaned. “Not *my* fans.”

I’d done a Google search and knew he was wrong. Jax had a growing fan base he didn’t want to acknowledge. Sure, he hadn’t released music yet. But these fans were anticipating his own album, and, if not that, hoping he’d see the light and join his brothers. It also didn’t hurt that he was GQ model hot.

“Anyway, it doesn’t matter whose fans they are. No one’s stopped you when you’ve worn the disguise.”

“I have to hand it to Regina. She did come through on this one.” Jax leaned back. “Maybe she’s not so bad?”

It had always been my motto, if I didn’t have anything nice to say, keep it shut. I pressed my lips together and nodded.

Jax took a long look at me and burst out laughing. “Was that painful for you?”

“You did that on purpose. You know Regina is . . .”

Laughing harder, he pulled me in for a hug. “She’s an evil bitch, yet I can’t get you to say a single mean thing about her. What’s up with that?”

"Betty sees something good in her. I'm still looking." I laughed along with him.

"Just avoid her. I don't trust her." He became serious. "Really, Sivan. I have a bad feeling about her."

Once we landed in LaGuardia, my heart began to beat faster. This was happening.

Relax, Sivan. You can do this. Breathe.

"Just take a deep breath."

My eyes shot up to Jax's intense gaze.

"It'll help. I do it all the time when I'm nervous."

"Who says I'm nervous?" A bluff was in order.

He shook his head and laughed. "I'm nervous, and I'm not even performing. I took a guess." He reached over and squeezed my hand. His was warm and comforting.

"Okay, well, maybe a little."

"See? That wasn't so hard." A huge grin lit up his face. "I'll get you to open up little by little."

Could I? Maybe this was as open as I would ever get. My stomach sank, but when I looked at him again, his good-natured expression and confident nod gave me a boost. My heart swelled.

"Come on, let's go. We don't have all day." Jax pulled me from my seat.

"Pushy bastard," I mumbled under my breath.

"Hey. I thought you didn't swear?" He laughed.

"I don't. In this case, it's a descriptive phrase."

He shrugged and slung his arm around my shoulder. "Well, this *pushy bastard* is going to get you to the audition on time."

A warm flood of emotion took over every square inch of me.

Maybe I can change.

After collecting our luggage, the three of us grabbed a cab and began our trek into the city. Dull brown and grey swampy areas were the first things I noticed about the landscape. Not what I was expecting.

"Once we get into the city everything will change. It's alive and vibrant." Betty's eyes sparkled.

The closer we got to the city, the more my body began to relax. The crowds of people fascinated me as we wound our way through the city streets. I breathed in the smells of coffee, roasted nuts, and hotdogs. The place buzzed with a distinct energy. Betty was right. I loved it.

Twenty more minutes and we pulled up to our destination.

"Wow, what a beautiful old hotel." The façade had a stone and brick exterior. "It's huge. Look how tall." I craned my neck to see all the way to the top.

"Henry and I would stay here on weekend trips. I thought it was time I revisited some of my fondest memories." Betty gazed up at the old hotel, and her eyes misted over.

"Betty, we could go—"

"No, no. I'm looking forward to it. Once I get past the front doors, I'll be fine. No, better than fine. This'll be good for me." She got out to pay the driver.

Jax caught my glance, and we both sat frozen for a moment. Before getting out, he leaned toward me and whispered, "Betty has good instincts. You gotta trust her."

"I do, but she's making this trip for me. I don't want it to be something she has to face before she's ready."

"It's been three years since Uncle Henry died."

"I know. But everyone has their own timeline." I hoped he understood my double meaning.

Betty met us on the other side of the cab. "First, we'll unpack. Then we can head out to the audition, and afterward, to Shake Shack. Sivan, you must try the portabello burger. It's crisp-fried and has melted Muenster and cheddar cheese. Jax, they have something called a Shack Attack with chocolate custard and fudge sauce."

Jax chuckled.

She flung her purse over her shoulder. "Sound good?"

Yep. Jax was right. Betty would be just fine.

"Sounds great," Jax and I said at the same time. We all laughed and headed into the lobby.

"Aunt Betty, you went all out." Jax stood in the middle of the room and turned in a slow three-sixty.

"Beautiful, isn't it?" Betty's smile held a tinge of sorrow as she let her gaze fall over the elegant surroundings. She turned to me. "I'll get us checked in, and then we can head up. I booked a two-room suite; I hope you don't mind bunking with me for the next two days."

"Mind? This is fantastic. I hope everything works out after all you've done to arrange this." Would I choke when the time came for my audition? My hands trembled, so I tried stretching them out a few times. "I don't want to let you down."

Betty took me by the shoulders and looked into my eyes. "You could never let me down. Do you hear me? There's nothing you could do that would ever disappoint me."

Total and complete acceptance. I relaxed and let the warmth

flood through me. I'd forgotten what that felt like.

Jax took my hand and gave it a gentle squeeze. "You're gonna kick that audition's ass."

Getting to Juilliard was a whirlwind of activity. We checked into our room, which was beautiful and elegant, just like the lobby, unpacked, and immediately set out for my audition. A two-hour cushion buffered us, because Betty warned traffic could be unpredictable.

Jax held my cold, sweaty hand all the way there. They began to shake again, so Jax squeezed tighter and whispered, "You've got this."

We stopped in front of a two-story, triangular, glass front entrance.

"We're here." I gulped.

"We still have an hour. We can walk around the campus so you can get a feel for things." Betty patted my other hand. "I'll get our guest passes, and we can get started."

After we walked through a few buildings, I began to relax. The sound of musical instruments being tuned and the smell of books and pizza put me at ease. The muscles in my shoulders and neck started to unwind.

The three of us walked the halls as Betty played tour director. "Juilliard has 850 students in total, representing music, dance, and acting. There are six concert halls, ninety-eight practice rooms in the school, and twenty-eight in the dorms. This is an all Steinway school. If you're interested in math and science, Columbia and Barnard offer joint and exchange programs.

"So you can get your math fix," Jax teased.

I rolled my eyes.

"Are there any outdoor areas?" Jax asked Betty.

"Yes, this way. We're close to Hearst Plaza and the Milstein Pool, where you can see Henry Moore's *Reclining Figure*. Wait until you see it. It's really cool."

Once outside, my breath escaped in a rush. "Wow." The sculpture sat in the middle of the pool with the city as the backdrop. I imagined sitting on the grassy lawn during the warmer months.

"See that bench over there, next to the tree?" Betty pointed to the pool area.

A large, red maple provided a canopy over the bench. "Yes, it looks peaceful." I loved it instantly.

"That's where I came between classes. It's one of my favorite places in the world." Betty looked down at her watch. "Showtime, Sivan."

I took a deep breath. "I'm ready."

Jax pointed in front of him. "I'm gonna hang out on the bench. I'll keep it warm until you get back."

"I'll take you to room 414." She rubbed my shoulder. "I'll come back and wait with Jax. After you're done, you can meet us there."

Jax gave me a gentle hug and took me by the shoulders. "Kill it," was all he said.

I laughed and gave him a little shove.

Betty and I walked down the light-filled halls in silence. We stopped in front of the door. She smoothed back a piece of my hair. "Forty-five minutes will go fast. Try not to think about the outcome. Just enjoy the music."

"Okay. That's what I'll do." Well, maybe that's what I'd try to do.

"Beethoven and Mozart are great choices. That's what I would have chosen."

With a nod, I gave a final hug to Betty and opened the doors.

Breathe.

Three sets of eyes, each behind glasses, peered at me from behind a long wooden desk. They held pencils perched over opened notebooks.

Turn around and go home.

"Good afternoon, Miss Holt. Please take a seat." The man sitting in the middle motioned to the bench sitting in front of the Steinway.

"Okay." I sat on the bench with my back to the keys.

"Whenever you're ready." The woman on the left smiled.

"Oh." My face heated, and I turned back around to face the piano. Awkward. I guess the interview process came after the audition.

I took one last cleansing breath as my hands hovered over the keys. The black, mahogany sheen of the piano's music rack brought a flush of memories.

After playing the last note, I asked, "Mom, was that okay?" I held my breath and waited.

"Was that okay? Oh, my darling, Sivan. It was perfection!" My mother's proud smile brightened the entire room. She hugged me tight, and I felt her joyful tears against my face.

My family was gone, but I felt their presence as I prepared to play.

My soul ached and rejoiced when I touched the ivory keys. The room, the audition, the instructors blurred into the background. I closed my eyes and became one with the music.

Images of dancing with my father after my fifth-grade graduation swept in, filling me with love. It was a spring day, and we whisked around the outside terrace. My dad's proud smile, the fading sun that warmed our cheeks, and the happiness of the day came back in a rush. I connected with the memory, letting the power of the emotion drive the tempo. Peace, freedom, and exhilaration filled me until the last note vibrated into silence. I was home.

With a deep breath, I turned back around.

Silence.

The woman on the left stood abruptly. "You. You don't move. Stay right there." She turned and hurried out of the room.

The two remaining panelists stared at me with their mouths hanging open.

"Is everything okay?" I asked. They were starting to freak me out.

"Betty told us you hadn't played in over six years," the man said.

"That's right."

"Why not?" he asked.

"Because . . ." I shrugged. No way would I talk to two strangers about the reason.

The woman shook her head. "Incredible," she said. She began tapping her pencil on the table.

"Did you warm up?" the man asked.

"No. We came straight from the hotel." Uh oh. "Should I have warmed up first?" Had my presentation been stiff?

"Yes. You should have *had* to warm up. All this," he pointed to the piano, "is a little incomprehensible."

"Why?" I blurted. Ugh. I didn't want to hear the answer right now. My thumb slid across my forefinger.

The two remaining panelists looked at each other, and their intimidating posture cracked a little for the first time as they both smiled.

"Are you auditioning at any other schools?"

"No." My pulse kicked into high gear.

"Good. I think it's time we introduced ourselves."

Chapter Nineteen

Jax

"Pacing won't make time go faster." Betty's eyes followed me as I attempted to burn off my anxiety.

"She's good, right? They won't reject her?" I wiped my sweaty palms on my jeans.

"I spent four years here, and I've never heard anyone play as well." She patted the bench. "Now sit down and relax."

I plopped down next to her. "It's just that, I want this for her, you know?"

Betty tilted her head. "You love her."

She knew? "No!" My voice cracked, and I cleared my throat. "I mean, no. Sorry for yelling." I didn't want to talk to Aunt Betty about this before Sivan.

She chuckled. “Doth thou protest too much?”

“We haven’t been together all that long. It’s too early for that.” Oh God. My heart thumped triple time.

“Mm hmm.” Betty looked up toward the sky.

Sivan can’t find out. Not yet.

“Aunt Betty, I think it’s probably best not to bring this up to Sivan. I have a feeling she’d run in the opposite direction.” Great, now I dripped in sweat.

Her face softened. “And here I was worried about Sivan getting hurt.”

I got up to start my pacing again. “I know you haven’t read her file, but I think something horrible must have happened to her family. Whenever I bring up the past, she freezes and shuts down. I don’t think she trusts life not to hurt her again. Not yet. If I had to guess, she’s worried if she loves again, she’ll be abandoned, or we’ll die.”

“Oh, Jax.” Betty’s eyes misted over. “You’re spot on. But you know what? She already loves us. I can see it all over her face. She just can’t acknowledge or accept it yet.”

“How long do you think it’ll take?” I held my breath.

“It depends. But I already see progress.” Betty smiled.

“What progress?” Sivan had snuck up from behind the tree.

Betty jumped up. “You scared me.” She hugged Sivan. “Don’t just stand there. How’d it go? I’ve been on pins and needles, and I think Jax has worn a path on the grass from all his pacing.”

Sivan giggled. “Okay, I guess.”

“What do you mean, ‘I guess’?” I searched her face.

“If a full-ride four-year scholarship is good, then I guess I did all right.” She squealed and started to jump up and down.

"Oh my God!" Betty shrieked. "That's why it took so long?"

"Yes. After my audition, one of the judges left the room and came back with an admission official and the scholarship committee. We had an interview, and they made the offer. I still have some paperwork to fill out, but they said it was routine stuff."

"Wow, that's great!" I picked her up and twirled her around. Warmth expanded in my chest.

She laughed and caught her breath. "I get to start in the summer. They have a summer camp to prepare, and I'll be able to stay in the dorm and get everything in order before the school year begins." Her face dropped, and she stilled.

"What's the matter?" Aunt Betty asked.

"It's just that, I don't know. I think it hit me I'll be leaving all of you." Tears started to form in her eyes.

"Oh, honey. You won't be leaving us for good. We'll still see you for all the school breaks." Betty rubbed Sivan's arm.

"You will?" She wiped her eyes.

"Of course. I wouldn't have it any other way. Emily and Alice will also insist. They love you, you know." Aunt Betty smiled warmly.

Betty, don't go there.

"Like we all do," she added.

Ugh. She went there.

Sivan bit her lip and looked down at the ground.

"Who's hungry?" I nearly shouted. "I want that attack thing Aunt Betty was talking about."

Sivan raised her head slowly. She stared at me a moment, almost as if she were in a trance. "What?"

"You know, the restaurant Aunt Betty mentioned earlier. Remember?"

Her eyes stayed unfocused as she stared over our shoulders.

Betty's calm voice asked, "Sivan? Are you okay?"

She blinked rapidly a few times. "Sure. Yes. I'm good."

But I was almost certain she wasn't. I approached her cautiously and took her hand. She tried to pull away, but I held it firmly. Our eyes met, and what I saw made my heart sink. Fear. "One day at a time, Sivan. Let's go celebrate your scholarship."

The crease between her eyebrows gave way to a small smile. "I always believed I was smarter than you, but you may have just surpassed me."

Thank goodness.

Betty pulled Sivan into a hug. "This is a great day. I'm so proud of you." She caught my eye over Sivan's shoulder and mouthed, "Sorry."

Two in the morning and sleep still eluded me. Betty had snagged the perfect room for us, a suite with two bedrooms. I decided to trade my tossing and turning in the large king bed for an overstuffed chair in the living room overlooking the city's twinkling lights. Might as well enjoy the view.

"You can't sleep either?" Betty whispered from next to me.

"Shit!" I jumped about a foot. "I mean, Aunt Betty, you scared me."

She chuckled. "Sorry. I was trying not to wake Sivan." She adjusted her robe and sat on the couch.

"Yeah. I think she needs the sleep. She looked exhausted by

the time we got back." I rubbed my eyes.

"Jax, you were right about her. I think I've lost my touch." She let out a long breath.

"Nah. I think you're just too close to the situation."

"I'm seeing what I want to see." She gazed out the window.

"Maybe a little." I smiled.

"I told Sivan I wouldn't look at her file. But, sometimes, when I'm next to the file cabinet, my fingers actually tingle." She laughed a little, and then became serious. "I thought she would've opened up to me by now. I hope I made the right decision."

"You did. Sivan trusts you."

"Still, I'm worried. When she shut down today, I felt a little out of my element. Like I needed to know where she was coming from to help her." She sighed.

"She says she doesn't want to wallow in the past, just look to the future. That makes sense, don't you think?" I believed the same thing, but I was also concerned there were things she should be talking about.

"Yes, but, sometimes, if things from your past aren't resolved, it can creep into your future. Sometimes even poison it." Aunt Betty rubbed her chin.

"What can I do?"

Her gaze turned back to me. "Keep trying to get her to open up. I think it has to happen before she'll be able to truly move forward. She's tough. She'll let you know when you've pushed too much."

"She's already kicked me once. I'm not looking forward to a repeat."

She raised an eyebrow. "She kicked you?"

Oh hell. "Um. Forget I said anything."

Her eyes narrowed. "I can probably make a good guess what led up to that."

I could smile now at the memory instead of cringing.

"Well," Betty continued. "She has fire and spunk going for her."

"No shortage there." I chuckled, and put my feet on the ottoman.

She stood. "I'm going to try to grab a few more hours of sleep. I think it would be a good idea for you and Sivan to go out on your own tomorrow, or I guess it would be today." She glanced at the clock on the table. "You still have a few hours before dawn."

"You don't want to come with us?" I'd thought the three of us would hang for most of the trip.

"I want the two of you to enjoy the city on your own. I have some places I want to visit. Alone."

"Oh. Uh . . ." My stomach dropped.

"And yes, if you're wondering, I'm going to revisit places I went to with Henry. It's my way of working out the past. It'll be cathartic for me."

I nodded, hoping it wasn't what I suspected; Aunt Betty still actively struggled with the death of Uncle Henry.

"I want to let you know I'm proud of you, too." She ruffled my hair.

"Who, me?" I pointed to myself.

She leaned against the chair. "Yes, you. When you first came to the farm, you were a little . . . How should I say . . . Angry?" She cringed a little.

I chuckled. "It's okay. Yes, I was pissed at the world."

"But look at you now. You've grown up before my eyes. You're a terrific help around the farm, your grades are straight As—"

"You know why."

"Sivan."

"Yep. She's scary smart with math."

She smiled. "More importantly, you seem happy."

"I am." Which made me a little nervous. I didn't want to go back to the old me. The guy who blamed everyone else for his problems.

"Which makes me happy." She gave my shoulder a rub. "Goodnight." She turned with a smile and crept back into her bedroom.

I reclined the chair and continued to stare out the window. After a few minutes, my eyelids became heavy.

"Sivan, give me your hand!"

Sivan stands in the middle of the Milstein Pool, and a huge, swirling whirlpool is only a few feet away. Her arms flail as she tries to swim away from the middle. She splashes and goes under. She's going to get sucked in!

"I can't. The current is too strong."

I need to save her! She'll drown.

I try to jump in, but two strong arms hold me back. "You'll get sucked in with her if you go in."

"I'll die trying. Let me go!"

"Jax!"

Hands shook my shoulders.

"What?" I spluttered as my eyes opened.

"You're having a bad dream. Are you okay?"

Sivan. She was okay. I grabbed hold of her and hugged her tight. My body shook, but I didn't care. I just needed her close. "Oh my God, Sivan. It was the worst dream I've ever had. A huge whirlpool was sucking you in, and I couldn't save you."

The dream seemed to last forever, but the sun had just come up, displayed by the shadows on the wall.

She stilled in my arms, and her breathing quieted. She slowly pulled away. Why did her eyes look so cold and distant?

"You said you'd die trying." Her voice was emotionless.

"Yes, I would." My pulse and rapid heart rate spiked. Something was wrong. "What did I say? Are you upset with me?"

"No. I need a breather. I'll be back." She jumped up, grabbed her coat and shoes, and walked out of the hotel room.

Shit. Shit. Shit.

Where were my shoes? Damn, I needed to catch her. Or should I give her space? Brain, work, damn it!

No. There was something wrong. I raced into the bedroom, threw on a coat, and jammed my feet into a pair of tennis shoes. I'd tie them later. After grabbing my cell, I checked the time and scribbled out a quick note to Aunt Betty that we'd be back soon. No need to worry her if Sivan was just hanging in the lobby. I slipped out the door before she could question me.

After a sweep of the lobby, I knew she'd left the building.

Where would she go? I skidded through the revolving doors out onto the crowded New York street and did a three-sixty. Nothing. She'd disappeared.

Wait—Times Square. It was a five, maybe ten-minute walk from our hotel. Sivan had told me it was the first place she wanted to visit.

Where the hell was it?

"Sir?" a bellman asked.

"Time's Square?"

"Two blocks down to your east, then turn right, after—"

"Thanks," I shouted and took off running. When I took the last corner, I knew I was in the right area. Bright neon lights, tourists, and a large costumed Elmo, all at eight in the morning.

A glance at the stairs confirmed it. Sivan sat hugging her legs halfway up on the Red Stairs with the large Coca-Cola sign looming in the background. She didn't notice me as I drew closer. Tears trailed down her face as she stared off into the distance.

I sat next to her, relieved she was safe. "Sivan."

She put her hands over her face. "I can't talk about it now." Her shoulders began to shake.

I put my arm around her. "No talking. We'll just sit. Okay?"

"Okay," she stuttered.

Ten minutes later, and she was no better. Her crying hadn't even paused between breaths. What could I have said to upset her so much? My dream? How much of it had I said aloud?

I rubbed her shoulder. I wanted to hug her and take away her pain. I'd sit with her all day if needed, but my ass was freezing.

"I'm cold," she finally said.

"Thank God. I can't feel anything from the waist down."

She gave a little laugh. Progress. "A few things came rushing back today. I'm sorry."

Her blotchy, tear-stained, red-eyed face was so damn beautiful. I smoothed her hair back. "You don't need to apologize. Maybe I should? Was it my dream?"

"No, you shouldn't apologize. This was all me. This doesn't happen often, but I had a flashback at the hotel about my . . . about my. . . ." She placed her head in her hands. "This is so embarrassing."

"Why?"

"I don't want to be the clichéd foster child with emotional problems." She rubbed her forehead. "I'm strong, dammit."

"You are. You're allowed a timeout."

"That's a nice way of putting it. I think it's referred to as a meltdown."

"Okay. Meltdown. I've had a few of those, remember?"

A small smile formed. "You had an epic meltdown. It was great." She wiped the remaining tears from her face.

"I did. Thanks in part to your cooldown by the fire extinguisher."

"Yeah. You needed that." She rested her head on my shoulder.

"I did." I chuckled. "What do you need now? What can I do?"

"I'm scared," she blurted.

"What scares you?" I rubbed her back.

"Well, for the first time in what feels like forever, I have a home. It doesn't feel like a foster home. It's real. I'm scared to leave. I don't want them to forget me." She stopped and took a deep breath. "I'm scared my past might always prevent me from moving forward. I'm trying to push through it, but . . ."

"Do you want to talk about it?"

"No." She bit her lip. "Here's the thing. I might never be ready." She looked down. "For instance, today, when I had that flashback, it's like it happened yesterday. It's fresh and painful and awful and . . . well, I don't want to go back there. I can't go back, maybe never." She looked me in the eyes. "If we're going to be together, that's a part of me you'll have to accept. If you push or try to find things out on your own, I'll walk. For good. That's a deal breaker for me. It has to be when or even if I'm ready."

I tried to calm my body that was still freaking the hell out. "I agree. You never have to worry about that, I promise. I can wait until you're ready. I hope, though, you'll trust me enough one day with the burden you're carrying."

She closed her eyes and whispered, "Thank you." After a minute, she moved onto my lap and put her arms around my neck. "You've already helped so much. Thanks for coming out here to find me. I feel better."

I kissed her, and all the tension melted. This was where we belonged. Together.

The familiar flashes of light and clicking sounds alerted me to a crowd starting to form at the bottom of the stairs.

Oh, shit! Forgot my disguise.

"Sivan, we have a situation."

She looked up. "Uh oh."

"Yeah." Before I'd been concerned about myself. This time all I could think about was Sivan. They'd seen us kissing and would follow her if she tried to walk away.

"You'll have to stick with me. I'm so sorry, Sivan. This is the last thing you need right now."

She waved me off. "I have pepper spray."

Hmm. Maybe the threat would work?

She examined the crowd. "They look harmless. We should walk slowly down, pose for a few pictures, then walk away."

"Are you crazy? They could rip us apart!"

"This is New York. Even the tourists are savvy. Think about it. You've been out of the public eye for almost five months. In fan years, that's at least thirty-five years." She smiled and patted my arm.

"Is there some logic I'm missing?" How could she be so calm? I was supposed to be comforting her, not the other way around.

"Remember, I'm the math whiz." She got up and straightened her clothes.

I did a quick sweep of the area to look for escape routes. Even though it was still early, a few stores were already open. "Okay, we'll try it your way. If they make a move toward either of us, I want that pepper spray out and flowing."

"Deal."

Ten minutes later, we walked at a normal pace back to the hotel, arriving in one piece. Remarkable.

I slung my arm over her shoulder. "You were right. We didn't get mobbed, and they turned out to be pretty cool."

"Sometimes, when people smell fear, it can set things into motion that otherwise wouldn't happen. Not that you shouldn't be cautious, but I don't think every mob will react like the one in the airport."

"I'm gonna buy some pepper spray. Maybe a Taser, too."

She rolled her eyes and slapped my arm. "Paranoid much? No wonder we're together. We both have issues." Her eyes crinkled as she chuckled.

"I'm still not sure if we just got lucky with that crowd, or if you were the calming factor. I think I'll need to bring you everywhere I go from now on to make sure I'm safe," I half-joked.

"Sounds good to me." She squeezed my hand.

Even though she smiled and said everything was okay, I still worried about her past.

Would she run next time and not come back?

Chapter Twenty

Sivan

"HAPPY VALENTINE'S DAY," JAX WHISPERED in my ear.

I jerked awake. "Where'd you come from?"

He chuckled. "The stairs and then through the door."

My heart hammered in my chest. *Brain, wake up.* "You're not allowed in my room. Betty will kill you." I'd fallen asleep in my sweats and t-shirt, but still.

"It's Valentine's Day. I think we should get a pass." He lay down on top of the covers, took my face in his hands, and kissed me, long and slow.

"Yeah. I think you're right." Rules? Right out the window.

"I have two gifts for you today." His eyes sparkled as he

reached over and grabbed a bag from next to the bed.

"Two?" I swallowed. Oh no. "I haven't bought your gift yet."

"Don't worry. I don't need anything. Just you."

"I feel so bad. That chemistry final was a killer. Betty wanted to spend some time together today, so I figured I could buy you a little something when we were out." I twisted the bedcovers in my hands.

He scooted closer on the bed and brushed his lips softly against mine. "That right there. That's all I need."

My insides turned to mush. "Are you trying to win the award for Most Perfect Boyfriend?"

"Yes. And there's my gift. That's the first time you've called me your boyfriend."

That slipped. My face flushed hot. "Ummm—"

"And here's the first gift for my *girlfriend*." He set a small velvet box in my hand. My eyes almost popped out.

He laughed. "You can start breathing again. It's not that." He leaned back in for another kiss. "Maybe one day, but not today."

I covered my face. "Well, that's embarrassing. I know it's too early, but you're always surprising me."

I had to admit, even though he acted beyond spoiled when he first arrived, I fell for him hard and fast. How could I help it? Like now, with him looking at me, those intense green eyes, a handsome smile that lifted just a little on the left side, and the mischievous glint whenever he was up to no good. I was hooked.

And totally okay with it.

Jax had become my everything, and I knew he had the same feelings for me. But we decided to take it slow. No sex or the

"L" word for us in the beginning. Although, Jax tried to work around both. He'd start to say I lo—oiiike you. We'd both laugh, knowing he almost slipped.

That was the easier part. The no-go for sex—a different story. We'd spent too many long kissing sessions on the family room couch when everyone was in bed. It would start off innocent enough; within minutes, though, we'd be lying on the couch kissing, pressed close with arms and legs tangled. Jax would switch back and forth between "this feels so good," to "I'm going to die," which always broke the tension and made us laugh. He had a daily countdown to summer going. Once we were eighteen and out of Betty's house, he had big plans for us. Our chemistry was off-the-charts, which was a great thing, but incredibly difficult.

Which gave me lots of time to adjust to our relationship. Jax understood this was a big deal for me. The closeness. The ability to let someone in. The risk of love. Too late, though. I already loved him. He'd snuck in there, taking little pieces of my heart with his smiles, encouragement, integrity, stupid jokes, and goofy grin. His eyes gave him away. He looked at me like I was the most important person in the world. We worked. We fit.

He nudged my arm. "Open it."

"Almost forgot." I laughed.

"You spaced out. What were you thinking about?"

"Just remembering how much we didn't like each other when we first met." I couldn't hold back my chuckle.

"I always liked you, even when I thought I didn't." He winked.

"That's romantic." I suppressed an eye roll.

"You know what I mean. It's hard to acknowledge feelings when the other person sprays you down with dangerous chemicals, kicks you so hard you wonder if children will be a part of your future, and don't get me started on your epic glares. I know where the phrase 'If looks could kill' came from."

I snuggled closer. "Yeah, it's a big lesson for me not to judge before making a decision about someone."

He slung an arm across my middle. "For me, too. Remember, I thought you were a goth-emo girl, all darkness and angst."

I poked his arm. "Hey, I have some of those."

He smoothed back my hair. "I think you want the world to believe that. But, remember, I know you best. You're the opposite."

A lump formed in my throat. I whispered, "So I can't fool you."

Another sweet kiss. "Nope. Because I'm also incredibly intelligent."

I snickered. "Oh, the arrogance makes another appearance."

Jax drew closer so we were only inches apart. His smile dropped. "But you love it."

I knew what he really asked. I took a deep breath and answered, "Yeah, I guess I do."

"And I love your black hair and blue eyes." He tucked a strand of hair behind my ear.

"I love your knock-knock jokes." My heart about thudded out of my chest.

He pulled back, and his mouth gaped open. "Really?"

I smiled. "Okay, maybe it's more like some of your knock-knock jokes."

"I love how you put little notes of encouragement into Emily and Alice's lunchboxes every day."

"What?" How did he know that?

"I'm all seeing, all knowing." He waggled his eyebrows.

"Ugh. I don't love how I can't keep any secrets around here." I stuck out my bottom lip and pretended to pout.

"Nope. You're my open book. Well, except for . . ."

My heart pounded. He hadn't brought up my past since New York. "I know. I'm getting there." The dark part of my past had become a physical being, a beast pounding at the gates of my memory.

Go away. I'm not ready for you yet.

I needed to keep all the bad stuff shoved down so I could keep pretending. Would the emotions devour me and ruin my relationship with Jax, and maybe everyone else?

"Open it." He picked the box up from between us.

I sat up and slowly cracked the lid open. The light from the windows illuminated the silver, making it sparkle. "Oh, it's a charm bracelet!"

"Not just any. Look."

I lifted it out of the box. The four charms included a J and a guitar, an S and a piano. "Oh, Jax. This is perfect." I shut my eyes so the tears wouldn't slip through. We'd be together, at least on my wrist. Next year, I'd be in New York, and I had no idea which college Jax would attend. My chest squeezed, and my heart took a dive.

"That takes me to my other gift. Well, I hope it's a gift."

"Now I'm curious."

He took a deep breath. "I've been accepted for the pre-vet program at NYU."

I jumped up off the bed. “What? Are you joking? Because, if you are, I’m going to kill you!”

He chuckled. “No, I’m totally serious. I just got the letter last week. Do you want to see proof?”

I threw my hands in the air. “You waited a week to tell me?”

A lighthearted glint sparkled in his eyes. “Yes, I almost let it slip a hundred times.”

It occurred to me he might have changed his plans for me.

He stood and took both my hands. “I see that look in your eyes. No, don’t worry about it. I chose NYU because it has a great program, and I loved our trip to New York. The people there are chill, and I didn’t get mobbed. It’s a good fit.” He paused for a moment. “And we’re only three to four miles apart, depending on which classes we’re taking.”

“Oh, wow. We can meet for lunch and go shopping. Hey, we never got to see the—“

Before I could say another word, his lips pressed against mine. It started out soft, but with so many things stirring inside me, winding tighter and tighter around my heart, the kiss evolved into a heated and passionate one. I wrapped my arms around his neck, and we fell back onto the bed.

Between kisses, Jax said, “Sorry, you were so cute, I couldn’t help myself.”

“You’re going to need to help yourself. Have you forgotten our deal?” Betty stood at the door, an eyebrow raised and wearing a slight smile.

Oops. I rolled away from Jax and right off the bed.

“Shit, Sivan. Are you okay?” Jax jumped up to help me.

“Best day ever!” I jumped up and adjusted my clothing. “Jax, tell Betty.”

He looked at me, back at Betty, then me again. "Um, well, I haven't told my mom yet." He turned back to Betty. "Can we keep this between us until I get a chance to call my parents?"

She nodded. "Sure."

"I'm going to NYU next year. I've been accepted into their Veterinarian Medicine program."

Betty took in my flushed and excited face and smiled her warm smile. "That's wonderful news. Congratulations, Jax. I know you've worked hard for this. It's a great school."

"Thanks, Aunt Betty." He slung an arm around my shoulder. "Couldn't have done it without my math tutor."

"Yes. It was all me." I gave him the elbow. Jax decided now would be a good time to tickle me. I moved back and slapped at his hands. "Don't you dare!" I was laughing so hard I almost didn't hear Betty.

"Sivan."

"Yes?"

"I have something important I need to talk to you about." She remained smiling, but my stomach dropped anyway.

"Is everything okay?"

"It's great. Can you come to my office in a few minutes?"

"Sure." This time, my heart pounded for a different reason.

After she left, I asked Jax, "What do you think that's all about?"

He rubbed his jaw. "No idea."

"Has it been a few minutes?"

He chuckled. "No, but I'm sure she won't be surprised if you show up now."

"I'll report back as soon as I find anything out." I started down the hall and turned back to where Jax stood. "Oh, Jax? I forgot to say congratulations!"

He grinned and shook his head.

I loved Betty's office. It was just like her, warm tones with bright sunlight streaming in. The colorful books lining the shelves almost matched her hair. By far my favorite spot in the entire house.

"Sivan, I have some news. Well, a few pieces I want to discuss with you." She folded her hands under her chin.

My stomach took a dip. "Okay."

"I'm starting the process to adopt Emily and Alice."

I bolted out of my chair. "This day keeps getting better. That's awesome news. I'm so happy for you and the girls. Do they know?"

"Please sit down. There's more." She smiled and met my eyes.

"Good stuff?"

"I hope, yes. Anyway, I did talk about this with the girls already. They're a little young and don't fully grasp all the details. But they're on board and are actually very excited."

Tears welled behind my eyelids. Emily and Alice would never feel alone in a house with strangers who only allowed their presence because of a check from the state. They'd never be attacked in the middle of the night because "Daddy" was a pervert.

I put my hands over my face and cried tears of relief. "I'm sorry, Betty. I'm not sad. This is a happy cry."

Get it together, Sivan. She's going to think you've lost it.

Betty walked around the desk and gave me a tissue. That's when I noticed she was crying along with me. "I knew you'd be happy for them. You are so special, Sivan. I hope you know that."

"Thanks." I hiccupped. "Emily and Alice deserve you."

She nodded slowly. "Sivan?"

My crying had slowed, and I took a cleansing breath. "Yes, I'm all right. Sorry for the outburst." I laughed and cried at the same time.

"I'm going to come out and say it. I want to adopt you too." Her warm eyes searched mine.

My body froze. "What?"

"I love you, and I'd be honored to be your mom." She held up her hand. "I'm not trying to replace your mom. I'd just like the opportunity to fill in."

Oh my God. The tears returned, and I started shaking from head to foot.

"Knock knock," Dad called from the front seat.

"Who's there?" Danny bounced and clapped his hands.

"Olive."

"Olive who?" Danny asked.

"Olive you." Dad laughed.

"Mom, you have to stop him." I giggled.

Mom smiled from the passenger side. "You know you love it."

I squeezed my eyes closed. Not now. I took a deep breath.

"Are you okay? Please, don't feel pressured if it doesn't feel right." Her eyebrows bunched together.

I'm sorry, Mom, Dad, and Danny. I'm going to try to move forward with Betty.

"Yes, I'm okay. It feels right," I choked out. "But I'm turning eighteen in May. Legally I'll be an adult."

"There are a lot of adult adoptions, mostly for financial reasons. My reason is because I want you to be part of this family. I want you to be my daughter."

I'll have a family again.

"Betty," was all I could say. My chest surged with happiness.

She hugged me close. "I don't know what your past was like. But I do know your future will be brighter. We were brought together for a reason."

"I'd love to be adopted." I hugged her back. The love I had for her filled every inch of my soul.

"I love you, too," she answered, almost telepathically. But I guessed she knew by the tight squeeze I had her in.

A knock and the door opened slightly. Jax popped his head in. "Sorry to interrupt, but the girls want pancakes, and I don't know how to make them." His eyes glanced back and forth between us, focusing on my face, which was probably red and blotchy. "Are you okay?"

"Better than okay." I tried not to jump up and down like a five-year-old. "Betty is adopting me, and now I'll be part of the family." A realization struck. "Which means we'll be cousins!" I started laughing.

Betty joined in and we dissolved into a fit of giggles.

Jax stared at us like we'd lost our minds for a few moments, and then broke out into a huge smile. He crossed the room and took me in his arms. "Welcome to the family, cuz."

"I'll fill you in on the details later," Betty called over her shoulder. "First, there's a pancake emergency I have to tend to."

The door closed behind Betty, leaving us to digest our new family status.

"You don't feel weird about it, do you?" I asked.

"Not at all." A tear slipped from his eye.

I wiped it away. "Are you upset?"

"No. I'm happy for you. You belong here, with or without an adoption. But now it's official. Welcome." He pulled me close and said so quietly I almost missed the words.

"I love you."

And then, "So much."

Chapter Twenty One

Jax

"We're both eighteen now, and you're leaving in two weeks," I whispered in Sivan's ear.

She pulled back a little and shook her head.

This wasn't the first time I tried to get Sivan to change her mind. I was going freaking crazy. We were in the loft in the barn, our favorite place when we wanted to be alone. I tugged her back into my arms.

"You're the one driving me to school. And we'll have five full days. More importantly, my roommate won't join me for at least a week." She raised one eyebrow. "And the best part—we won't break any of Betty's house rules."

I brushed some hay from her hair. "I can't tell you how excited I am to have you all to myself without having to hide away in the barn."

"Ah, we'll always remember our youth." She laughed and looked around the loft area. "I'll miss it here though."

"Don't worry. Betty will be flying you back and forth every opportunity." I'd overheard her making plans with my mom.

She bit her lip. "How about you?"

"I've talked to my mom. She's okay with me hanging here for the smaller holidays. But she insists I come home for Christmas. Here's the good part—she's talking Betty into all of us coming to Seattle this year for Christmas."

"Seattle? Where it rains all the time?" She pretended to pout.

"Hey, that's my hometown you're trashing. And it doesn't rain as often as you might think. We Seattleites spread that rumor so we don't get too many people moving to the area."

She nudged me. "I'm only teasing. I'd love to see where you grew up."

Perfect opening. "So, where did you grow up anyway?" I asked as casual as I could.

She cocked her head. "Good try. I'm getting there, Jax. Before I leave, we'll talk. I'm almost ready."

Relief washed through me. I wanted her to trust me with it.

"But it's not pretty. I'm warning you."

"Okay. I'm ready when you are." I rested my head on her shoulder.

"I appreciate you not pressuring me all these months. I trust you, I really do." She let her hand run down the side of my face.

"I'll never let you down. I promise." I sat and held up three fingers. "Scout's Honor."

She giggled. "Oh, so now you're a Boy Scout?"

"When I was ten."

"No way. You helped little old ladies cross the street?"

"Well, I would have. We usually just did rope tying and stuff." I shrugged.

"Did you wear the cute, little uniform with the merit badges?"

Time for a change of subject. "Enough. We have to get ready for our celebration dinner tonight." I stood and brushed off the hay.

"I'll bet you were the most handsome Boy Scout ever." Her eyes sparkled.

I chuckled and shook my head. "Not going there," I said while checking the barn entrance. "Aunt Betty will call out a search party if we don't get back inside." I reached out and grabbed her hand. "Here, let me help you up." Once she was standing, I stopped her. "Wait a sec."

The sun streamed in through a little window at the edge of the loft, and, like a spotlight, lit up Sivan's face and hair. I gazed into her eyes, and it hit me, like a punch to the gut. I knew I loved her, but this was more. A connection—pure and physical, but at the same time deeper, more meaningful. Something deep inside my heart clenched.

"You're so damn beautiful," was all I could get out.

She reached up and pulled a piece of hay out of my hair. "So are you."

I pulled her to me and kissed her like I'd never see her again. I couldn't get enough.

We finally broke apart. "Come on, let's get a snack."

Her cheeks were flushed, and she looked a little dazed.

"Okay, whatever you say."

"I'll have to remember this strategy to get you to do what I want."

She chuckled. "Anytime."

When we entered the kitchen, it smelled of cornbread and chili. "I know what I want."

"We're going out to dinner in an hour," Sivan reminded me.

"Yes, to celebrate your graduation and leaving for New York. Such a shame," Regina said from behind the counter. She glared at Sivan.

"What's your problem anyway?" I asked.

Sivan's face reddened and her nostrils flared. It appeared she'd also had enough of Regina's attitude and passive-aggressive remarks.

"Let's just go." I placed my hand on Sivan's arm to steer her out of the kitchen.

"No." She pulled back. "I want to know. I've been listening to her snide comments since September, and I'm sick of it." She turned back to Regina. "What have I ever done to you?"

Regina put her hands on her hips. "You want to know? You really do? Because I'd be happy to tell you."

By the looks of her, she was ready to come unleashed. This was a bad idea.

"Never mind." I needed to get Sivan out of this mess. "Come on," I coaxed.

Sivan stood, unwilling to budge.

"You asked. Now I'm going to tell you." Regina narrowed her eyes and stared down Sivan.

Damn. *What did I start*?

"You." Regina pointed at Sivan. "You come here in your black hair, black clothes, black everything and play the 'Oh, I'm a foster child. I've had it so bad. Everyone feel sorry for me.'"

Sivan straightened.

Regina kept going. "You have everyone here fooled, but not me. Poor Betty doesn't know you're just after her money. You even got her to adopt you. And Jax." She looked back at me. "You're famous. You can have anyone, but you pick her?"

"That's enough, Regina." Betty had entered the room. Her face appeared calm, but the fire behind her eyes gave her away.

"Betty. I didn't mean . . . You weren't supposed—"

"I think it's time we sat down and had a talk about this." Betty glanced at me, then at Sivan. "I'll meet you at the restaurant in an hour."

"Sure, we'll see you there." Sivan's shoulders relaxed, and she was even able to pull off a little smile. Betty always seemed to have a calming effect on her.

After they left the room, I asked, "Are you okay?"

She combed her fingers through her hair and took a deep breath. "Yeah. I usually don't let her get to me. Regina's treated me like I was the enemy since the beginning. I could be the most perfect person on the planet, and she'd still hate me. I think she took one look, decided she didn't like me, and that was that. I'll go back to my usual and ignore her."

I pulled her into a hug "You are the most perfect person on the planet."

She slapped at my arm. "Ha ha. Very funny." Her face flushed, and she smiled.

Warmth filled my chest. "You are to me."

"Cheers!" Betty held up her glass.

"Cheers," Sivan and I said at once. We were seated at the fanciest restaurant in the county. Sivan and I sat on one side of the booth, Betty on the other. The décor was how I liked it, clean lines with lots of beige and grey. It had opened only a few months ago, but everyone and their best friend wanted reservations. Betty had pulled it off in her I-can-do-anything type of way. I was pretty sure she knew every influential person behind the scenes in every state, maybe the world.

"Except, shouldn't this be champagne, not lemonade?" I asked.

"Nice try, Jax. That'll be served at your twenty-first birthday, not your graduation celebration."

"Spoilsport," I teased. I'd had my fill of drinking in my sophomore and junior years of high school. Couldn't say I missed it.

Betty smiled. "That means I'm doing my job."

Sivan cleared her throat. "I have an announcement."

"Oh yeah?" I asked.

"Yeah." She winked. "I just wanted to say I'll miss you both this summer."

Dread dropped like a dead weight in my stomach. Not seeing her from June to August made my insides clench. How long could I go without her warm laugh and soft lips?

"If you get homesick, you can fly back for the weekend." Betty offered.

"Thanks, Betty. I might take you up on that." Sivan turned to me. "Jax, do you think you can survive the sixty-five days?"

"No," I said, but I smiled.

Both girls laughed.

"Betty will make me eat tofu and vegetables." I pretended to gag.

"I guess I could get some cage-free, organic chicken if you get too desperate before you leave for Seattle in July. I know you've been sneaking out of the house with Sivan to go to that horrific chicken restaurant where they serve birds full of antibiotics and fried in that toxic grease. Not to mention they're crammed into cages so they aren't even able to move."

"You've convinced me. No chicken unless it's free range. If I'm going to become a vet, I'll need to help protect animals, even if they aren't considered a pet."

"My job here is done." Aunt Betty held her arms up high.

"You still have lots of work with me." Sivan giggled.

I always loved to see Sivan and Betty together. They had a best friend vibe, but they also had a love and respect thing going on. Now that the adoption had gone through, and Sivan was officially her daughter, she'd always be safe.

Betty's eyes softened when she looked at Sivan. "Such an exciting time for you. Do you know your schedule?"

"I think I wake up at seven a.m. and I'm done around ten p.m. every day." She wrinkled her nose, but the excitement behind her eyes shined bright.

Betty's eyes widened. "I don't remember such long hours."

"That's just for the summer. It's an intensive program to get me prepared for the fall." Sivan fidgeted in her seat, looking like she was raring to go.

"You should be well prepared, then." Aunt Betty patted her hand.

"I'm looking forward to it." Sivan's smile lit her entire face.

"I'm not." I hugged her shoulder. "But I am looking forward to driving you out and staying for five days. That part will be fun." We hadn't told Betty that Sivan's roommate wouldn't be joining her for at least a week. I couldn't wait to have Sivan all to myself.

Always one step ahead of us, Betty said, "I don't want to hear too much about that type of fun."

Sivan's face turned beet red, and she gave me a shut-the-hell-up glare.

"Sightseeing. That's what I was talking about." A quick save.

Betty didn't buy it and shook her head. "Just remember my 'be safe' talks."

She'd taken us both aside and gave us the sex talk, which made me laugh because I'd had it from my parents and school when I was in the fifth grade. Aunt Betty knew this, but said I needed a refresher.

"We'll be safe. No worries there," I assured her.

The waiter set down plates of lobster in front of Sivan and Aunt Betty. I got the prime rib. "Looks great!" I wolfed it down in record time. The girls were close behind with their "yum" and "delicious" comments.

Betty pushed her plate to one side. "Let's get down to business for Sivan's move. Jax, you'll take the truck and get Sivan and her things all squared away. I'll fly in with the girls the next weekend for a visit before your classes start. Does that still work for you?"

"Yes, that works perfectly. I'm so excited for Emily and Alice to visit. By the time they get to New York, I'll have all the best places already scoped out for them." Sivan was almost bouncing out of her seat.

"If there's a Disney Store, I'm sure that's all they'll need." Betty laughed.

"I saw one right in Times Square." Sivan's face clouded slightly. No one would notice, but I looked for it. That day in New York started bad, but Sivan had quickly changed things around.

"Then it's settled. We'll come out, and you can be our director."

The two met eyes and smiled. There was a long pause.

"I'm going to miss having you around every day." Aunt Betty teared up. "But I take comfort knowing you're in the best possible place for your talent. I'm so happy for you."

"Thank you for arranging it and always wanting the best for me. You're my mom in every sense of the word. Not only because you adopted me, but because you've had my back ever since I walked into your home last summer."

"Our home," Aunt Betty said warmly. "And speaking of having your back, I had a nice long chat with Regina today."

"Ugh," I said. "She's a bi—"

"Jax," Aunt Betty interrupted me, one brow raised.

"Okay, she's a brat. Better?" I was sick and tired of everyone trying to look for the good in Regina. She had a cold, evil heart.

"Yes, a little better." Aunt Betty smiled, but her eyes seemed a little sad. "Regina, she isn't exactly what she puts out into the world. There's more to her."

Sivan nodded. "I guessed that. You wouldn't have someone taking care of the girls unless you trusted them. And she's good with them. I've observed her a few times when she didn't know I was watching. I think there's something about me she doesn't like."

"I wish one of you would have told me it had gotten to this point, where Regina was openly rude to you." She studied Sivan. "You're right. But it's not that she doesn't like you. She's jealous and feels threatened by you."

Sivan put her hand on her chest, her eyes large. "Of me?"

"Yes, you have an innate self-confidence she doesn't have right now. She knows you've been through adversity, but you've come out on top. She's going through a hard time. I hope you'll have patience with her while she works her way through it."

"What's her deal anyway?" I asked. It'd be hard to be nice to someone like Regina.

She paused, seemed to do an inner check, and continued. "Did you know Regina's parents are wealthy?"

"No, but it doesn't surprise me." She always wore clothes better suited for a Paris runway, not looking after kids.

"Did you ever wonder why she works for me?"

Sivan tilted her head. "No, but now that you mention it, it does seem out of place for her."

"I met Regina through her parents at one of those society functions when Henry was alive. He was trying to raise money for a new wing at the hospital. Anyway, Regina sat in the corner all by herself. We began to chat and hit it off."

"Is that why she works for you?" Sivan asked.

"In part. The other reason is, although she has parents on paper, she really doesn't."

I frowned. "What does that mean?"

"Her parents spend most of their time traveling the world. They really haven't acknowledged her existence for many years. Regina told me once she felt like an inconvenience."

Sivan's face paled. "I know how that feels."

I grabbed her hand under the table.

Betty's eyes softened. "She feels like the girls and I are her family. When Sivan came, she believed—"

"I stole her family," Sivan finished.

"In a sense, yes." Aunt Betty met Sivan's eyes. "But this isn't your fault. You know that, right?"

"Yes." Sivan started to rub her finger against her thumb. I hadn't seen her do that in a long time.

"I hope I got through to her today, so please, let me know if she continues." Aunt Betty sighed.

"She's been making bitchy remarks to Sivan every time we see her. She won't change." She didn't have my sympathy because of all the crap she'd pulled on Sivan.

"Give her time. Now, on to more pleasant subjects. Who wants to go to the Ice Creamery after dinner?"

Sivan held her stomach. "Not me. I'll burst."

"Jax?" she asked.

"I'm always game for ice cream." I could almost taste the pralines and cream.

"I'll head back to the farm and try to start my packing. I got the cutest set of red luggage at Target on my way here," Sivan said.

"Which car did you drive?" Aunt Betty asked her.

"I drove the Escape, and Jax drove the truck. He didn't want to shop at Target. Imagine that." She shook her head.

"I drove the Buick. We didn't do a very good job with our carbon footprint today." Aunt Betty sighed.

"No, but we all came from different directions. You still

going to get that manicure later?" Sivan asked.

"Yes. I wish you'd come. We could make a girls' night of it."

Sivan looked down at her nails. "I could probably use a change." She shrugged. "But not tonight. Tonight, I tackle the big suitcase."

"Okay. Let me walk you out, and I'll buy Jax the ice cream he's already drooling over."

"Hey, there's no drool." I paused. "Yet."

Both girls laughed as they went to Sivan's car. I watched them talk, but couldn't hear the words. Aunt Betty wiped a tear from Sivan's face and gave her a hug. I wondered what that was all about?

She beamed as she walked toward me.

"Is Sivan okay?" I asked. If she weren't, I'd drive straight home.

"More than okay." Aunt Betty glowed. "She told me she loved me for the first time. I know what a huge step that was for her." A tear rolled down her cheek. "And I'm pretty sure you're next."

Chapter Twenty Two

Sivan

I SAT ON THE SUITCASE, BUT it wouldn't shut. Ugh. I had just the one when I arrived at the farm. Now it looked like I'd need ten. *Betty*. She loved to shop for me.

The doorbell rang, interrupting my fight with the luggage. I gave it one more bounce, but it stubbornly remained at least three inches from closing.

Thankful for the break, I headed toward the front door. I hoped the noise didn't wake Emily and Alice. Once up, they were almost impossible to get back to sleep.

I peered out the peephole and swung open the door. "Mrs. Thompson. How are you tonight?" As I finished the sentence, I frowned. Worry lines marked her eyes and mouth. Another woman stood next to her, her expression also somber.

"Sivan, this is my sister Nancy. She's looked after the girls a few times. And you can call me Mary. Is Betty home?" Her eyes darted around the foyer.

"Hi, Nancy. Um, no she's not here. She's getting her nails done." I paused. They glanced at each other, but remained silent. "Okay, well, um, it was nice meeting you. I'll let Betty know you stopped by."

Mary wrung her hands. "I brought Nancy with me just in case."

"In case of what?" Their body language put me on high alert.

Breathe, Sivan.

"Sivan, I need to take you to the hospital. Nancy can stay here with the girls," Mary blurted.

"Why?" My blood turned cold.

"Betty may have been involved in an accident." Mary continued to twist and fidget with her hands. "I was hoping someone else was driving—"

"No. There has to be some mistake." I backed out of the doorway. "I just left them a half hour ago at the restaurant." Or had it been longer? Dread crept up my spine.

"I heard over the police scanner there was an accident on Highway 4. Sivan, you need to brace yourself."

"Why?" I whispered. My body shook, and my legs had turned to rubber.

The two women looked at each other.

"Why?" I shouted.

"Betty's truck. It rolled twice." Mary paused and lowered her voice. "I called the sheriff's office to make sure. There's been a fatality."

No. No. No!

"Jax was driving the truck." As the words left my mouth, the realization struck. I stared past them.

"Sivan, listen to me." I hadn't noticed her approach until she shook my shoulders. "Nancy will stay with the girls. We'll get to the hospital and get this all sorted out. The fatality could have been the other driver involved in the accident."

I nodded, but I knew deep in my soul my life had been forever changed. Again.

"I didn't tell Jax I loved him. I was waiting for the right moment." I grabbed her arm. "Jax is going to be a vet. He's been accepted at NYU." My soul was being wrenched apart.

"Oh dear. I think she's in shock," the sister said. What was her name? They continued to talk, but their voices sounded muffled and incoherent, as if cotton balls were in my ears.

A hand clamped around my arm, and my feet followed as Mary pulled me toward her car. She placed me in the front seat and attached the seat belt.

"This can't happen again," I said. "How many minutes to the hospital?"

"We should get there in about ten minutes, Sivan. Hold on until we hear something from the sheriff. If anything happened, Betty—"

"No! Please don't talk right now." I needed silence. I put my head in my hands and squeezed my eyes shut.

God, are you there? I need your help right now. I'm sorry I've been so mad at you. I'm sorry I blamed you for my family. I'm sorry I haven't gone to church. Please, God, please save Jax. I'm begging you. I don't think I can live without him. I'll do anything. Anything.

We parked in a space close to the emergency room doors.

"Here we are. I'll go in with you and stay until we get this all worked out." Mary pulled me from the car.

I nodded, distracted, because I was still bargaining with God in my head.

We walked through the doors, and the first person I saw was Regina. Her face, red and blotchy, crumpled with grief.

She ran toward me. "Oh, Sivan." She threw her arms around me and started to sob. "I'm so sorry. I'm so sorry."

I pushed her away. "No." He was not gone. Jax had not died. But her face told a different story. "No!" I shouted at her. "You're a liar! Get away from me!" I turned from her, but she grabbed my arm.

"Betty talked to me today. She asked me not to give you a hard time and to back off," she said through sobs. "I'll make this up to you, Sivan. I'm so sorry about the way I've treated you. Oh God, I can't believe this has happened to you again."

"Quit lying. It was someone else! Someone else died," I screamed. Deep down, I already knew. The lights in the emergency room were too bright. The room started to spin.

Regina shook her head. "I've talked to the doctors. There wasn't anything they could do." She reached for me again.

I pushed her away. "Don't touch me!" Paralyzed and cold, I needed to get away. I was going to be sick. Nausea whipped through me, and my vision blurred.

"Sivan, honey, let's take a seat. I'll get you something to drink. You look a little pale." Mary took my arm again. Her fingers hot like fire on my cold skin.

God, please let this be a nightmare. I want to wake up.

Mary turned to Regina. "Can you please find Betty and ask her to come to the hospital?"

"W-What do you mean?" Regina's eyes grew large.

As though speaking through a tunnel, I heard Mary say, "Sivan needs her. I think she might be going into shock."

"I can't. I can't get Betty." Regina burst out into another round of sobs.

I clutched onto Mary and whimpered, "Find Betty. I want her right now. Can you get her?" Betty was my lifeline. I couldn't handle this without her. My body shook uncontrollably.

"Of course, honey. I think Regina is too distraught." She pulled out her cell phone and pushed a button. "I called her earlier, but she didn't answer. Maybe this time."

"Mrs. Thompson!" Regina yelled.

Mary jumped and dropped her phone.

"Betty can't answer. It was Betty. She di . . . she died." Regina bent over sobbing, clutching at her stomach.

"Betty? Betty, too? They both died?" Raw pain exploded inside me, surrounding me in a degree of agony I hadn't felt in six years. My world, gone. Destroyed by those few words. *Emily and Alice.* Oh my God. I thought they were safe. My chest froze. I couldn't breathe. Oxygen . . . I sucked in, but the air had gone thick. My lungs were concrete, I gasped for air. Black dots swirled in front of my eyes.

Please, God, please, just take me now. I can't live through it again.

And the world went dark.

The smell of chemicals and a rhythmical beep woke me. My body was lead. I couldn't move. Grogginess had taken over my brain.

Where am I?

The emergency room. Oh God. *Betty and Jax.*

No. I squeezed my eyes shut. It was a bad dream. The machine next to me made a faster beeping sound.

"I gave her a sedative with her IV. That should help a little when she wakes up," an unfamiliar voice said.

I cracked open an eye. Jax's mom sat next to my bed. I hadn't felt it at first, but she had a hold of my hand.

"Should I ring the nurse when she wakes up? I'm not sure what I should do." Tears choked her voice.

"That's a good idea. She's been through a huge shock. She might need another sedative. The most important thing for you to do is let her know she's not alone."

"Okay." Charley sniffed.

I kept my eyes shut. I wasn't ready for the world. I'd probably never be ready again. *Why couldn't I just die?*

Emily and Alice. I must protect them.

I tried to swallow, but my tongue was too thick.

"Hi, Charley. How is she doing?" Who was that?

"Not awake yet." Charley sighed.

"I can stay with her for a while so you can take a break. You've been awake all night with the flight and sitting with Sivan." Regina's voice.

"No, Jax asked me to be with her when she wakes up. He should be out of the MRI in an hour."

Wait. *What?*

I opened my eyes. "Jax?"

Charley stood. "Oh good." She wiped her face. "You're awake."

"Did you say Jax?" My heart began to pound out of my chest. The monitor beeped so fast, it set off an alarm.

"Yes, he wanted to be here when you woke up. The doctors insisted he get checked out before they'd release him."

"He's alive?"

Her eyes softened. "Oh, honey. Did you think he died?"

"Yes." Tears streamed down my face.

She leaned over and hugged me. "This must be so awful for you."

"Betty?" Maybe it was all a bad dream. Maybe . . .

She looked down, her face giving way to grief. "We lost Betty, yes."

I squeezed my eyes shut again and choked out, "I'm sorry." *Oh, Betty. Please don't leave me.*

She hugged me again. "Hush. We all need each other right now."

We held on tightly and cried onto each other's shoulders. Both of us for different reasons, but the searing pain was the same.

Betty. Beautiful, lovely, happy Betty. Gone.

"The girls. Oh God. The girls." I sat up in bed. My breath caught.

"I'm spending the rest of the day with them. Emily knows what's going on, but Alice doesn't seem to be grasping it." Charley squeezed my hand.

I covered my face and let the tears fall. I ached for those sweet, innocent girls. They just lost their entire world.

Charley put her arm around me. "I'm adopting them."

"What?" My head shot up. My brain was still foggy. Did I hear her right?

"Betty would've wanted it, and I already love them."

I nodded. "Thank you." Her words calmed me a little, and I swallowed. "And you're sure? Jax is really going to be okay?"

Her eyes glanced at the doorway. "You can ask him yourself." She gave him a nod. "Jax, I'm going to go get the girls now. You can take over here." With one last hug, she left the room.

Oh, Jax. He didn't look like himself. His clothes were wrinkled and blood stained, and his beautiful face was covered with scratches. And those beautiful green eyes were different. Instead of his usual mischievous glint, they held sadness.

As soon as his mom left the room, he approached the bed. "Sivan. God, I'm so sorry. We drove together to get ice cream. I shouldn't have—" Tears streamed down his cheeks.

"No, don't say that. It's not your fault." I scooted over, and he sat next to me. I unraveled the twisted IV tube and put my arms around his neck. "I didn't pray for her."

"What do you mean?" He rubbed my back.

"When I heard about the accident, I thought it was you. I couldn't . . . I couldn't think straight. I prayed so hard, Jax. I didn't know I had to pray for Betty." I sobbed and clutched onto his shoulder. "I would've prayed for her."

"Shhh. It's okay. She knows." His hands continued to run up and down my back in an effort to soothe me. "You told her you loved her. That meant a lot to her."

"She told you?"

"Yes, it made her very happy." He stopped and shut his eyes.

"Jax?"

He kept his eyes closed and blew out a large breath. "Yeah?"

"Please look at me."

His head rose slowly.

"I love you."

He looked into my eyes, and his hand cupped my cheek. "I know. I've known all along. And you probably know I love you."

I nodded.

"We'll get through this, Sivan. We're together, okay? We're a team. You aren't alone this time."

A tiny beam of light shined into my darkness. "Okay. And Jax?"

He kissed me gently on the lips. "Yeah."

"I'm going to try to help you, too. I know you loved her as much as I did."

"I did. It's funny how I didn't want to come to stay with her at first." He shook his head. "I would have missed so much."

"Me too."

He lay down on the bed and put his arm carefully around my stomach. "The other driver was a teenager. The police told me she got her license a few months ago. She was texting and ran the red light."

"It didn't have to happen." Betty should be with us. She shouldn't have died.

"No. It shouldn't have happened." He wiped tears from my face with his thumbs.

"I wonder if she knows how great Betty is." I couldn't use the past tense. It wouldn't go past my lips.

"The sheriff's office has charged her with vehicular manslaughter."

I sat up because the room had started to spin again. "She could have taken both of you."

He pulled me close and hugged me tighter. "I'm here for you. I'm not going anywhere."

Could I trust that? Would he be next?

Was I really cursed?

CHAPTER Twenty Three

JAX

SIVAN LOOKED SO SMALL AND fragile in her bed. Tangled hair, pale cheeks, and mascara smeared under her eyes made my heart seize. How could I make this better? How could anyone?

Waves of grief, fear, and anger had taken over. She'd be crying one minute, and the next she'd clutch onto me for dear life. After that, her hands would form into fists, and she'd want to track down the teenage driver to tell her exactly what she'd done.

She was a mess, but so was I.

I'd pull it together so she could lean on me. There was no way I would let her down.

God, what I'd give to talk to Betty about it. She'd become so much more to me than an aunt this year. When I needed advice or a sounding board, she'd always make time for me. She also knew Sivan better than anyone. She'd know how to help her.

I watched Sivan's sleeping face. She had a crease between her eyebrows, and her mouth seemed to be forming words. She should look peaceful, but her face still held the trauma of the last two days.

My mom came back into the room. "How is she?"

"I don't know, Mom." I straightened her blanket.

"Betty really loved that girl. She loved all of them, but Sivan, she was special to her." Her eyes gentled, and she wore a sad smile.

"I know." My mom had dark smudges under tired, red-rimmed eyes. "How are you? I'm sorry I've been tied up with Sivan."

"No, honey. You take care of Sivan. I have your dad and brothers." She patted my hand and said quietly, "All she has now is you."

"I know. I'm worried about her."

"You have to take care of yourself first, okay? I know you and Betty had become close this year. You'll also need some time to grieve."

"When's the funeral?"

"In two days. It'll be in the same church as Henry's. Because he died young, Betty made sure all her wishes about burial were clear and written down, just in case." Her voice caught, and she looked down. "All her wishes will be . . ." She couldn't continue.

"Mom." I motioned. "Let's go to the kitchen. I'll make coffee."

"Oh, honey." She grabbed my hand and whispered, "I don't

know if I can stand this. I can't say goodbye to my sister. I'm not ready."

I patted her back as she quietly sobbed. When she calmed down, I led her into the kitchen and pulled out a stool next to the counter. I started to prepare the coffee.

A memory of Aunt Betty dancing around the kitchen table to an old Beatles song came back. "I don't think any of us are ready. She was something."

Mom smiled. "Yeah. She really was." She wiped her face and took a deep breath. "I need to go talk to the attorney about the adoption. He said it shouldn't take too much longer because of the switch. All the basic legwork and red tape have been done. I think we should have this wrapped up in a few months."

"Are you okay with adopting two girls? It's a big deal. They're great, don't get me wrong, but Betty had her hands full." I prayed she'd say yes.

"Am I okay?" Her eyes widened. "I don't think you know how much I've wanted to dress a couple of frilly girls. I'm beyond thrilled." She perked up for the first time in days.

Relief flooded through me. "You know, Mom? You are more like Aunt Betty than you think."

She smiled and placed her hand over her heart. "That's the best compliment you could give me."

She took the cup of coffee and gave me a tight hug before she left.

"That was sweet." Sivan's voice startled me from the hall doorway.

"Hey, you eavesdropping?"

"Yep." She walked into the kitchen. "I'm so thankful for your mom. I don't know if the state would have allowed it, but I would have dropped out of school to take care of Emily and

Alice."

"My mom will do a great job with them."

She smiled, but her blue eyes revealed sadness. "I know she will. Betty will be . . . I mean, Betty would be relieved. She really loved those two."

My chest ached. "I don't think I'll ever get used to it."

She blinked slowly. "What?"

"Talking about her in the past tense."

"Me either." She paused. "I don't know if I can go to the funeral."

I took her hand. "I'll be with you. We'll do it together. Emily and Alice will need us there."

"Sivan, you need to get some sleep. The funeral is tomorrow." I didn't think she'd slept more than a few minutes at a time.

"How did you know I was awake?" she asked.

"Your breathing." When she slept, her breathing slowed and had a quiet rhythm.

I'd cleared the way with my parents so I could stay in Sivan's bedroom. They gave us the space we needed to take comfort from each other.

She turned over and slung an arm over my chest. "I think once we get past the funeral I'll be able to sleep."

"Yeah." I wanted to put this part behind us, not only for me, but especially for Sivan. It was taking a toll on her.

Eight hours later, we sat together in the church pew behind a veiled curtain, listening to friends and neighbors talk about Aunt Betty. The church was beautiful, old, probably a hundred years, with stone archways, hand carved wooden pews, and flowers everywhere. People crammed into the pews and aisles. Everyone loved Aunt Betty.

Ray sat one pew over with his head in his hands. My throat constricted seeing him like that. He was always such a badass—a strong guy. Mom sat next to me and held onto Dad's hand for dear life. My brothers sat lined up next to Dad. Emily and Alice squirmed next to Sivan, while she tried to distract them with a puzzle.

We had to say goodbye to Aunt Betty.

Sivan hadn't fallen back to sleep, and the fatigue seemed to roll off her in waves.

"Are you okay?" I whispered in her ear.

She shook her head. "They're telling stories about her, but they haven't captured her spirit."

"It's okay." I squeezed her hand. "We know."

"No, it's not." She stood abruptly.

Before my shocked brain could put it together, she strode up to the front of the church and adjusted the microphone.

"Um, I didn't prepare anything to say today, so this is, uh, . . ." She swiped at the tears raining down her face. "I want to do this." Her voice wavered.

Pain for Sivan, and grief for Betty, about killed me. My heart tore, ripped from my chest by an invisible force.

A hush came over the church.

She stood for a moment, still and quiet. After taking a deep breath, she spoke again. "The truth is, I didn't want to talk today. I mean, that would make it real, right?" She cleared her throat. "So, I'm going to talk to you about my Betty. The . . . the Betty I know." She wiped the flood of tears and continued.

"Have you ever known anyone who, when they walk into the room, it changes, becomes electric, more alive? That was Betty. She made everything fun and happy and . . . good."

Sivan glanced my way, and then back to the main gathering. "Betty took one glance at me and saw through all the barriers I'd put up to keep the world at a distance. She looked into my soul and went right in and pulled me out. I began living again because of her. I learned how to love again."

She wiped her forehead and grabbed onto the podium. Should I go to her? I sat forward in my seat, ready to act.

She straightened and seemed to gather strength. "So now, I'm going to tell you a few things about Betty you probably didn't know." Her eyes searched the crowd and landed on an older man in the second pew. "You run the hardware store, is that correct?" she asked.

He nodded slowly. "Yes."

"Do you remember about two months ago, a mysterious bunch of flowers were planted in front of your store?"

Realization dawned, and he smiled.

"Betty and I had gone to town to find some flowers for the farm. She noticed your store and said, 'That could use a pop of color.' Well, she dragged me out of thc housc at one a.m. to help with her little plan. It took two hours until Betty was happy with how it looked. She laughed all the way home, anticipating your surprise when you discovered them."

Her eyes went back through the crowd and focused in on a woman about Betty's age. "Mrs. Upton?" The woman nodded. "After your husband died last year, it was Betty who deposited the twenty thousand into your account. I wouldn't have known about it, but the banker let it slip during one of our errands. Apparently, she'd gone to a lot of trouble making sure no one knew."

She pressed her fist against her chest. "That was Betty's way. She didn't need a thanks or gratitude. She gave because she wanted to brighten up the lives around her. I hope I can follow along in her footsteps and be half the person she was."

God, she was brave. But part of me wanted her to stop. This must be taking a toll on her. I wanted to go to her, wrap my arms around her, and tell her they knew. It was okay.

"And Betty?" She looked up. "I want to thank you for trusting me, for never pushing. Time didn't allow me to tell you everything, but I know it didn't matter. You accepted and loved me, not knowing anything about my past. Thank you for being there when I needed you the most. Thank you for setting the example of what every person on this earth should strive for."

She bit her lip and closed her eyes. "I was honored to call you mom, even if it was only for two weeks."

She trembled from head to foot. I sprang up and went to her. She nearly collapsed just as I got my arm around her and led her back to the pew.

The rest of the day went by in a blur.

"It's been eight days, Mom, I'm worried."

Her eyebrows creased. "Is Sivan still sleeping?"

"Almost around the clock. She wakes up and barely eats, and then goes back to sleep."

We were in Betty's office, going through all her files. I loved it in here; I could still feel Betty's presence. Sivan hadn't come in here yet. I was concerned she was avoiding it.

I was helping Mom get everything in order before she headed back to Seattle with Emily and Alice. My plan was to take Sivan to school early, then come back to the farm and close everything down before I left for school in late August.

Mom frowned. "That's not good. I think we should call the doctor."

"The doctor? Do you think something's physically wrong with her?" Anxiety gnawed at my gut.

She put down a box. "She's been through quite a shock, and she probably went through something similar with her family. I assume that's why she was in the foster system before she came to Betty."

"Yeah. We knew something bad happened, but she never told Aunt Betty, and she hasn't told me yet either." I picked up a box of files and put them by the door.

Mom sighed. "I think whatever went on with her family has probably been brought back up, and she's reliving that along with Betty's death. It must be overwhelming for her. Sleep is what the body does when it can't cope. Sivan might be going through a depression, and sleep is her escape."

My chest tightened. "What can a doctor do to help?"

"Well . . ." She took a deep breath. "Either recommend medicine or counseling, or both. I think, at the very least, she needs a professional she can talk to."

I rubbed my hand over my face. "Should I try to get her to talk to me?"

She shook her head. "I wouldn't push her right now. It might be too much for her to open up. I think she probably needs professional help."

I paced the room a few times. Frustration gripped me. "If I knew what happened to her family six years ago, I might be able to help her more. I feel useless. All she does is sleep, and I'm not doing anything for her."

Mom stopped packing, came over, and placed a hand on my

arm. “You are, honey. Just being by her side will do her a world of good. I’m sure, when you drive her to school, she’ll perk out of it. I haven’t heard her play yet, but Betty said she’s the best she’s ever heard, and that’s saying a lot.”

“That’s part of what I’m worried about. Whatever happened with her family was so painful she didn’t play for over six years. She loves the piano. You should see her, Mom. The music becomes part of her.”

“The music will probably save her this time.”

“*If* she goes. Right now, she can’t even get out of bed. We’re supposed to leave in four days. She quit packing. She isn’t even talking about school anymore.” I ran my fingers through my hair and tried to calm my racing heart.

“Maybe we can get the doctor over today. If he recommends it, we’ll look for a good counselor in New York. I can call Betty’s doctor and at least get some ideas on how to proceed.”

“Okay, I think that’s a good idea.” A plan. The tension eased from my shoulders.

She dropped another box by the door. “I’m going to start lunch for the girls. You want anything?”

“No, I’m good.” My eyes scanned the office. We were almost done.

“We still need to find the original Foster Care Parenting Adoption Application for Emily and Alice.”

“I’m on it.”

“Thanks, Jax. You’ve been great picking up the slack around here. I don’t think . . .” Her eyes filled with tears. “I don’t think I could’ve made it this last week without you.”

I crossed the room to hug her. “You’ve been a big help for me, too. Thanks for the ideas for Sivan.”

"Good. Please remember to eat later." Her eyebrows drew together.

"I'll fix myself something as soon as I'm done here."

She kissed me on the cheek and headed for the kitchen.

I took a deep breath and sat behind the desk. I closed my eyes and remembered the first time I saw Sivan and Aunt Betty together. They laughed, talked and joked, and were so in tune with each other. It was like they'd known each other for a lifetime instead of a few weeks.

Sivan is devastated, and I'm not helping her at all.

I scrubbed my hands over my face. I wished she'd talk to me. I was scared for her. Could she pull herself out of her depression before it was too late? Would she be able to cope with another huge loss in her life? And what type of loss had she experienced six years ago?

My eyes landed on a small file cabinet we'd dragged in from the kitchen.

Sivan's file? Sivan had mentioned that Betty never looked at her file. That must have meant that the file was somewhere in the house. If I could find out what Sivan was dealing with, maybe I could be of more help, say the right things, give her the help she needed.

The house was quiet. Sivan was sleeping, and everyone else was in the kitchen. Time to break a lock.

I approached the file cabinet like it was a living, breathing thing, ready to pounce. I wanted to find the file, and yet I didn't. Sivan had asked, no, insisted I wasn't to dig into her past, but this was an emergency. Information was power. In this case, information might save her.

A tug on the handle a few times confirmed it was locked. Sivan's file must be here. My palms started to sweat.

Am I doing the right thing?

I was doing the only thing. I had to help her in any way I could.

The key. Where would Betty hide it? I sat back down behind the desk and let my eyes scan across the room, landing on various objects. The plant. No, it would get dirty and maybe rust. Behind a frame. Again, no. It might fall out. Desk drawers? After emptying them out, it was clear she hadn't picked the obvious.

I sat and propped my head on my hands. *Think.*

The picture of Uncle Henry's smiling face. It wasn't a huge frame, but it was her favorite thing on her desk. It made sense. I grabbed it and slid off the backing. When the key hit the desk, it made a metallic ping. I smiled. Aunt Betty had put the two things she loved together.

I had mixed feelings as I opened the cabinet. Sivan would never know I'd invaded her privacy. God, I hated myself. But what choice did I have? Watch her wither away before my eyes? Let her dreams of attending Juilliard slip away? Let *her* slip away?

No. I'd help her in every possible way. If I knew what she was dealing with, I could help her.

I unlocked and opened the drawer. Sure enough, Sivan's file was the only one in the cabinet. I lifted it out and flipped it open, not even bothering to go back to the desk.

After reading the first paragraph, my heart seized.

"Oh, Sivan," I whispered. A lump formed in my throat, and my body broke in a sweat. No wonder she's hanging on by a thread. I couldn't imagine—

A gasp came from the doorway.

Oh God.

Please, don't be Sivan.

I looked up to Sivan's wide eyes. Eyes that had gone from feisty and alive, to dull and lifeless since Betty's death. Her beautiful, injured eyes stayed locked on mine, wounding me as sure as if she'd shoved a knife in my gut.

What had I done?

This was a mistake. The biggest one of my life.

CHAPTER Twenty Four

Sivan

JAX'S EXPRESSION GAVE IT ALL away. I would have thought he was doing routine paperwork, but when he looked up from the file, his face had a familiar look.

Pity.

I stood still. My hands clenched tight, hot tears forming behind my eyelids.

"You read it, didn't you?" I asked in the calmest voice I could muster.

His face turned pale. "Just the first paragraph. I wanted to help—"

I held up my hand. "Stop. I don't want to hear your excuses."

"But—"

"No!" I shouted. A seed of rage started to sprout. I hadn't felt anything except for a sleepy numbness, and this out of control escalation scared me. "How could you? No, don't answer that." I studied him. "I see your expression. All the foster parents looked at me like that at first. Pity. Then they would use it against me."

"I would never use this. I wanted to help you. I didn't know what to do." His eyes pleaded with mine.

"Maybe you could've listened to me. Maybe you could've respected my wishes. Maybe you could've been supportive instead of sneaking behind my back."

"Sivan, you have to listen—"

"No, you listen to me." I pointed a finger at him. "You've betrayed me in the worst way. It should've been me telling you this in my own time. You promised, remember?"

He looked down and muttered, "The Boy Scout pledge. Shit." He looked back up. "This is different. I'm worried about you."

"So that gives you the right to dig out my file? We're back where we started last fall. This is all about you. You have to control cvcrything. Everything has to go your way."

He shook his head. "I just wanted to help you. I didn't read all of it. I don't know everything."

"That's only because I caught you. You want information? You want to uncover everything about me?" Fury and rage took over. "Here it is." I grabbed the papers from his hands and shouted. "You want it, you got it." I held up the first page. "My parents, brother, and I went to the ocean almost every weekend."

He held up his hands. "No, Sivan. You don't have to tell me."

"On August 25th, the year I turned eleven, we decided to go for a picnic. Mom and Dad went for a swim. They'd done it a thousand times, but that day was different. They got caught in a riptide and were pulled out past the reef. I told my brother to stay put while I ran down the beach to pull up the flag to alert the lifeguards. When I came back, my brother was gone. At eight years old, he thought he could save them." Pain stabbed like a knife piercing my chest, but I kept going. "You know what I did?"

"Sivan." He shook his head and looked down.

"I'll tell you. I stood there, staring at the waves, praying they were safe."

"That's all you could've done," he said softly.

"I know. I don't blame myself. If I would've gone in, I would've drowned with them." I threw the first page on the floor. "Sometimes I feel like my brother did the right thing. He was the lucky one."

"No, Sivan." Jax held out his arms to me.

I backed up. "I'm the one left living with it. The loss, the aftermath. I thought I was given a second chance when I came here, but I wasn't. It's starting all over again."

"Sivan, I want to help you."

Heat flushed through my body. "Help me? When I needed you the most, you betrayed me. I only asked one thing."

"I couldn't get you to stay awake! You weren't eating or even talking. I'm so damned worried about you, I can't think straight," he shouted. His face crumpled. "I didn't know what to do."

My hands formed fists. "Then you should've asked me."

He averted his eyes.

I grabbed page two. “After my family died, I was placed in the foster care system. My parents didn’t have any extended family, and I had nowhere to go. I ended up with the Lawson family. They put on a good show at first. That was the year I became a cheerleader. But six months later, the *real* children decided I was no longer welcome. They bullied me, thinking I’d run away. When that didn’t work, they decided rat poison in my oatmeal was the way to go.”

“What the hell?” A vein in his forehead pulsed, and his nostrils flared.

“Luckily, when I ended up in the hospital, a smart intern tested for it. The police were called, the kids were thrown in juvie, and I was sent along to home number two.”

I held up page three. “The Hartle family. They hadn’t wanted a foster child. They wanted a housecleaner and cook. I was okay with it. At least they weren’t trying to poison me, right? But the dad started gambling, and they’d fight constantly. I tried to go to school, but I was too exhausted. Then the drugs started. Cocaine, meth, whatever they could get their hands on. They never slept and were always screaming and swearing. You know how I don’t like swearing? It was from this house. One day, my caseworker came by for a spot visit. There was no food in the refrigerator, lines of cocaine on the table, and cash laying around.”

“No more, Sivan.” Tears were in his eyes, and he rubbed at his chest.

“You don’t want to hear about my childhood? Because that file in your hand says you do.”

“I only wanted to find out about your family, how they died, to see if it was similar.”

The grief, fresh and suffocating, cascaded over me, and I barged forward. “You wanted the information.” I held up page four. "Family number three. This time I was placed in a beautiful home with a church-going dentist and his lovely wife. Kinda like those 1950s shows they play on the Lifetime Channel. The mom wore a dress every day, and the dad would come home promptly at six, and we'd all have dinner together. They held charity functions, were on the school board, and said a prayer before every meal. This should've been my forever home, right? But 'Daddy,' . . ." I paused to do air quotes, " . . . decided he'd rather be a boyfriend. He came into my bedroom—"

"Sivan, stop. Please. Don't do this." Tears streamed down his face.

"I got away and called my caseworker. She removed me immediately. I taped a video testimony for his trial, and Daddy Dearest is now serving time and must register as a sex offender for the rest of his life.

"You can imagine what it was like for me coming here after six years of hell. And now you want me to pop out of it in a week? How dare you! How dare you come in here and invade my privacy because I don't fit into your timetable of when I should be over it. Yes, I'm sleeping a lot. You didn't trust me to handle this. Betty trusted me. She would never have done this." I cried into my hands. "Now I can't trust you anymore. I can't be around you. I'm packing and going to school early. Without you."

"Please wait until you calm down. You need to understand why I got the file."

I pointed to the file. "I will never understand why you did it. You've lost my trust. And now you've lost me."

He shook his head.

I turned and left the room. Jax didn't try to follow. He knew me well enough to know I wasn't going to change my mind in a few minutes.

One suitcase was packed, but I needed at least four more. I'd already gathered them and dragged them out of my closet.

I had to say goodbye to Emily and Alice before I left. They were already prepared for me to go, and they'd be well cared for by Jax's parents. I'd keep my promise and FaceTime them every week so we could keep the bond. I could fake a smile for that long. I hoped.

The numbness returned as I packed my last belongings. Betty had already transferred the title to the Escape and put money into my account, so I was all ready to go. I took a last look around my bedroom and took a moment to remember Betty. All the late-night talks, the advice, the hugs . . . the love. That part would never die.

"I love you, Betty," I whispered. I left the room and my old life behind.

New York was crowded, messy, and chaotic. And I loved it.

"You staring out the window again?" my roommate, Darby, asked.

"I still can't get over this view. It's beautiful." Our dorm window had a fantastic view of the city.

She glanced out the window, her face scrunching in disgust. "It's raining."

"It's still a spectacular city even when it rains. And if you go outside right after, there's a fresh concrete/rain smell."

"You mean the odor that's mixed with the rotting garbage? 'Cause that's all I can smell."

I rolled my eyes. Darby wasn't a fan of the city. She was,

though, the greatest cellist on the planet. We'd shared a dorm room since I arrived four months ago.

"Okay, so maybe you need to go out after garbage pick-up." I chuckled.

A knock sounded at the door.

"Oh God. Tell me it isn't her again." She pretended to gag.

"Okay, I won't tell you." I smiled and walked toward the door. I braced myself for the whirlwind.

"Sivan! I'm so glad you're home. How are you doing?" She wrapped me in a tight squeeze.

"Good, except you're choking me again." I laughed.

"Oops. Sorry." She looked around the room. "There you are, Darby. I brought you your favorite cookies. Peanut butter with chocolate and butterscotch chips, right?"

Darby's mouth turned into an O.

That's the way to win her over. I kept my laugh silent.

She handed Darby the plate and said to me, "Let's sit. I need to talk to you."

"Listen, Regina, you don't have to do this."

"What?"

"Come over almost every day. I appreciate you looking after me, but I'm okay now."

"We're friends, right?"

"Yes." Strangely enough. I shook my head, remembering how Regina transferred to NYU right after Betty died. She moved to the city a week after me to "help me along" as she'd put it. She'd drag me to movies, Broadway musicals, and out-of-the-way restaurants. If it weren't for her, I'd probably be a social recluse, alone in my room right now. She also found a great counselor for me to visit once a week. It was her love for Betty that motivated her, but I appreciated it.

She plopped down on the couch. “Sit. I have news.”

My stomach sank. “Good news or bad?” I sat next to her.

“Good, I think. Well, I don’t know how much you’ll like it, but I wanted to prepare you.”

Uh oh. Never words I wanted to hear.

“Okay. So, it’s been four months since you left Iowa.”

“Regina—”

“I know, I know. You don’t want to talk about it. You need to listen to this part.”

“What?” I couldn’t hide my annoyance.

“Well, I’ve told you about Jax.”

My heart stilled. “Is he okay?”

She smiled and patted my hand. “Yes and no. He’s still waiting for you to talk to him.”

I took a deep breath. “I know.” I missed him so much sometimes, it made it hard to breathe.

“You know he’s in the city right now.” She studied me.

“Yes, I know you’re both attending NYU. Is that what this is all about? You two plotting on campus?”

“No, I actually don’t see him. I talk to his mom, Charley. Did you know we’re really good friends now?”

“I’m not surprised.” Regina’s complete turn-around was across the board.

“Anyway, Jax has been respecting your need for space and hasn’t contacted you. But he did send a message for you.”

“Wait. I told you, Regina. No messages until I’m ready.”

"Not from me."

"Who's he sending the message through?"

"The world." Her face glowed.

I tilted my head. "Um. That doesn't make sense."

"Did you know Jax wrote most of his brothers' number one hits?" She lifted an eyebrow.

My breath caught. "He never mentioned it."

"Well, he did. Charley told me."

"Okay." I couldn't keep my heart from racing.

"He's releasing his own song this week. It's called, 'Black Hair, Blue Eyes.'"

My body froze. I sat and stared at her. *No way.*

"But . . . but Jax hates the industry. He doesn't want to be famous," I stuttered out.

"I know. But I think sending a message to you was more important."

"Oh my God! Are you two talking about Jax Jayne?" Darby asked.

Ugh. Roommates. I hadn't told her about Jax because of this very thing.

"Yes!" Regina clapped her hands. "Isn't it exciting?"

"And he wrote a song just for Sivan?" She looked at me like I'd sprouted wings.

"And it's the best song you'll ever hear. It's about love and loss and heartbreak—oh, so romantic. I cried the first time I heard it." Regina clasped both hands over her chest.

That numb feeling started to return.

Relax, Sivan.

"The song is also about hope." She raised an eyebrow.

Time to visit Jolene, my therapist.

"Let's go over what you've learned or discovered in the last four months." Jolene leaned forward in her chair.

I sat in the recliner, but I never used the recline function. It felt too much like I was in a therapist's office. But it was one of the ways I could keep coming. Denial. Might have to work on that as well.

Her office was decorated to calm the nerves of her patients. Comforting shades of pale green and beige, overstuffed furniture, an antique, carved desk, a diploma from Yale. All the essentials.

"I've learned if I don't deal with my grief, it'll eventually come out. Sometimes in unhealthy ways that could make things worse than if I would've dealt with it in the first place."

"That's right." Jolene beckoned me on. "What else?"

"That once I deal with my grief, I'll be able to remember the people I loved with happiness instead of pain."

"How are you coming along with that? Any progress?"

"Yes. My parents and brother. Once I quit blocking all the memories of them, some happy ones have come back. I'm able to remember some of the good times growing up."

"Excellent. And Betty?"

"I remember everything about Betty. But I still have pain."

"It hasn't been very long in terms of grieving. The important thing for you is to not shove away or try to run from the memories or people associated with her."

"Regina visits almost every day, and I FaceTime with the

girls and Charley weekly."

She cocked her head. "You're leaving someone out."

Jax.

"I can't. I'm not ready." I crossed my arms.

"You've tied him up in your grieving process. He should be separate."

"What do you mean?"

"When you think about Betty's death, what do you remember?"

My throat constricted, and I broke out into a cold sweat. "I remember her dying and then Jax's betrayal."

"Exactly. They've become one in the same with you. Your emotions were heightened, perhaps that's why you felt the betrayal so intensely? If Betty hadn't died, would you have had such a strong reaction?"

"Maybe not quite as strong. But he promised. He knew I was in bad shape, but he did it anyway." I looked away. Betrayal washed over me like it was yesterday.

"Have you entertained the thought that the only reason he read your file was *because* you were in bad shape?"

"He did say that."

"I'm sure it's true. We haven't spent a lot of time discussing Jax, but I believe it will be hard for you to move forward, past all your pain from losing Betty, until you resolve the conflict with Jax. He made a mistake, and you'll hold on to the anger and grief indefinitely if you don't forgive him and move on."

I'd become an expert at shoving out the things that caused pain. First, my family after they died, then Jax. If I forgave him, would the love come rushing back? If I let go of my anger, would I be able to let him go again? If I let myself love him again, would he die?

"I don't want him to die," I blurted.

"What do you mean?" She leaned forward.

"The people I love. Well, they die." I bit my lip, but couldn't stop the tears.

"Oh, Sivan. You can't live that way. Don't deny yourself love because of fear."

I sat up. "That's what Betty said to me. I almost forgot." The pain shifted a little, and a warm memory of Betty's smile replaced it.

"How do I let go of the fear?"

"It's a choice. You choose fear, or you choose love."

I nodded. Not sure if I could even think about it, let alone actually accomplish it.

"When you're able to push aside the fear and face your grief, all the obstacles you've been wrestling with will surface. Your darkest wounds, your mistrust, along with any lingering triggers might pose a challenge." She squeezed my hand. "I'm not going to lie. It won't be easy."

"Do you think I left Jax not only because he betrayed my trust, but because of my own fear?"

"Fear. Tell me what that word means to you."

I answered quickly. "Protection."

"From what?"

I shrugged. "From life, from pain."

"I want you to do something. Close your eyes, and think about how the sun's warmth causes moisture to release from the earth."

"Okay." I smiled because that was my favorite time to be

outside. The earthly and fresh smell I loved.

"If you're open to love and forgiveness, a light will shine on the places in your soul where you've shut down, and you'll be able to transform back to your natural state—love."

I let her words sink in for a minute. "Do you think I'm ready?"

CHAPTER Twenty Five

JAX

"I CAN'T STAND IT ANYMORE. I'm going to find her." I paced across my small dorm room.

"I thought you were going to wait for her to contact you," Gage said.

"She still hasn't called. The song released last week and still no word. I'd hoped to get through to her with that song. Maybe if I see her in person?"

Gage had come to stay with me for a week between tour stops. It was nice to have my twin around for moral support.

"Hey, man, you have to prepare yourself for the possibility she might not want to see you."

I stopped and stared at him.

"Sorry, bro. I have to tell it to you straight."

"Thanks a lot." I groaned and resumed pacing.

"Would you stop that?" he shouted.

"What?"

He threw his hands up. "The damn pacing. You're driving me crazy."

I flopped down on the loveseat and ran my fingers through my hair. The headache I'd had

for the last month wouldn't leave.

"Mom's really worried about you. Hell, we're all worried. You've been dragging around ever since . . ." He stopped and examined me before continuing. "Ever since Betty died and Sivan left. I've been here a week, you've barely slept, and I had to bribe you to get junk food. What's up with that?"

My heart stalled. "You haven't told Mom, have you? I don't want her to fly back out here again."

"No, I covered for you. I knew she'd freak. She's tied up with ballet classes and shopping for pink." He laughed and shook his head.

Relief flooded through me. Missed that bullet. "Thanks."

"All you do is go to school and study."

"It's my first month, and I'm veterinary pre-med. What else am I supposed to do?" I rested my head on the back of the loveseat.

"I don't know. Go to a couple parties, get to know people?"

"People? You mean girls?"

"Yes. Because you need a back-up plan if this doesn't go the way you want. It's been over four months. You need to move on."

Anger and frustration exploded within me. I jumped out of my seat and got in his face. "Back-up plan? What the hell am I supposed to say? That I'll be fine? That the girl I love more than anything in this world is lost to me forever? That I should go on and date an imitation of her? No! There'll be no dating. I won't try to put this behind me because I'll never meet anyone like her. She's it for me, Gage. You don't understand."

He crossed his arms and stared at me intently. "I'm starting to. Well then, I think it's time you went out and got your girl back."

I threw my hands in the air. "How do you propose I do that?"

"Stalking."

My mouth dropped open. "You want me to stalk Sivan?"

"Yes. Our fans do it all the time. I found a girl in our hotel closet last month."

"Oh God. I don't even want to hear about it."

"I was good." He laughed. "We had security escort her out. But we did give her some signed pictures for her ingenuity." He scratched his chin. "Okay. Here's the plan. We'll need to get into her school as guests."

I crossed my arms. "We'll?"

"Yeah. You think I'm going to miss out on this?"

"Yes, you'll be staying here." I gave him my best don't-mess-with-me look.

"Oh man," he whined.

"I'll be nervous enough without you looking over my shoulder."

"How will you gain access to the school without my expertise?" He waggled his eyebrows.

"I'll figure it out. I can stand out on the curb if I have to."

“And look like some creepster? You gotta have a plan. If she sees you outside, she might turn around and take a back exit or something.”

“I hadn’t thought of that.” I needed a different plan.

“Call them, and set up a campus tour. Like you’re a prospective student.”

I narrowed my eyes. “Your mind is starting to scare me.”

“I’ve been chased around for the past two years. I’ve gained a little insight into the stalker mind.”

“Again. Scary.”

“At least something positive will come from it.”

“I thought you liked the spotlight, all the fame and fortune.”

“It’s okay. It’s part of the package. But sometimes I envy you. I thought you were nuts when you first refused to join the band, but now I can see why. You’re going your own way, and that’s cool.”

“I think going to Aunt Betty’s was the perfect thing for me to do. Out of sight, out of mind. I can walk around campus, and no one bothers me.”

“Not for long. Your song is climbing the charts.”

My stomach dropped. “I hope you’re wrong. This is the only song I’ll ever release, so if I do get some attention, it’ll hopefully be short-lived. If not, it’s worth the risk.”

Sivan is worth it.

Gage glanced at the darkened sky. “You aren’t going out in this storm, are you?”

“I am.”

"I changed my mind then. I'm back to thinking you're nuts." He motioned to the window. "Why the hell would you go out there? Is today the tour?"

Sheets of rain pounded the sidewalks. The earth vibrated every time thunder rumbled.

"Yep. I'm taking a taxi, and I'll be indoors for the tour."

"You know, I'm going to write a song about this. I'll name it, 'Desperate Love.'"

"Ha ha." I shoved him. "Just wait until it happens to you."

"It'll never happen. I'll be a bachelor until I die. I'm having too much fun."

"Out of the mouth of babes."

"Hey, I'm ten minutes older than you."

"But many years younger in maturity. I'll ask Mom if she dropped you as a child."

He looked out the window. "Speaking of your head issues, I think your cab just honked."

I wiped my sweaty palms on my pant legs. "Okay. This is it. Wish me luck."

"Yeah. And I'll also wish you don't drown on your way to meet your princess."

"Why do I put up with you?"

Gage smiled and winked. "You can't get rid of your twin. No one's told you that?"

I laughed. "I think I've heard that somewhere."

"Good luck. Really, man. I hope it goes your way." He gave me a side hug.

I took a deep breath. "So do I."

I sat in the back of the cab and decided Gage was right. I was nuts. What was I doing? The worst storm of the year raged outside, but still, I had to keep my appointment. There was a good chance I wouldn't even see Sivan today. She could be tucked away in an off-limits room. She could be at her dorm or in one of the practice rooms.

I wondered how she was doing. Sure, she did the FaceTime thing with Mom and the girls. They said she looked good. But was she? Deep down?

Today, I'd find out. Maybe.

The taxi's engine sputtered and screeched to a stop.

"What was that?" I asked.

The driver hit his steering wheel a few times and shouted something in another language.

My tour was in fifteen minutes. I peered up at the darkened sky. The rain and wind hadn't given up. "I'll get out here. How much do I owe you?"

A few more shouted words I didn't understand and then, "Twenty bucks."

We'd only traveled a few blocks, but I decided not to argue. I slapped a twenty into his hand and stepped into the torrential rain. Could I make it in time? I scanned the streets looking for an unoccupied taxi. Nothing. Looks like I'd be taking my first subway ride. I pulled my hood tighter and began a hurried trek down the stairs and into the station.

It was like everyone in the city had decided to take the subway all at once. I stood still, trying to figure out which train line to take. Swarms of people passed me by, some of them knocking right into me.

I didn't have time for this. I purchased my MetroCard and hurried to the turnstiles. I'd ask someone once I got onto the platform. I swiped my card and pushed. Nothing.

"Are you f'ing stupid or something?" A short guy wearing a plaid shirt and khakis stared me down.

Really?

"First time." I turned back to swipe again. If he said anything else, I might just punch him and keep going. Thankfully, the next swipe got me through.

I checked my cell. Damn. My appointment was five minutes ago. This day kept getting worse. Deflated, I sat on a bench and put my head in my hands.

An elderly woman stopped in front of me. "Are you lost?" She wore a tattered, brown coat and had gentle brown eyes.

"Yes, I guess I am." I tried to smile.

"Where are you going?" She sat next to me.

"Juilliard."

She clapped her hands together. "Oh, such a beautiful school. Are you a musician?"

"Yes. But I don't go there. I need to see someone." I sighed. "It might be too late."

"A girl?" She smiled sweetly.

I nodded.

"It's never too late. Take the Line One to 66th Street at Lincoln Center." She pointed at one of the trains about to depart.

I jumped up, and took a few steps. "Oh, and thank you." But she was gone. How the hell had she moved that quickly? I searched the crowd, but she'd disappeared.

The train doors were about to close, so I made a run for it, slipping in at the last second. I grabbed on to the pole and tried to let the stress go before I got to Juilliard.

I closed my eyes and took a deep breath. *I'm so proud of you, Jax.* My eyes shot back open. Aunt Betty's voice. Sometimes the memories were so real, it was like she stood right next to me. It usually made me feel sad, but this time I smiled and whispered, "Thanks."

The storm had passed by the time I exited the subway. The sky was a deep blue with fluffy cotton ball clouds, and the sun warmed the sidewalks. The scent from the florists' buckets of lavender filled the air. People had left their taxis behind and strolled the streets with their coffee cups in hand. Everything was back to normal.

Except for me. I hadn't made it in time.

My feet pointed in the direction of Juilliard. I'd go and sit by the pool and plan my next move. At least I'd be in the same area. I could take a little comfort from that.

Or, maybe I'd find her. Aunt Betty loved the tree by the pool. It'd brought her peace. That's right. I'd bet Sivan would hang there whenever she had a chance. But today? Even though the sun shined down on the city, everything was drenched.

I rounded the corner from behind the tree, and, sure enough, someone was sitting on the bench. Could it be Sivan?

I took a closer look, and my stomach sank. Damn. It wasn't her.

The girl wore a blue wool coat and had pretty, light brown hair that shimmered in the sunlight. Her face tilted up toward the sun. I wasn't close enough to see her face, but I'd guess she was smiling.

She might know Sivan. I approached slowly, not wanting to scare her.

"Um, hello?" I said from behind.

The girl straightened and froze.

"I'm sorry, I didn't mean to startle you."

Her head went down, and she shook it. "I can't believe you're here." She stood and faced me. "Jax."

"Sivan?" Every molecule in my body screamed at me to take her in my arms. It took every bit of strength to stay standing in place.

"Jax." Tears escaped the corners of her eyes. "Jax," she said again.

"Sivan, I—"

She took the two steps that separated us and launched herself into me, wrapping her arms and legs around my body. "I'm so sorry. I'm so sorry." She cried into my shoulder.

I held onto her with everything I had, but the grass was slippery, and I couldn't keep my balance. We tumbled backward, with me ending up on my back and Sivan on her side.

"I guess I have something else to apologize for." She giggled. "Are you okay?"

More wetness seeped into my clothes, but I didn't care. "I'm glad to see things haven't changed. Always knocking me to the ground," I teased.

"Oh, Jax." She leaned over and smoothed the hair back from my face. "I can't believe it's you." Her eyes filled with tears again. She kissed my lips softly and whispered, "I really am very sorry."

"Tell me I'm not dreaming." I ran my fingers over her soft cheek.

"You're not. This is real."

"Sivan, I'm so sorry about what happened. I was an idiot." I turned to my side and pulled her close.

"It's my fault. I was scared." She trembled in my arms.

"I shouldn't have looked. That's on me."

She pulled back a little. "Jax."

"Yes?" I held my breath.

"I'm still scared, but I choose love." And then she smiled the most beautiful smile I'd ever seen.

I wiped the tears from her face, and said, "And I choose you."

EPILOGUE
Five Years Later

Sivan

"I'M SO GLAD WE DECIDED to keep the farm." I rested my head on Jax's shoulder.

"So am I. Aunt Betty would be happy we decided to raise our family here. She left you the farm because she knew you belonged here."

The pots on the front porch were filled with all the flowers Betty loved, the colors bursting in all the shades of a rainbow. "I couldn't imagine selling it. This place is so beautiful." We rocked slowly in the swing.

I patted my stomach. "Baby number one, almost ready for the world."

Jax placed his hand on my belly. "Hey, Bruiser. It's time to quit hiding. We have to get you in shape before the Seahawks season begins."

I raised an eyebrow. "Jax?"

"Yep." He smiled and flashed the smile I loved so much.

"First, we don't know if this baby is a boy or a girl. Second, we live in Iowa."

"It makes perfect sense since Iowa doesn't have a professional football team." Jax nodded as if that would convince me.

"And if we have a girl?"

"Well, I might quit calling her Bruiser. But she'll be a fan." He laughed.

"It's been five years today." I rubbed my stomach.

"I know. How are you doing?" He put his arm around me.

"I'm okay. It's weird because, in some ways, it seems like forever. In other ways, I can still smell her perfume and see her eyes light up, and her smile . . . wow. Wasn't her smile the best?"

"Yeah. But I also love your smile." He leaned over and kissed me gently.

I took a deep breath. "Do you think she'd be proud of us?"

He squeezed my shoulder. "I know she would be. She'd love that you played with the New York Philharmonic for a couple of years, getting all sorts of accolades. Now you'll be teaching children piano from our farm and giving them the gift of music. Not to mention all the animals you'll be helping with the rescue shelter you created in her name." He kissed the part of my neck that gave me tingles. "So, yes. I think she'd be very proud."

"And how about you? You'll be finishing up your veterinary training and starting your residency a year early, just like you planned." I nudged him. "Admit it, it was the math tutoring I gave you."

"Yeah. Had nothing to do with the fact I'm a genius at chemistry."

"Oh, the arrogance is alive and well." I giggled.

"I had to have a lot of confidence with the name that's followed me around." He rolled his eyes.

"You mean, The Singing Vet?" I continued to laugh.

He groaned.

"Your song for me stayed at number one for how long?"

He shrugged. "Too long."

Whenever I had a bad day, I'd turn it up full blast. His words of love and hope always made me ache with happiness. He'd risked a lot to get his message through to me.

"At least the fans have let up. We don't even need the wall we built around the farm." I looked out onto the pastures. Natural stones formed the fence and blended into the landscape.

"Yeah, I'm glad they're fickle in my case. Although, we still need it when my brothers visit. Remember last time?"

"Oh, that's right, the little crowd at the gate at Christmas. They've been at the top of the charts for what, six years now?"

"Seven. And I think they're ready to take a hiatus. All of them seem either exhausted or downright burned out." He pulled me to him as we continued to rock. "They can't figure us out."

"Why's that?"

"How we can be so happy all the time."

"Did you tell them we know what it's like to live without each other? That we treasure each day, or more like each moment?" I leaned back and put my legs on his lap. "Remember that day on the bench, when the rain cleared, and the sun warmed my face? I knew, in that moment, I would never allow fear back in. Love replaced it, and that's when I heard your voice."

"I remember." He smiled and started to rub one of my feet.

Ah. Heaven. Waves of relaxation swirled around my body, and tingles went up and down my legs.

"I don't know how much time we have. But you know, I'm going to live the hell out of life until it's over." I closed my eyes.

"Bruiser or Princess will be so lucky to have you as their mom."

"We have to pick out a name soon." I tapped my finger against my lips.

"I think we both know what our favorite name will be if we have a girl."

I blinked back tears. "Yes," I whispered.

"How about Bertrand for a boy?"

Bertrand? "How about we wait until we have a girl?"

He chuckled. "Sounds good. By the way, how many are we planning?"

"We talked about this before the wedding. Don't you remember?"

"Two?"

"No, silly. Five."

His face drained of color.

I wanted to draw it out, but he looked so panicked. "I'm just teasing. I'm good with seeing how it goes. But at least two. Can we agree on that?"

He let out a deep breath. "You'll pay for that." He started tickling the bottoms of my feet.

I kicked and laughed and held my stomach, and, uh oh, my water broke. "Jax."

"Okay, I'll stop. But you deserved it." He laughed.

"You know how our due date is Saturday?"

"Yeah?"

"Well, how does a Thursday baby sound? My water just broke."

He jumped up. "Are you okay? Are you having any pain?"

"Not yet. But I think you should call the doctor."

"Yes. And grab your suitcase. I'll get the car." His eyes jumped around.

"Jax."

He ran his fingers through his hair. "What?"

"We get to meet our child today." I looked up to the sky and mouthed, "Thank you."

A few hours of hand holding, back rubs, and soothing words later, tucked safely in my hospital bed, I had our baby girl snuggled in my arms. "I love you, Betty." Now it took on two meanings. Jax lay next to me in my hospital bed, sound asleep, but he had a smile on his face.

I had a slight tinge of fear, but I pushed it right out. It didn't belong in our family. I didn't need it anymore. No longer would I think about what I'd lost or what could be taken away. Only what I'd been given.

I'd already lived a hundred lifetimes of love with Jax. I appreciated every second and refused to taint the future with doubt.

I would treasure each moment going forward for what it was. Extra.

Peace and contentment settled around my heart like a warm blanket.

I kissed my daughter's sweet head.

Relax, Sivan. You've got this.

THE
End

ENJOYED THIS Book?

Would you leave a Review?

I highly appreciate the feedback I get from my readers. It helps others to make an informed decision before buying books.

If you enjoyed this book, please consider leaving a short review.

Visit http://eepurl.com/clLfBf for a Free Book!

INTERESTED IN contributing to a program that helps Foster Children?

An author friend put together a list of items you can put together yourself to donate to a program near you! Please see her message below:

Fostering Love is a simple program I started for foster children in my county. It's well known that many of these children are removed from their home for any number of reason, and because of that they often have few, if any, belongs with them. As these children move through the foster system their belongings are put in trash bags and moved from home to home. Fostering Love is a program to provide bags for the children who are pulled from their home with nothing of their own. I pack it all inside a duffel bag the child can use should they have to move from an emergency foster home to permanent one. No child in our country should feel unwanted and unloved, yet, so many do every hour of every day. The bag is a temporary solution to a long-term problem, but for the kids and the social workers who help them, often times they offer a bag of hope to a scared or sad child. Once you have your bags complete, contact your health and human services department and arrange a time to drop them off. That's all there is to it! These bags would be a fabulous project for churches, youth groups, school groups or families who want to make a difference. You can find the lists for each age group on my website: www.KatieMettner.com

ACKNOWLEDGEMENTS

It takes a village to write a book. I personally need a very large village. First, the beta readers. Famous was a challenge for me, and my betas kept me in line and nudged me when I got off course. Thank you to all my Scribophile Critters! Deidre Huesmann, Claire O'Sullivan, Anya T. Catmus, Kristina Luckey, Anne Howes, Maggie Penn, Lisa Born, Bobbie Tron, Michelle Freed, Rand Hill, Rodney Likes.

Thanks to BetaBooks for choosing Famous by Default for their Beta Pool: Kathy Knuckles, Karen Kumprey, Cheryl McMahan, Pam Burleson, Jennifer Ford

My other betas came to me through Facebook groups and word of mouth. They don't expect money or favors (But they deserve both!) Thank you for your dedication to the written word and helping me to shape Famous into what it turned out to be: Dana Oldgow, Kimberly Black, Jacqueline Sinclair, Jennifer Trevino, Leanne Hawkes, Jan Hinds, Melesia Tully, Donna Feyen, Maari Hammond, Heidi Petrone.

Francis Vanessa Valladares Duarte: You've been with me since the beginning. Your kind words and great insights have helped me immensely!

Christina Schrunk: You are a great beta reader! You went

the extra mile and caught so many things I would've missed (Like the girls being left in the bathtub forever -lol)

Nancy Thompson: You saved me from myself and that's no small feat. You pulled me in from the author ledge and breathed life into my deflated soul.

Julie Hartnett: You are a great friend – I wanted to acknowledge you for that! Where would I be without our daily chats? Probably mumbling, "lalalallalala" and it wouldn't be the movie– lol.

Laurel Harkins: You're the best sister ever! You always have great advice and wonderful suggestions. You make writing fun ☺

My family: You may not read my books (hint, hint) but you're always supportive! Thanks for putting up with my blank stares and missed dinners.

BOOKS BY M.K. Harkins

Intentional

***Intentional** is a real page turner which got me more and more involved. It developed into an intense situation which developed into another and then exploded into a great climax!* ~Amazon Reviewer

This book is a great read. It is very well written and I would recommend it to anyone who is interested in intense romance novels with a little bit of suspense in the process ~My eBook Café

Have you ever read a book and once you are finished you want to seek out the highest mountain to shout to the world "READ THIS BOOK?" ~ Lola Kay

Unintentional

I have to say in all honesty. . . . I LOVED this book!!!!! I actually liked it even more then Intentional. I thought this book flowed very well and I loved how she switched off the POV's during the chapters. I felt we got the full feeling of the story that way. This book is listed as a standalone and I truly believe it can be read as one. The author does a wonderful job of recapping the end of Intentional from Cade's POV , that you really don't miss anything from the first book ~ Jennifer from Book Bitches Blog

This story is great. I love how the author gave me a love story with some mystery thrown into it. This is one of those books that you don't want to put down until you've finished it, because you have to know what happens next. So in this book you have a great story, awesome characters, excellent writing, and a happy reader at the end. I highly recommend this book ~ Leigh Broxton

Breaking Braydon

I was left in complete awe after finishing this unbelievably heart-felt book. M. K. Harkins has stolen my heart, and I honestly don't want it back. This story left me wanting so much more and yet feeling completely content and satisfied. Watching these amazing characters love and support each other was beyond description at times at how it made my heart swell with pride and admiration. What a magnificent journey I was given the privilege to watch and take part in, and I will forever remember the story that made me cry tears of joy and rapture ~ Shadowplay (Amazon Reviewer)

I loved this book! It's hopeful and uplifting, emotional without being overwrought. And the author has made

incredible, jaw-dropping strides in her craft. The writing is clean, the plot swift, the characters engaging, and the dialogue snappy and often quite funny. Even the secondary characters have heart and humor, and it's my great hope the author will spin-off a story or two for each of them.

If you enjoy inspiring, witty romance with an upbeat, playful vibe, Breaking Braydon is for you. It's the perfect way to spend the day, curled up with Braydon and Jain ~ Story Girl

Taking Tiffany

This story has a lot of romance, adventure, mystery, intrigue, and surprises, one after the other. Just when you think you have it figured out it goes in a different way. It was a very entertaining read and I definitely recommend it. Of course, it has a HEA. ~ **Amazon Top 1000 Reviewer

This has quickly bumped up my favorite books list. I really loved it. Loved it so much, as soon as I finished, I went right back to the beginning to read it again!

I highly recommend. Lovable characters, surprising plot twists and smoldering chemistry all make Taking Tiffany a must read. ~ More Than A Review

Sweet with just enough mystery. I never would've guessed the outcome which was amazing. At the same time it was touching and adorable which made it the perfect romantic book. There's just enough romance and just enough mystery/suspense. ~ Amazon Reviewer

The Reader (The Immortal Series Book One)

"This story is incredibly original and really intense! Overall I would say that this is one of the books to watch, and I predict it will be huge!" ~ NetGalley Reviewer

"This is a fast-paced page turner that had me from the beginning. I read the book in one day as I could not put it down." ~ Amazon Reviewer

"The Reader is different, mysterious, & intense. A paranormal fantasy trip with secrets, suspense, romance, seers, immortals, hunters, much more! The characters are well developed & full of life. The plot is full of intrigue & twists." ~ Goodreads Reviewer

The Jack (The Immortal Series Book Two)

Coming 2017

WANT TO CHAT?

Places to find M.K. Harkins

Email - mkharkins@hotmail.com

Facebook - www.facebook.com/marilyn.wellnitz

Website – www.mkharkins.com/

Twitter - @mk_harkins

Newsletter – www.eepurl.com/baBOrz

BookBub - www.bookbub.com/authors/m-k-harkins

Goodreads -
www.goodreads.com/author/show/7067079.M_K_Harkins